Cornerstone:
The Delving

Book Two of the Cornerstone Series

by

K.A. Krisko

Publisher

First Edition
ISBN-10: 0-9976110-0-6
ISBN-13: 978-0-9976110-0-7

Edited by
Jay Howard

Cover art and design by

Visit my web page at:
http://www.kakrisko.com

Table of Contents

It is not the strongest of the species that survive, nor the most intelligent, but the one most responsive to change.

~Author unknown, commonly misattributed to Charles Darwin

The devil could change. He was once an angel and may be evolving still.

~Laurence J. Peter

Chapter One

Jack Bright lowered his binoculars and glanced over his shoulder. The quick look provided him with a view of Kyle's backside. His cousin's son was draped over the aft port rail, retching into the Pacific.

Jack turned away quickly. He knew he shouldn't have brought Kyle, but the young man had begged him, partly to show his girlfriend a good time and partly, he claimed, because he wanted to see where his brother had died.

The Boston Whaler Conquest rolled in a figure eight pattern in the swells that reverberated off the rocky cliffs. The girlfriend, Terry, sat on the forward deck, her back against the front of the pilothouse. Her expression was inscrutable beneath over-sized sunglasses. She didn't seem to share Kyle's nausea.

Jack braced himself against the pilothouse on the starboard deck and raised the binoculars again. He followed the cliff face to

1

the top, where the steeple of the castle's chapel poked into the sky: dark, Gothic and malevolent.

The castle. That damned castle.

"The end of Earth as we know it," Jack muttered under his breath.

Kyle staggered over, face pale, and gripped the grab rail. "You think he's still up there?" he gasped, nodding briefly at the castle. "Maybe just held captive?"

Jack shook his head. "It's been too long, Kyle. Korrin's gone. We have to accept that. And this is the closest we're going to get to that thing at this point."

The hairs prickled along the back of Jack's neck, and he looked up at the sky. There was a big black bird up there, flying lazy circles, gradually working its way down closer to the boat. Jack wasn't fooled by the shape; that was no natural bird, but undoubtedly the castle's Lorecaster, its wizard, flying his shadow-form in the shape of a raven. After what Jack had done, or attempted to do, to the castle, the young Lorecaster was a sworn enemy.

Jack strode over to the pilothouse, ducked through the door, and started the boat's motors. He swung it around and headed further out to sea, partly to relieve Kyle's nausea. But he slowed again just a quarter-mile south of where the castle loomed on the cliff. There, a huge slump littered the base of the cliff with debris, including the remains of five houses and some of their occupants. All of them had been Jack's friends, co-workers and employees of the environmental lobbying group Earth Natural, of which he was president.

Jack felt a twinge of guilt as the boat slipped quietly by the slump. After all, he had, at least indirectly, caused the slump when he'd tried to blow up that cursed castle on the hill. His only consolation was that all of the people who'd died had known what they were risking.

"Hey, there's a trail over there," Kyle said plaintively, pointing to the cliff near the slump. "Maybe we can take a little hike."

"That trail goes right up to the castle," Jack replied. But Kyle's pale face garnered some sympathy. Poor kid was still seasick.

"I can put the boat in around that outcropping past the slump," he acquiesced. "I've done it before. You can scramble up to the top of the rocks there, and it's far enough away from the castle to be safe."

"Maybe we can wait there, and you can drive back and pick us up after you bring the boat home," Kyle suggested miserably.

"The only road to this area runs past the castle and the Lorecaster's house," Jack said. "Sorry. You have to go home on the boat."

They puttered past the outcropping and Jack swung the boat around behind it, bringing the bow up close to a big rock in a sheltered cove. Terry threw the bumpers over and scrambled onto the rock holding the bow line. Jack cut the motors and followed Kyle out of the pilothouse. There were several trees rooted in the cracks of the rock, and he tied the boat off to one of them with a quick-release knot.

Terry scrambled easily over the rock and jumped down to a bit of sand behind it. Kyle, a little heavy around the middle, followed more slowly. Jack waited impatiently. He might be twice Kyle's age, but he was fit and agile.

Once off the rock, Jack led Terry and Kyle to the cliff and picked his way up through the boulders. He had visited this cove a number of times before. It was a way to get close to the castle, to observe what was going on there, without driving up to the isolated little neighborhood where it sat. He knew he could hike around the outcropping to the slump at low tide, but he'd also figured out how to scramble up to the top of the cliff.

Stunted firs clung to crevices here and there. Animal trails wound off through the deepening forest as they gained the top. The surge of the Pacific Ocean faded and the summer heat settled over them. A few insects landed on Jack's arms and neck.

They turned north at the top of the cliff. After a quarter-mile walk, Jack motioned Kyle and Terry to stop and he crept forward alone. A small neighborhood lay beyond, a few summerhouses in little clusters. Jack could see the raw edge of the residential road's pavement where the slump had taken the five houses closest to the cliff down to the sea below.

Kyle and Terry came up behind him and stood staring. The lower neighborhood, at whose southern edge they stood, was tucked in amongst the firs, drowsing in the mid-afternoon heat. The houses of the upper neighborhood were more exposed, and behind them the land rose steeply. On top of that rise stood the castle, sentient and malevolent.

Jack felt his pulse quicken. This was the closest he'd been to it in a long time, and he almost imagined it knew he was there. Involuntarily he stepped a little further behind the trunk of a tree.

"I can't believe Korrin walked into that thing," Kyle whispered. "He had a lot of guts."

Or he was an idiot, Jack thought, but aloud he said, "Remember it wasn't as complete then as it is now. The bigger it gets, the more powerful it becomes. I'm sure Korrin wouldn't have gone in there if he didn't believe he had the advantage."

"He took the sword," Kyle said, his tone reverent.

"Yes. I wish we could get it back," Jack muttered. "One of the most valuable tools we had, and now it's in their hands."

Terry stood with her hands on her hips, a slight smile on her lips. She was not, after all, one of the Knights of Earth Natural, like Jack and Kyle. Kyle had told her about the castle, but Jack didn't know if she believed it.

4

"You want me to walk up there and get your sword?" she asked. She grinned as she said it. "I'm not one of you, your castle won't bother me. Right?"

"I'm not sure about that," Jack warned. "Besides, we have no idea where the sword is. Somebody would see you if you went wandering around up there and would want to know what you were doing. Most likely the Lorecaster."

"I've seen him before," Terry said. "Kyle pointed him out once in Seaside Heights. He's not so scary. Just a skinny guy with a unibrow and a ponytail."

"Don't underestimate him," Jack growled. "He's young and he doesn't know his power yet. But it's there, and he most likely knows you're connected to us, too. He was flying his raven-shadow around earlier."

Kyle and Terry both looked up at the sky, but the raven was not to be seen.

"You feeling better now?" Jack asked Kyle. "We should get back to the boat. This is risky. I don't know how far the castle's influence has spread, but we're probably at the edge of it."

"I guess," Kyle sighed. "Just get us back to the marina as quick as possible, okay? I feel better when you're going faster."

Jack led them back through the woods to where the trail dropped off towards the ocean. He paused a moment, his eye caught by motion above them. The raven was there again, circling lazily high over the boat.

He let his eyes rest on the vessel a hundred feet below them. He'd taken the 27-foot ocean sport-fishing boat as partial settlement of a suit against a developer who'd failed to follow state environmental mitigation requirements. He'd named it the *Natural Seize*, a play on the name of his organization, Earth Natural. He smiled a little in satisfaction.

With a jolt of adrenalin, Jack realized that the *Natural Seize* floated free. It was no longer tied to the tree. The bow line floated in front of it, and it backed slowly away from the shore, bobbing and rolling.

"Hey!" Jack yelled, as though the boat might respond. He scrambled down the cliff as fast as he could, slipping and sliding on the loose dirt. Several times he went down on his butt. His hands scraped against rough rock. Small prickly plants clinging to the barren cliff side stabbed him. Finally he staggered onto the narrow gravelly beach at the bottom. He edged around the big rock on slippery stones. Waves washed back and forth, wetting his shoes. The boat floated just beyond his grasp.

Jack waded further into the ocean, the seawater shockingly cold. He felt his jeans grow heavy. He thought for a moment that if he was going to swim, he should take them and his shoes off, but he didn't have time. The boat was picking up speed as it floated further out of the cove. He needed to get to it fast.

He sucked in a lungful of air, braced himself, and dived forward into the surf. He felt his knees hit underwater rocks and was glad he'd kept his jeans on. He made some forward progress into deeper water with a breaststroke and then switched to a front crawl.

He was a strong swimmer, but open ocean wasn't his preference. Swells splashed him in the face and he tasted salt. The cold sapped his strength quickly, and his heavy clothes and shoes dragged at him. He flipped over onto his back for a few seconds to rest. Kyle stood on the shore, Terry on top of the big boulder, watching him. The raven circled overhead.

He flipped back over and started swimming again. The rocking of the boat became more pronounced as it reached the edge of the protected water of the cove and began to encounter the larger waves of the open ocean. It was drifting southward, too. There was another outcropping that way. Another couple of minutes and the boat would slam up against the cliff. If the motors were damaged too badly he wouldn't be able to start it and turn it into the waves, and it would eventually founder and break up against the rocks. The consequences would be dire. He was pretty sure he couldn't make it back to shore at this point. His only chance was to get to the boat and get aboard.

He poured the last of his strength into his efforts. Another two minutes and he reached the starboard side of the boat. The outcropping loomed, each wave washing them nearer. Jack grabbed one of the bumpers and hung on to rest for a moment. Then he let go and dropped back into the water. The ladder was around the back; he worked his way aft.

The dual motors stuck out at a steep angle as he'd lifted them to avoid any rocks on his way in. The burred edges of the propeller blades caught at his arms as he went around them. For a moment he had a nightmare vision of the motors coming on by themselves, but he didn't think the Lorecaster could do that. He was in more danger from the cliff, now just feet away.

Finally he grabbed the ladder and heaved himself up. He staggered forward and yanked open the pilothouse door. The boat shuddered as the starboard outboard struck the rocky cliff. A moment later the port motor roared to life and Jack spun the wheel to bring the lolling Conquest around into the incoming waves.

Jack steered the boat out into the ocean and swung around to make the correct approach to the cove. Bringing it alongside the rock was a little trickier with only one motor, but he didn't want to start the starboard one until he'd had a chance to take a look at the propeller.

Terry grabbed the rail and held the boat in long enough for Kyle to step aboard, then jumped on herself.

"You want me to drive?" she asked through the pilothouse window as Jack brought them out away from the cliffs. "You need to warm up."

Jack glanced at her. "You know how?"

"I'll be okay out here," she replied. "You'll just have to take over when we get to the marina."

He relinquished the wheel to her and stepped out into the sun on the back deck. He kept an eye on the castle retreating on the horizon as he stripped off his wet shirt and shoes. Kyle handed him a towel, and he roughed it through his hair and over his chest.

Drier and warmer, he stepped back into the pilothouse, away from the wind. Terry didn't seem to be having a problem piloting the boat. Jack leaned against the window to her right and allowed himself to consider how close a call that had been. He realized he was shaking, from the exertion as much as from the chill.

"You think that was a coincidence?" Terry said after a few minutes.

"Hell, no."

"You think the castle's trying to kill you?"

"Me and everyone else it doesn't like." Jack glanced through the back window of the pilothouse, but they were too far away now to see the steeple. "Can't say I blame it; I tried to blow it up once."

A long moment went by. "So you believe the castle's alive, then," Terry finally said.

Jack ran a hand through his wet hair. "Not exactly. It's inhabited by some sort of entity that lives in its stones. And it's evil."

Terry shrugged, but she kept her eyes on the ocean in front of the boat. "What's evil, after all?"

"Well, I'd say some alien intelligence that wants to change the Earth as we know it is evil," Jack said. "The castle's growing, and the more it grows, the more rocks it inhabits and the more powerful it gets."

"Me, I'd say that evil is something that can only be done to people by other people," Terry replied. "Maybe you should back off and quit pissing it off. Seems like it's got all the power in this relationship."

Jack sat down on the forward berth and rested his elbows on his knees as the *Natural Seize* cut the water smoothly up on plane. Backing off was one thing he couldn't do. There was Korrin to

8

avenge, and all his friends who'd been lost in the slump he'd created himself. That was the most important, because he had to prove to himself that their deaths were both unavoidable and meaningful. He couldn't agree with Terry; evil had to be an external thing. And he knew where it lay: inside that castle on the cliff, not inside his own mind.

Cornerstone: The Delving

Chapter Two

He was lost. Lorcas Felken stopped and pressed his back up against the cool, damp stone wall. His breath came hard and fast. He glanced behind, but it was too dark to see anything in that direction. Ahead was only the faintest gray glow suggesting a distant source of light.

He'd never been lost in the castle before. There had been times when he hadn't been sure where he was going or exactly how to get out, but he'd never actually been lost. But these tunnels seemed to go on and on, twisting, rising, falling, almost as if Rook was creating them or rearranging them as he went – which was, he realized, not unlikely. Rook himself was nowhere to be found within Lorcas' mind. Only the faintest inkling of the consciousness he'd come to identify as the spirit of the castle tickled the back of his brain.

The sword glinted faintly in his hand. The weight of it was comforting. Somewhere ahead – or maybe behind, now – the misshapen shadow that had taken Raine, that had attacked Zumar on the day of the Coronation, lurked and slithered.

"Zumar!" Lorcas whispered, but there was no answer. He took a deep breath of damp, earth flavored air and held it, listening. He turned his head sharply at the faintest hint of a hiss from somewhere up along the tunnel. The sound was followed by a strange hollow rumble from even further away and a momentary dim flash.

"Damn it, Zumar!" he muttered. His adrenalin was pumping and his mouth was dry, but he was fairly sure he himself was in little danger from the Bob-blob, as he'd nicknamed it. Zumar was in much more danger and was supposed to stick around where Lorcas could protect him if necessary while they hunted the thing.

Lorcas preferred hunting with Tomash, but Tondra and Alan had kidnapped him for the day, forcing him to help with some of the administrative duties of running the Coalition of Fell Ken, the fledgling organization they'd put together to support the growing community. Lorcas would have spent the day doing something else, maybe drawing, but Zumar had pressed him. Zumar, vengeful over the disappearance of Raine and in danger himself, had the most reason to hunt the Bob-blob, but he couldn't do it alone. He needed a corporeal being to wield the sword. Typically, he now seemed to have disappeared, just when Lorcas needed him. He couldn't help but wonder if the fickle Messenger had done it on purpose, hoping to lose him forever in the bowels of the castle.

Lorcas slid a little further along the passageway, one shoulder in contact with the wall to guide him in the twilight. Abruptly, the wall opened away from him and he fell sideways. He tried to catch himself, but solid stone reaching to his knee tripped him up. He landed heavily on his right side, scratching himself across the left wrist with the sword.

He sat up quickly and felt around. The opening he had fallen into for all the world resembled a large window casement, but they were underground. There was a sill, what felt like glass behind him, and a pointed Gothic arch overhead. It was suffused with a dim golden light.

He felt warm blood trickling down his arm. He set the sword down and felt in his pocket for his keys. He kept a little LED flashlight attached to the key chain for emergencies, though he didn't usually use a light while they hunted for fear of alerting the Bob-blob. He preferred to let his eyes adjust to the dim ambient illumination and keep one hand free.

The key chain had a red-light function on it, and Lorcas switched it on and squinted at his wrist. The cut was not serious. He caught a drip of blood with the fingers of his right hand and wiped it on the sword blade. No harm in baptizing the sword with more of the Lorecaster's blood; it was, after all, his blood that made it able to reach into the shadow-world, or so he'd been told.

A dark presence passed in front of the window opening, blacker than the twilight, and Lorcas froze. He clicked the flashlight off quickly. Then he scrambled to his feet and eased out of the casement, the sword leading the way.

"Watch it, Lorecaster!" Zumar hissed from the darkness.

Lorcas stumbled to a halt. He could barely see Zumar's shape, like a ripple in the dark.

"Don't swing that thing around!" Zumar said. "You poke me and I'm done for."

"Don't sneak up on me and you won't be in danger of getting poked," Lorcas growled. "Was that you just now or the Bob-blob I saw?"

"Dunno," Zumar replied. "I didn't see anything."

Lorcas pocketed the flashlight. "Where the hell did you go?"

"There's another little tunnel just back off there." Zumar waved back down the passageway. "You missed it in the dark. It doesn't go far. It's kind of an odd shape, like something built into a corner."

"You mean triangular?" Lorcas asked. "That doesn't sound like something we've seen before."

"No. These tunnels are getting more and more complicated. I can't tell if I'm retracing the same territory or not."

"What's Rook doing, anyway?" Lorcas grumbled. "He's ignoring me. I haven't talked to him since we stopped building up above."

"Not talking to me either." Zumar shrugged. "He's busy. Doesn't give a rat's ass for the rest of us when he's got a project going."

Lorcas sighed and lowered the sword. "Can you find us a way out of here? I'm done."

"Yeah, I think so," Zumar said, "if Rook doesn't change something on us while we're going."

Lorcas followed Zumar along the dark passageways, up and down staircases and through doorways. Halls opened left and right, some of them giving off a soft glow in one color or another. As they rose, the walls became smoother and more finished in appearance and the ceilings higher.

The area began to look familiar. Lorcas was pretty sure they would come into a kind of long, vaulted space at the top of the next set of stairs. He trudged upwards, his legs feeling the burn of too much up and down. Soon they would be out and he could relax with a beer or a glass of Marek's wine. But just as he neared the top, the steps seemed to crumble beneath his feet. He felt himself falling, felt the stairs semi-supporting him as they plummeted like a giant falling snake. Then the staircase snapped into place, with what had been the top now the bottom.

Lorcas tumbled head over heels to the last riser and fell over the end into space. He hit a number of things on the way down, sills and ledges and other bits and pieces sticking out of the walls. They would have hurt a lot more, but he could tell that Rook's power was slowing his descent, even if the castle didn't seem to be paying attention to him. He thought briefly about switching to his raven form, but his body, he knew, would keep falling even if he did so. A moment later he smacked into a stone floor, which gave slightly beneath him like a box springs.

The sword skittered away. Around him it was pitch black. The faint light from above showed as a circle, none of it reaching where he lay. He barely had time to push himself to a sitting position before a powerful fetid draft like a giant exhalation surrounded him and the air seemed to pulse and waver.

Lorcas fumbled around the floor, searching desperately for the sword. His hand encountered the blade, and he quickly patted up it to the hilt and grabbed it. He leaped to his feet, the sword before him, and turned about, peering into the dark. He couldn't tell from which direction the wind came. It was accompanied by a hollow rushing sound that ebbed and flowed like the tide. It seemed to be all around him.

His eyes settled on a spot that seemed lighter than the surrounding dark. As he stared, the spot grew in intensity. A yellow light emanated from it as it slowly took the shape of a gigantic, slit-pupiled eye. The eye blinked languidly, cold and reptilian. It looked to be about the same height as Lorcas himself, some six feet tall, and about two-thirds of that across.

Lorcas was pretty sure he didn't want to be in the same room with that eye, whatever it was attached to. He backed slowly away, holding the sword out in front with both hands. His back slammed into a wall, and he stepped sideways slowly, still watching the eye. There was a passage to his left, and he crept into it. The eye did not move, except for a slight narrowing of the pupil.

The edge of the passage wall cut off Lorcas' view as he continued. Once he was entirely out of the eye's field of vision, he lowered the sword and scrambled along the hallway half-sideways, looking back and feeling forward. He stumbled noisily over things unseen on the floor, bounced off door-jambs and buttresses. Other things seemed to dart away from him down the dark passages, things soft and formless and things with hard claws skittering on the floor.

After about fifteen minutes he stopped. He had absolutely no idea where he was, how to get back to where he had been, if it was even possible, or where Zumar had gone. He did know he had no inclination to yell out and draw attention to himself. Whatever was lurking down there in the depths of Rook's basement was significantly more alarming than just the Bob-blob.

He found an outcropping of stone and sat down for a minute to rest and try and get his head together. He knew he needed to go up; he'd fallen down, so that made sense. The other possibility, though, would be to go sideways, if he could figure out in which direction the ocean lay. If he hadn't descended all the way down to below the level of the bottom of the cliff, perhaps there would be an exit along the sea side.

That was well and good, but which way was the ocean? At least he could tell which way was up, so perhaps that was a better plan. He stood and began to feel around the chamber he was in, searching for any kind of staircase or ramp.

There was only a down staircase, as far as he could tell. He backtracked into the room he'd been in just before entering the chamber, and there he found an upward-sloping ramp. In the next room there was an up staircase, but it dead-ended in a chamber with no outlet. Lorcas went back down a level and tried another room.

By only going up, and backing out of any room in which there was only a downward stair, Lorcas began to make his way higher. He realized he could see a little better. He began orienting himself towards the lightest hallways and staircases, and finally he saw true daylight. It was a low-set window in the side of the castle, down a little passageway, but it was covered with a thick, ornate grille of metal. It was as though someone had created a knot from iron bars, and one bar on each side was sunk deep into the casement.

Lorcas grabbed the bars and tested them, but they were solid and the grille didn't even rattle. He knelt and peered out the window. He was in an area he didn't recognize, looking not towards the sea but towards some heavily forested area. He guessed he was north of where the body of the castle stood, where the landscape rose in a series of hills and cliffs. At least he was above the dungeon-like tunnels where strange things crawled and breathed.

He thought of the key he still carried within his chest but the window seemed to have no lock or hinge. The bars were buried within the stone itself. As he crouched near the casement, considering what to do, he heard the strange intake of air behind him again, almost like a breath. The bodiless sound caused the rise of an uncontrollable panic in his chest.

There was motion outside the window and a face appeared on the other side, inches from his. Lorcas jumped back, but the face belonged to Tomash. Zumar crowded up beside him.

"Hey, Lorcas." Tomash grinned. "Zumar thought you might need a hand."

The sound echoed behind Lorcas again, louder this time. It seemed to be getting closer. The hairs stood up on his arms with the rush of what was left of his adrenalin. "I need out, now!"

Tomash sobered. "Okay, we'll see what we can do. I've never been in this area before. Maybe there's a door or something. We'll take a look around."

"Hurry up!" Lorcas said. Faintly he heard the scrape of something hard on stone. "There's something in here, and I don't want to find out what it is!"

"Can't you get Rook to let you out?" Tomash asked, peering in through the bars.

Lorcas shook his head. "He hasn't been answering me." He paused and concentrated for a minute. "I can feel him. I can feel him real strong, but I can't hear him. I can't explain the difference. Just please look for a way to get me out, and hurry!"

Zumar appeared beside him, inside the castle wall. "You stay here," the shadow said. "I'll go see what I can find."

Lorcas glanced down the dark corridor again as the scraping and hissing got closer. "Tomash, don't you have a hacksaw or something?"

"Sure, back at the house," Tomash said. "I don't have it with me. What about your sword?"

"It won't cut metal. I don't think," Lorcas amended. He stuck the tip of the sword between the bars and slid it gently along the base of the bottom one. To his surprise, a faint scratch appeared.

"We only need to get two of these cut, and we could probably rotate it and you could fit through," Tomash said. "Here, give me the sword and I'll work on it."

Lorcas stuck the sword hilt-first through the window. He didn't like handing it over; it was his only source of defense. Tomash pulled it through and began working at the top bar where it intersected the sill. Lorcas crouched, listening. The scraping of the sword mirrored the noise behind him. It sounded like metal being slowly dragged across the stone floor.

Tomash paused. "What was that?"

"I don't know. It's getting closer, though. Keep sawing!" Lorcas urged.

Tomash employed the saw with renewed vigor. The sounds seemed now to be just down the corridor, a few bends away. Lorcas pressed up against the side, out of the way of the tip of the sword but as close to the outside world as he could get.

The sword sliced through the top bar. Tomash paused and yanked on the grille hopefully, but it remained in place. The bars were thick, and it was too firmly anchored. He picked up the sword again and started on the bottom bar.

A dark shadow fell across the end of the passageway, heralding the arrival of whatever-it-was. The sword cut through the bar. Tomash dropped the blade and grabbed the bar with both hands, yanking in an attempt to pull it outward and rotate the grills.

"Watch out!" Lorcas yelled. He sprawled on his back and kicked. The bar moved slowly, bending a fraction of an inch at a time. Small bits of rock flaked away from the attachment points of the two side bars. The grille rotated in agonizingly small increments.

A giant exhalation, hot and dank, ruffled Lorcas' hair. He abandoned his effort and forced his head and shoulders through the gap. Tomash grabbed him under the arms and pulled. The end of the bottom bar raked down Lorcas' back. He twisted sideways and jerked his feet through. An instant later he lay tangled in the vegetation on a slope beneath the sill.

Lorcas scrambled to his feet. "Zumar!" he yelled, his panic for himself transferring to concern for the shadow. He crouched and stared back into the gloom, but he could see nothing. Hoping Zumar had removed himself from the castle altogether, the two men scanned the wooded slope, but there was no movement, no answering shout. Then Lorcas' eye caught motion and Zumar appeared, striding through the woods atop the mound in which the window was set.

"Right here!" he announced, jumping down across the window to join them. "Good thing you found a way out. I didn't see another one you could get to without going right back the way you came."

Lorcas picked the sword up off the ground and examined the blade. There was not a mark on it, despite having been used as a saw.

"You look a little the worse for wear," Tomash said. "You okay?"

"Basically." Lorcas examined the cut on his wrist. It was still oozing. His clothes were tattered and dirty, and he could feel bruises on his legs and arms and the burning of the scrape down his back. "I could use a drink."

"What the hell was that coming up behind you?"

"I don't know." Lorcas looked back to the window, but nothing showed behind it but deep darkness. "There are more things down in there than just the Bob-blob, though."

"Maybe hunting it isn't a great idea anymore," Tomash said. "Definitely not just you alone."

"I was with him," Zumar said in a hurt tone.

"Lot of good you were," Tomash commented.

Lorcas looked up at the sky where heavy clouds scudded, heralding a coming storm. A large drop hit his face. But even standing outside in the rain was preferable to standing in the dank dark of the castle's basement with that giant eye staring at him.

"Let's get going before we get drenched," Lorcas said.

They contoured around the hill from the casement, and in a few minutes the castle itself came into view. Lorcas had never seen it from that angle. They were north and east of it, inland from the sea cliffs. The castle looked small and pointy. It was not a large structure, especially compared to the castles and fortifications Lorcas had seen in the books of medieval construction he'd been studying. It consisted of the small, Gothic chapel, with a steeple only four stories high, and the Keep, a larger building with a steep-pitched roof and multiple turrets. The grounds around the two buildings boasted the tiny cemetery, with the graves of the Knight, Bob, Raine, and Bishop the cat, and a limited garden. There was a short stone wall surrounding the two structures and continuing down into the neighborhood, but nothing in the way of a major building had been added since the disastrous Coronation the previous fall.

The rebuilding had gone fairly quickly. But after things were restored to where they'd been prior to the Coronation, Rook seemed to lose interest in creating much more, at least above ground. Rather than repair the waterway they'd built as a ruse to cover the van's tracks, he'd created a large pool below the castle, inland from the chapel at the base of the hill. It had slowly filled with dark water

20

from below, and now, from certain angles, reflected the castle in creepy parody.

He'd also directed Lorcas to obtain the materials to erect a few oddly-placed spires, which now stuck up here and there around the perimeter like bare trees. Then he'd retreated, leaving Lorcas feeling oddly empty and purposeless.

Obviously Rook had been busy underground, though. It was just as well, Lorcas thought. Perhaps Jack Bright and the rest of the Koen, seeing no further development, would think Rook was discouraged or stalled. Maybe they'd leave him alone and quit spying on him from Jack's boat. Lorcas had seen Jack and two other people he didn't know, and couldn't identify from the height he'd maintained, out on the *Natural Seize* the day before. It wasn't the first time. It bothered him when Jack prowled around the base of the slump. His mother's body still lay buried under tons of rock and mud down there somewhere.

They rounded the lower part of the hill upon which the castle sat and the neighborhood came into view. It had changed somewhat since the year before. All of the houses that remained now belonged to the Fell Ken, and somewhere close to a hundred and fifty people lived there. A stone path connected all the buildings, and many of them, including his own, exhibited stone walls around the foundations and stone facades. The neighborhood was beginning to resemble a medieval village, or perhaps a fantasy version of one. Some of the new residents had taken a cue from the theme and added embellishments like covered stone wells, horse-drawn carts (with no horses), and flower pots made from wine casks. One of the larger houses had been developed into a meeting hall resembling a church. Lorcas could see a group of children running around one of the new modular houses in the lower neighborhood. That building had been turned into a school, he knew.

They passed along the shore of the strange little lake, its surface disrupted by raindrops. It was coming down fairly hard by the time they crowded into Lorcas' entryway, although only he and Tomash were actually wet. Lorcas opened a beer for himself, forgoing the wine, and one for Tomash, and they settled in the living room as the storm really got going outside. The downpour pounded on the roof and distant thunder rolled.

Lorcas tossed Tomash the TV remote and set his half-finished beer on the coffee table. "I'm going to grab a shower. Help yourself to more beer."

Upstairs, he examined his shirt and pants. The pants were salvageable, but the shirt was too ripped and dirty. He tossed it in a damp pile on the floor. He turned his back to the bathroom mirror and examined the scrape from the bar down his back. It oozed small drops of blood. He swallowed a couple of ibuprofen tablets before jumping in the shower. Afterwards he stuck a bandage over the cut on his wrist before heading downstairs again, feeling warmer and more comfortable.

"Since you're up…" Tomash said, gesturing with an empty beer bottle.

Lorcas fetched him a fresh one and a second for himself. He brought the sword and a handful of paper towels into the living room and dried the weapon carefully, looking along the edge of the blade. Even in good light, he couldn't see a nick or burr on the blade, which was decorated with delicately etched scales. There was no sign of the blood he'd wiped on it, either.

"Why are we still walking around in the castle anyway?" Tomash asked after a few sips of the fresh beer.

"Obviously we're looking for the Bob-blob, and for Raine," Lorcas said with a glance at Zumar. "You know that."

"Yeah, but I mean, what are we doing walking? Can't we use the van?"

Lorcas stared at him. He stuck the tip of the sword into the carpet and balanced it with a hand on the hilt. "Is the van still accessible?"

Tomash shrugged. "Dunno. It was parked by the dungeon last I saw it. I don't know why it wouldn't still be there. The explosion caved in the doorway but that doesn't mean the dungeon didn't survive."

"Wonder if it still starts?" Lorcas mused. "If it doesn't, a new battery would probably do it, as long as it hasn't been chewed up by mice or whatever else is roaming around in there."

"A lot of those passageways are definitely wide enough," Zumar put in. "Headlights would be nice."

"And it's automatic protection from attack. Genius, Tomash! No wonder you're the King." Lorcas laughed.

"Shut up." Tomash slumped back in the couch.

He was uncomfortable with his title, and Lorcas knew it. Tomash had never expected to take on leadership of the Fell Ken so soon. They'd all expected Perry and Delva to be around for at least a few years more. And in actuality, Tondra, Tomash's sister and co-ruler, and her consort Alan, did most of the management of the clan.

"Got the keys?" Lorcas asked in a minute.

"Should be in the ignition," Tomash said. "We didn't want anyone finding them on one of us."

"Right," Lorcas remembered. "You want to go for a cruise?"

"Scenic drive," Zumar replied. "I'm up for it any time."

"Count me in, if I can get away from Tondra for a day," Tomash agreed.

Lorcas crossed an ankle over his knee and grinned. He took a slug of beer. "I'll feel better being contained in something solid anyway. There are things down there, I don't even know what."

"Obviously," Tomash said with a grimace, "otherwise we wouldn't have had to saw through a couple of iron bars to get you out. You could've come out the normal way. But I've only ever heard rats and things like that."

"Definitely scuttling noises, like little claws on stone," Lorcas agreed. "But some scuttling sounded bigger. Then there was something that went by me that I thought was the Bob-blob, but now I'm not sure. It could've been anything. Not something natural, though. I could feel it. Then there's the whole matter of the inside of the place shifting around while you're in it."

"That's an issue," Zumar said. "I mean, if I need to I can walk right through walls, but it's not all that comfortable to do anymore; I'm getting more solid."

"Yeah, and the staircase changing directions while I was on it was no joke, either," Lorcas said. "But that wasn't the freakiest thing, not by far."

"What's freakier than little ratty scuttling sounds and haunted blobs?" Tomash asked.

"What I saw at the bottom of everything, when I'd been dumped down there by the stairs," Lorcas said. "I was in this chamber and I started hearing and feeling this moving air, like hot breath. And then this thing started glowing from the opposite wall. It got brighter and brighter, and it was huge. I'm talking, like, six feet tall. And you know what it looked like? An eye. Like a huge, yellow, glowing eye with a reptile pupil, you know, one of the elongated ones."

"That is freaky," Tomash agreed. "I wonder what in hell that is?"

"Well, we've known there are weird things living down in the depths of the castle for a while now, but that takes the cake. I have no idea what it is."

"Um," Zumar said, "yes you do."

"No, I don't," Lorcas snapped.

"Yes, you do. Maybe you just don't know that you know, you being you. Or you don't want to admit it."

"What?" Lorcas looked at Zumar with the combination of a sneer and a frown he often reserved for the shadow. "What do you mean I don't know that I know? What the hell is it?"

Zumar looked slowly back and forth from Tomash to Lorcas. "You didn't expect him to just stay in the rocks forever, like some sort of spirit, a shadow like me, did you?"

"What do you mean?" Lorcas demanded again, a cold feeling washing over him.

"I mean," said Zumar, "that is Rook down there. And you better get used to it, because I'm pretty sure he's not going back into the cornerstone any time soon."

Cornerstone: The Delving

Chapter Three

Jack sat on the edge of the desk in his office, his toes balanced on the floor, pitching bits of torn-up and crumpled paper towards a wastepaper basket a few feet away. Behind him huge windows looked out over the Pacific Ocean, framed by dark, looming firs. The building was not tall, but its position allowed it a sweeping vista over the sea in which he'd recently taken an unwelcome swim.

"You sure the Lorecaster loosened that bow line?" his cousin Don asked again. Don, shorter than Jack, a few years younger, with the broad shoulders and beefy upper arms of a weightlifter, sat sunk into a couch against the wall opposite the windows. "You sure you actually tied it off properly? You know the movement of a boat could work a bad knot loose."

"I'm sure," Jack snapped. "I've been tying knots longer than you've been alive. And no, I didn't see him actually fooling with it, but he was there, flying his shadow-form."

"But how could he have done it?" Don wondered. "If he was in his shadow-form, he wouldn't have the ability to interact with the physical world. Not enough to untie a rope, anyway."

27

"Maybe we've underestimated him." Jack tossed another piece of paper. "But he's young and doesn't have a good tutor, with his dad dead and Perry dead now too. Zumar's not a Lorecaster, so he can only teach him so much. It would take a very strong relationship for Lorcas to absorb power and information directly from Rook without a more experienced tutor. It would definitely have to be stronger than what I felt when we met Lorcas in Lafayette last year."

"Relationship could've been strengthened by that disaster of a destruction attempt," Don pointed out. "All it did was strengthen the Fell Ken's resolve."

Jack glanced at him. He still felt guilty, but he pushed the emotion down. There were going to be casualties in this war because that's what it was: a war. A war to preserve the Earth in its natural condition, without Rook's inexorable creep into its very bones. He shuddered at the thought of the horror a world controlled by Rook would be, with its risen dead and its abomination of a shape-shifting Lorecaster.

"Obviously Rook is far too advanced at this point for normal, physical means of destruction to have much of an impact," Jack admitted. "We're going to have to figure out another way to stop him. We've got to get inside, become a virus that eats away at his power from within."

"Well, that's going to be harder than it sounds," Don said. "Rook can tell if you're Fell Ken or Knight, and there's no way he'll let a Knight get inside his walls ever again. Korrin blew that for us. And after the thing with Lorcas' mother, he'll probably be real careful even with unfamiliar Fell Ken."

"Yes," Jack mused, "it'll have to be someone who's neither Fell Ken nor Knight. Someone who's not freaked out by Rook but believes what we say and has the guts and maybe the naivety to do as we direct."

28

"Sounds like our own personal Lorecaster," Don replied. "But we don't have what it takes to mold someone into what we want. That kind of power flows to the Fell Ken through Rook."

Jack shook his head. "No. But throughout history people have been able to get things done through natural means, without relying on unnatural powers. We can do the same, and in the end we'll win. We have to win."

He got up and went around the desk. He sat down in the leather chair and leaned forward on his elbows, grabbed the cordless phone out of its base, and punched in a number from memory. He tapped the desk with the fingers of the other hand, waiting for someone to pick up.

No one did. When a message came on, Jack leaned back in the chair. "Kyle, hey, Jack here. Give me a call when you get this. I need some information from you. And your help. You want to avenge Korrin? This may be your chance to get involved."

He punched the phone off and stared at it for a minute before placing it back in the charger.

Don smiled at him somewhat grimly. "I know what you're planning. You sure that's a good idea? It will be dangerous."

"Yes, but I still have hope that we can change the course of events and even extricate Lorcas before he's consumed by this evil," Jack said. "We owe it to Condra to try. She came to us in hopes that we could help save her son, and she sacrificed her life for that hope."

"I'm not sure why you give a damn about the Lorecaster," Don sneered. "He's not a very likable person, if you ask me. He's let himself be manipulated by everyone from Perry to the Messenger."

Jack turned to him quickly. "Well, yes, of course, that's the point, isn't it? The Lorecaster has to be malleable. He has to give himself up for Rook. He has to allow himself to be used. Lorcas is perfect for the role. Even his father couldn't do it: he was too independent, too strong in himself. As much as he wanted to, he

29

could not be the Lorecaster. He couldn't give himself over completely. Eventually his attempts killed him. But Lorcas is the perfect storm. That's why Rook's grown so fast, and why we have to stop him now."

He got up and strode to the bookshelf that lined one wall of the office. From high on the shelf he chose a large volume with a frayed, faded spine. He brought it back to the desk and plunked it down heavily. He bent over it as he flipped through a few pages in the middle. Then he stabbed a finger at an illustration.

Don got up and joined Jack at the desk. "George and the Dragon?" he asked rhetorically after a glance at the page.

"It's an illustration of one of the stained glass windows in the chapel, and if that's George, he's losing badly. But I'm actually interested in this other window." He tapped the opposite page. "This is where the key lies, I believe."

"But you can't read it, can you?" Don confirmed.

"Of course not. No one can. None of us, anyway. It's in code."

"Old, created by someone who spoke a dead language, and in code," Don corrected. "No one has been able to decode it. Kyle's been working on it for years, and his father before him."

Jack shrugged, but he continued to stare at the page. "Yes, written in the days when Zumar's castle still stood, probably by Paracel, the Lorecaster at the time. At least it was written in his hand, although the words may have been dictated or suggested to him. No one can decode it because it's not only encoded, the underlying language isn't human. It's alien, Rook's language. And we don't have the key."

"But you have some guesses," Don said. "I know you've studied this book. I've seen it out before."

Jack nodded. "This window is a kind of control panel for Rook," he said, circling his finger over the illustration of a window featuring what appeared to be a clock face made of gears, with what

30

looked like a plan of some alien solar system above it. "It looks like stained glass, but it's much more than that. It survived the explosion and collapse, for one thing. No ordinary glass would have been able to do that."

"Of course, I remember the stories," Don said. "I grew up with this stuff, too. The window contains a map of his universe, a map back to where he came from, and a means for him to access it, a kind of navigation panel." Don crossed his arms and sat back down on the arm of the couch. "But if it's that important, Rook isn't going to let it be damaged easily. He'll be wary."

"Of course." Jack leaned on the desk again. "I don't think we can just destroy it by, say, smashing it. But I also don't think we need to destroy it. That's not my plan. I'm more interested in this area below it."

Don leaned towards the table again and Jack tapped the illustration below the window. "See this area? The illustration is pretty detailed. Somebody took a lot of care drawing it, and if you look on the following pages, you'll see specific segments enlarged, with text that appears to relate to them." He flipped a few pages over slowly, allowing Don to look at each one for a few moments.

"Well, it almost looks like some sort of machine," Don observed. "There are slots and gears that could be used to control something. It could be part of the window, or it could be something separate."

"Right," Jack said. "This part of the castle appears to have been first created during Paracel's time, in Zumar's last castle. Older illustrations we've found of what we believe to be previous castles, previous incarnations of Rook, show the window but not this section below it. These illustrations are explanations of how it works and why it was created."

"What's your theory?" Don asked. "I've never heard this before."

"I think it contains a mechanism that allows Rook to be shut down by the Fell Ken in emergencies, to stuff him back in his rock, so to speak. It would be a way for the Fell Ken and Rook to disappear quickly if they were under siege, for their own safety, as a last resort."

Don raised an eyebrow. "You're saying the Fell Ken have a failsafe of sorts, some built-in process they can follow to hide Rook without his express permission."

"Basically that's it. There's precedent, you know."

Don snorted. "You mean Atlantis. Castles rising and falling, all that stuff."

Jack crossed his arms. "Traditionally we've claimed Atlantis as an ancient victory over Rook. He rose to become a formidable power at that time. Somehow he was overcome, and the entire structure and all the rock he'd co-opted up to that time sank and disappeared. He didn't pop up again until thousands of years later."

"And that event was either triggered by his enemies to disable him, which is what our tradition has held, or, you're saying, by his supporters to protect him and themselves when things were getting bad. But you said this mechanism was created in Paracel's time, thousands of years later. The Knights and the Fell Ken didn't even exist in the time of Atlantis."

"Correct," Jack agreed. "I think Atlantis truly was a victory for our side, whatever we called ourselves then, and it was probably that experience that persuaded Rook to allow the Fell Ken to create this mechanism in Paracel's version of the castle."

"But why would Rook allow the Fell Ken to have something that powerful, something that could shut him down like control-alt-delete on a computer keyboard?" Don argued.

Jack smiled at the analogy. "Because he has to. He has to interact with humans. We know that, because otherwise he just wouldn't. He'd just do everything himself. But he had to have human help to start to move out of the cornerstone, and he knows he'll have to have help in the future. The Fell Ken provide that interface with the human world.

"Yet Rook doesn't understand human beings very well. He might not be able to interpret aggression or respond to it appropriately. I don't think he really understands how most humans would view him if they knew about him or the kind of defense they might mount against him if they believed he was real. So I think he agreed to create this device that could be activated by the Fell Ken to conceal him quickly if they felt it was necessary. At the same time, it would save or at least temporarily hide members of the Fell Ken, and they'd be available to start over again quickly. Win-win."

Don considered. "This is an important discovery if you've interpreted it correctly. If it was triggered by the Fell Ken at Paracel's castle it might explain how the cornerstone itself survived and was rescued, and why so many other artifacts survived as well."

"And it's our ace in the hole now," Jack said. "It brings everything back to square one so Rook can't be found, but it also limits his power drastically."

"You think just anyone can activate this device and make Rook retreat to his cornerstone?"

"Not anyone, no. You'd have to have the specific items to activate it. Those items, and the way to employ them, would be known only to the Fell Ken. I'm not clear on what the items are yet. That's part of what we need to find out, part of why we need someone on the inside. We have to figure out what things we need and obtain them."

"And when you have these items, you can activate this device. Or someone can. Rook goes back in his cornerstone, and then what?"

"Then we're back where we started. We'll have Rook contained in the stone, Zumar will be stuck there as well, Lorcas' power will wane at least temporarily, or if we're lucky he'll just quit, and we'll have the advantage. Then we can move decisively, the way we should have in the past."

"We didn't know where the cornerstone was in the past," Don said. "And there's still one issue I see. Didn't some of these books come from the Fell Ken?"

Jack stared at the volume for a moment. "Yes, they did. This one did. They were taken in the past when Knights were able to get their hands on them, like we took the castle stones when we could. They've always been viewed as extra valuable because they contain information known only to the Fell Ken."

"Or not," Don said. "I doubt the Fell Ken would allow such information to fall into our hands easily. I know we supposedly got these books when the Fell Ken were scattered and depleted, but still, I think there's the possibility that they're a plant, a set-up. You expend a lot of energy plotting and planning, and it turns out you've wasted your time because what's in these books is meaningless."

"I know that's been suggested," Jack replied, "but I've studied these books for a long time, and I've consulted with our allies in Europe, as you've certainly guessed." He glanced at Don. "We don't see any signs that they're propaganda: they're too complete, too well done. I believe they show the reality of Rook's interior workings."

"I'm still not convinced, but I see you've got a plan and that you're set on following it. I'll go along with it, but I think we should continue to explore other options."

Don moved a hand to his cell phone, which was clipped to his belt in a holster. The cell phone case, Jack knew, concealed the clip of another holster, the body of which sat inside Don's waistband. That holster held a dagger, curved, sharp-pointed and well-honed. It was an item passed down through many generations, said to be infused with the blood of a previous Lorecaster. It was allegedly the knife that had killed Paracel, and was thus able to reach into Rook's world as well as into the guts of flesh-and-blood humans. The Knights called it simply the Dika. Don was well trained in its use.

"Ah, yes," Jack sighed. "The Knights have always had their assassins. Better you than me. I'd rather blow things up, keep things large scale and impersonal. You can have the face-to-face."

"You'll give me permission to employ my skills if I get a chance?" Don asked. "In exchange, I go along with your harebrained scheme and support it to the rest of the Knights."

"Fair enough," Jack said. "You know the rules, Don. Don't lead anyone back to us. If you get caught, you go down alone."

"Understood," Don said. "That's the way it's always been."

"Alright," Jack said, "it's going to take all of us to accomplish this. I need you on my side when I present this idea to the rest of the Knights."

"Are you actually going to present it to the Chamber?" Don asked skeptically.

Jack thought for a moment before answering. "Maybe not. Sometimes these things go better when fewer people know."

"The fewer people in a conspiracy, the less chance someone will spill the beans. Is that it?" Don grinned. "That's the way I figured you were going to play it. Will you need my help setting things up?"

"Maybe," Jack admitted. "And I need someone to bounce ideas off, so you're in."

"Well, I better get fortified, then," Don grinned. "I'm gonna grab some lunch. You want me to pick you up something?"

Jack shook his head. "No, thanks."

He walked out of the office building with Don and stood in the parking lot for a minute, watching as his cousin pulled away in his gunmetal gray Hummer, a new acquisition and, Jack thought, a good match for Don's personality. Then he turned to the ocean. He walked across the office building's lawn to the cliff's edge and stood looking to the west, the wind tousling his hair. He could smell the salt in the air. He loved this place, this part of the U.S. and the world, with its violent surf, rocky cliffs, and dark fir forest. He wanted more than anything for it to continue on into the future along whatever course it was naturally meant to take. He couldn't stand the thought of some alien presence usurping the very bones of the place, corrupting its soul and spirit.

He was snapped out of his reverie by his cell phone. He pulled it out of his pocket and glanced at the face before answering.

"Hi, Kyle, thanks for calling me back. Listen, I need your help with something. I need you to make a phone call for me, and I need your cooperation. It's not going to be easy for you, but it's a way to avenge Korrin. Keep that in mind when I explain."

He turned away from the wind and walked back to the building as he spoke. In his office he grabbed a pen and a piece of paper and made a quick note. "Thanks, Kyle. You won't regret this. It's what a true Knight would do. But keep it to yourself for right now. I haven't presented it to the rest of the Knights. You, Don, and I are the only ones who know about this plan."

Jack swiveled the chair around and stared out the window. The wind was coming up and the tops of the firs swayed. To the north, clouds gathered as though responding to his threat. He felt the little prickle of doubt he always felt when he was about to put some plan into action that would endanger the lives of others. Certainly those plans had gone awry in the past. But he had to continue to try; it was his duty as a Knight and as a human being and natural resident of the Earth.

Many people, if they knew what he believed, would think he was insane. Very few would believe in a sentient castle bent on reshaping the Earth. He was putting himself out there, risking ridicule or worse. But it was worth it. What was it Terry had said on the boat? "Evil is something that can only be done to people by other people." But she didn't understand what Rook was, what he represented. If she did, she'd have to admit that evil could come from an external place, and that it could be something done to the Earth as well as to people.

He was startled from his thoughts by the office phone. He took a deep breath before turning to pick it up.

"Thank you for calling," he said. "Did Kyle explain what's up? It's dangerous. I want you to know that up front. And if you don't want to do it, I will completely understand. We'll figure out some other way."

He listened for a moment, tapping the chair's arm nervously with his fingers. "It's no joke," he continued after a minute. "It's real and it's deadly. And even if you do start this project, you can back out any time. I'm asking. I'm not telling you to do anything. You understand that?"

He waited again. "No, I'm not offering you money. You do this out of curiosity, or interest, or for whatever reason. The first part won't be dangerous. It should be fairly simple. We'll go from there." He leaned forward, staring into the room now instead of out the window. "I'll get you what you need to start. Anything you think you need, you tell me. We'll fund it. And I've got some books to give you. You'll need to do some reading. No, it's not on-line. You'll have to read real books, yes. I'll drop them off this afternoon if that's okay."

Don came back into the office while Jack was packing some books into a cardboard box. He slung a plastic bag with a wrapped deli sandwich in it onto the desk.

Jack eyed it. "I told you I didn't want anything."

"Yeah. You need to eat. Life goes on."

Jack pulled the bag towards himself reluctantly. Don was right, of course. Jack tended to get so wrapped up in his plans and schemes that he didn't take care of himself. It was important now, of all times, to make sure he was in the best shape he could be for what was to come. And he was still healing from his swim in the Pacific. He could feel the bruises and scrapes on his knees when he moved, and there was a series of scratches on his forearms from the propeller blades.

"I've got to run down to the marina and pull that prop off the boat," he told Don as he unwrapped the sandwich. "I want the *Natural Seize* ready to go whenever we need her. You gonna come give me a hand?"

Don shrugged. "Sure."

"I've got to drop this box off in Lafayette, too. I can drop you back here before that if you don't want to come, or you can follow me to the marina in your truck."

"I'll jump in with you," Don said. "I'd like to meet our ace in the hole." He grabbed the box and followed Jack out to the black truck.

In the truck, Don pulled out a few of the old volumes and flipped through them while Jack drove. "You have any idea what you're looking for, or are you just planning on playing it by ear?"

"Oh, I have an idea. You look further in that book I showed you, the one with the diagram of the failsafe, and you begin to notice that certain items are featured more than others. There's the sword we once had, that Korrin took with him. We know quite a bit about that, since it was in our possession for more than four hundred years. But there are a couple other things as well: a staff that appears to come apart, and particularly an object located within it, a caduceus or rod; a key; and a ring. There are a few other things, like a silver goblet, but they don't feature as prominently. All of them are likely held by either the Lorecaster or the King at this point. Finding them is job one; getting them, well, that's further down the line. We'll cross that bridge when we get to it."

"Or somebody will cross that bridge. That's what you're throwing into the mix." Don shook his head. Jack didn't reply.

The marina was less than fifteen minutes from Jack's office. The route took them past the shuttered antiques shop that had once belonged to Perry, shadowed beneath firs, the front yard neglected now. Jack glanced at the building and felt a prickle at the back of his neck. It was a feeling he often got in the presence of the Fell Ken but, as far as he knew, there were now none in Seaside Heights at all. Oddly, though, he did not have the same reaction when they drove past the turnoff to Delva's house, where she'd lived with her granddaughter Raine. A 'For Sale' sign could be seen planted in the front yard. Jack suspected the house had been left to the Fell Ken as a whole or to a specific representative, which he knew to be traditional among them. They likely had little use for it, since all of them seemed to be massing in the area of the castle itself. 'Cliffview Estates', they were calling it. A joke, an obvious front, if you asked him. But it gave him some comfort to think that they might come to Seaside Heights only incidentally now, rather than being planted in the middle of the town like a weed in an otherwise manicured garden.

Jack didn't keep the *Natural Seize* in the water, but rather on its trailer, parked under a canopy covering a space he rented from the marina. He parked his truck close to the boat and pulled his tool kit out of the steel box in the back.

"Hold the engine," Jack directed.

Don grabbed the shank and steadied it for him. In a few minutes Jack had the propeller removed. He examined it briefly, then put it in the back of his truck and climbed up in the bed. Don handed the tool kit up to him and Jack stowed it. Then he stood up, hands on his lower back, and squinted around the storage yard. Something was bothering him. He watched disinterestedly as a cat ran along the top of the marina seawall, his mind elsewhere.

"You sure you want to come to Lafayette to drop off these books?" he asked Don.

"I'll come along," Don said with a grin. "You'll seem less crazy and more believable if I'm with you."

"Because you come across as less crazy, or because more than one person believing in something makes it seem less crazy?" Jack wondered aloud as he climbed out of the truck bed.

"Both," Don said. He opened the truck's passenger door. "Is Kyle going to be there?"

"I don't think so. I think he'd rather not hear about this particular plan any more than he has to," Jack said. "Things have been rough for him lately, with his mom sent off to Europe, his brother gone missing, and now this. I'm sorry about it."

"Yeah, me too," Don agreed grimly. "Let's hope we don't get sorrier."

Chapter Four

Lorcas was sitting in the den poring over his father's books when he got a strange sensation. He ignored it at first. He was determined to find some inkling of what he'd seen in the bowels of the castle. Zumar had immediately become evasive after his revelation, muttering about how it wasn't his place to tell the Lorecaster what he should already know.

Tomash had been just as bewildered as Lorcas. "I thought Rook was the cornerstone," he said after Zumar departed.

"Well, I guess I always knew he was something that dwelt in the cornerstone, rather than the rock itself," Lorcas admitted. "I just didn't think about it much. I never thought about him physically coming out, or what he would be like if he did."

Without Zumar's help, or the help of Perry or Delva, and with Rook seemingly preoccupied and unwilling to make direct contact, Lorcas retreated to the library. He was sore and bruised from his fall and his escape through the barred window anyway, and he didn't feel much like doing anything physical for a few days. But it was slow going; many of his father's books had been collected in Europe and they were in Slavic languages Lorcas didn't know. His father had translated some of them by hand, slipping scrawled pages into the leaves, but the handwriting was difficult to read and the translations incomplete. Lorcas had continued to work at it despite the frustration, and had created a dictionary on his computer with Zumar's assistance. Still, he didn't so much read the books as stutter through them, one word at a time.

Something tickled Lorcas' mind again and he looked up from the book impatiently. It wasn't exactly like when Rook was trying to get his attention. It was more like a trespass alarm, some kind of warning. It occurred to him that it might be Jack or one of the Koen approaching the area. He had felt the same thing when Jack and the *Natural Seize* had approached along the coast. He'd flown over them and watched as they climbed the rocky trail to the southern edge of the neighborhood and, with some amusement, seen Jack's desperate swim to rescue the errant boat. The boat, bobbing in the swells, had apparently loosened its own knot, though he wasn't sure Rook hadn't had something to do with it, reaching fingers of influence out to the rock to which the boat was moored.

He got up and moved quietly into the living room, then into the far end of the kitchen where a row of high, narrow windows looked out towards the front of the house. Keeping close to the wall of the entryway, he peered out cautiously.

There was someone standing along the spur road that came in to the neighborhood from the T intersection. The road itself was technically not closed to the public, but the neighborhood next to it was gated now that it was exclusively the home of the Fell Ken.

Lorcas went around the half wall into the entryway and out the front door. He walked casually towards the person. A low stone wall swept around from the main gate to the south, off to his right, a visual deterrent rather than a true physical barrier. It enclosed the neighborhood and continued around the hill upon which Rook sat until it turned towards the sea, encompassing the cemetery and a part of the woods beyond. There was a metal garden gate between

Lorcas' house and the entry road. Lorcas flipped up the latch and pushed it open, keeping his eyes on the stranger.

As he got closer, he could see that it was a woman. She had a slender but athletic build and straight, dark-blond hair hanging to just below her shoulders. She wore a ball cap and large sunglasses, obscuring her face except for a somewhat enigmatic smile.

"Can I help you?" Lorcas asked.

"Just looking. Isn't this that place that blew up last year?"

Lorcas glanced over his shoulder at the castle. "Yes, it is."

"Looks like someone's done a good job getting it back in order."

"We're working on it. I'm afraid it's not open to the public right now. Safety considerations, you know. We're being extra careful."

The woman gestured in the direction of the castle. "Oh, I'm not interested in touring it or anything. I'm actually looking for a way to get to the southern part of the state forest that's just north of here. I've been to the rest of it, but the southern part's kind of hard to access. I'm looking for good hiking and mountain biking areas."

Lorcas relaxed a bit. "The road you came in on curves around the base of the hill and keeps going up that way. Eventually it does go into the forest, but it's dirt from here on out. It can get kind of rough."

"Oh, I've got a Ford F-250 pickup truck, four-wheel-drive. Got chains, even. I think I can do it. I'm a good ol' farm girl." She grinned at Lorcas, revealing slightly crooked teeth that Lorcas found inexplicably attractive. "I've even got extra clothes and food in case I really get stuck and can't get anyone to help me out. And I can ride out on my bike if I have to."

"Well, cell phone reception's not too good up in there," Lorcas warned her. "If you do get stuck, this will be the closest civilization. Ride out to here and come knock on my door. That's my house right over there."

The woman reached up and pulled her sunglasses down a bit. She looked over the top of the frames with gray eyes. "That's an… interesting looking house."

Lorcas turned and looked at it himself. The house appeared to be wrapped in rock, as though it was being swallowed by some giant slowly-moving stone. A bit of clapboard stuck out in the front and near the garage.

"Yeah, well, it's supposed to look creepy, you know? The whole theme of this place will be mystery weekends and haunted houses and the like when it's open."

"Well, it does look creepy, maybe kind of like something out of *The Hobbit*."

A lot creepier than that, Lorcas thought to himself, but he smiled in response. "Don't worry, I'm not a troll. Or an orc."

The woman pushed her glasses back up her nose. "No, you look more like a young wizard."

Lorcas smiled uncomfortably as she touched a bit too close to the truth for his liking.

"Well, thanks for the info. I'm sure I'll be fine. See you later!" She turned with a brief wave, walked back down the road towards the T intersection and disappeared off to the right.

Lorcas remained where he was, and a minute later a big dark-red pickup with bicycle handlebars sticking out of the bed roared up past the trees and bounced off the pavement onto the gravel road leading past the castle. He watched until it disappeared around the hill.

Lorcas stuck his hands in his pockets and walked back to his house thoughtfully. It was the first time since the destruction of the castle that he could remember feeling a glimmer of interest in anyone. Mostly lately he'd felt angry, simmering, restless, resentful. This was a welcome break. Of course, he'd probably never see her again, but at least something had been awakened within him.

The feeling held on through that evening. For the first time in months Lorcas felt like drawing. He pulled his tilt-top table into the living room and spread out a sketch of a fish he'd never finished, one with rock-like scales and castle structures hidden within it. He worked on it for several hours with music in the background, pausing only for a few sips of wine.

The next morning he took a look at the drawing in the light of day. He always liked to look at them in various lights before deciding whether they were done or not. He stood off to one side and then another and paced around the room a bit, coffee in hand. It was still early and the neighborhood was quiet, few other people up and about.

A curious squeaking sound came from outside. Lorcas froze. He wasn't sure what he was hearing, but it wasn't something he was familiar with. The squeaking was followed by a sound he could identify, that of the gate latch clanging into place. He set his coffee down carefully and quietly walked to the kitchen window.

The woman he'd talked to the day before was coming towards the door with her bike. She was walking it, but controlling it with the handlebars. As she applied the brakes and brought the bike to a stop he heard the squeak again. He felt a little adrenalin rush as he went to the door.

"Hi!" the woman said. "I hope it's not too early!"

"No, I've been up for a while. You didn't get stuck, did you?"

She leaned the bike up against the wall of the garage. She was wearing jeans, a T-shirt, and hiking shoes, with a sweatshirt tied around her waist. She took the sunglasses off as she approached.

"Yeah, I did. Good thing I brought extra stuff. You were right about the cell phone coverage." She stuck out her hand. "Terry Bell."

"Lorcas Felken," Lorcas replied. "Come on in. You want a cup of coffee?"

"I'd love one," she sighed. "I'm a little muddy." She gestured to her pants.

"Don't worry about it. I'm not exactly a fastidious housekeeper." Lorcas led her to the living room. "Have a seat. I'll get the coffee going." He went into the kitchen, poured more water into the machine and added a coffee module.

"Nice drawings," Terry said. "Did you do these?"

"Yes." Lorcas walked back into the living room. "That's what I do for a living. I illustrate technical manuals and the like. Mostly I specialize in fish and birds. I've drawn stuff for the Fish and Wildlife Service, done signs for the state forests. Done a few reptiles here and there, too."

Terry flipped a few pages over, looking at the drawings. Lorcas watched her. She was tall and she moved confidently. She was not beautiful, exactly, but she had an open, natural look, with no make-up and an amused expression. The fact that she'd spent the night out in the state forest alone and didn't seem particularly bothered about it was interesting. She was a lot different from Carol, more akin to Tondra, maybe, but less abrasive.

"Coffee's ready." Lorcas returned to the kitchen and got the mug out of the machine. "You want cream or sugar or anything in it?"

"Nope." Terry moved from the drawings to the old secretary's desk near the entryway. She examined the few objects Lorcas had obtained for the castle which he'd set on the back of the desk.

Her back was to him, and as he walked into the living room he caught motion out of the corner of his eye. Zumar, partially opaque and obviously inhuman, stood near the door to the den. Lorcas frowned and shook his head briefly, and Zumar disappeared from view. Bishop the cat, less cooperatively, scuttled from the den up the stairs.

"Here you go." Lorcas offered Terry the mug and she took it and wrapped her hands around it with a smile.

"Thanks. What should I do? Should I call for a tow truck or is there someone around here who could tow me out?"

Lorcas considered for a minute. "Well, I've got a dually flatbed. It's four-wheel drive. Depending on how bad you're stuck, I should be able to get you out."

"You got tow chains or a strap?"

"Got it all," Lorcas said. "You want to throw your bike on the back or pick it up on the way back through?"

"I'll leave it here for now, if that's okay," Terry said.

"Why don't you stick it in my garage? Here's the key. I've got to change my shoes and grab a jacket."

Terry nodded, took the key, and headed for the door with the coffee still in one hand. Lorcas waited until she was outside, then turned to the den. "Zumar!"

"Right here, boss," Zumar said, materializing through the den door.

"What do you think? You feel anything weird about her?" Lorcas asked.

Zumar considered. "Nope, not really. She's definitely not Koen. Not Fell Ken, either. Seems to just be a normal human being." He shrugged. "Nothing to worry about as far as I can tell."

"Good." Lorcas nodded.

Zumar grinned. "Oh, very good. You have fun out there!"

Lorcas snorted but couldn't help responding with a grin of his own. He grabbed a pair of work boots from near the door, jammed his feet in, and laced them up quickly. He snatched a jacket from a hook near the door as he went out.

Terry pulled the door of the garage down and followed him around the side of the house to the truck he'd bought the year before. Lorcas checked the toolbox behind the cab to make sure his chains and tow straps were in there, locked the hubs, then hopped in to the driver's side and fired it up. It was a diesel and a manual shift, but he'd come to enjoy the power and control it gave him. He jammed the clutch down and shoved the shifter up into first with a grin at Terry.

He pulled around in a half circle and headed for the main gate down the road. It was an electronic gate, incongruous in the medieval-style entry arch. It began to open as they approached and after a short pause Lorcas pulled the truck through and turned back the way they'd come, following the neighborhood spur road past his own house again and north towards the forested hills.

The improved gravel road, laid down to help with the castle's construction, continued for several hundred yards past the pavement until it turned up the slope upon which the buildings sat. Lorcas kept going straight, and the truck bounced into the ruts of the two-track dirt route that led towards the state forest.

Lorcas kept his hands on the wheel, but he glanced sideways at Terry. "So, where do you live? Seaside Heights?"

She smiled. "No, down in Lafayette. Not in town. I live on my parents' farm. Told you I'm a farm girl."

"Right," Lorcas remembered. "Is that what you do for a living?"

"No, my mother runs the farm with help from our manager and some other employees. I live there because it's convenient. I work part-time in a bike shop and part-time as a paralegal, mostly just digging up old cases and copying them for the firm. They specialize in environmental law and construction mitigation agreements."

Lorcas nodded and concentrated on the road. Cliffview Estates had no mitigation requirements that he knew of, but if they did, well-positioned Fell Ken would take care of what was needed.

They passed the barred window in the side of the hill. He glanced that way quickly, but he didn't want to draw attention to it. Past there, the track became even worse, the ruts deep and muddy as the road wound through dark fir forest. Grass grew on the center hump, along with a few shrubs that scraped along the skid-pan of the dually. The track was seldom used, due partly to its location and partly to conditions. When it was wetter it could become a real morass, Lorcas knew. His father had taken him up there when he'd been a boy a few times, but he hadn't paid much attention to it since moving back to the summerhouse.

A half-hour in, they arrived at a wire gate. Terry hopped out and peeled it back while Lorcas drove through. She closed it behind the truck and climbed back in. A sign posted just behind the fence informed them that they were entering the state forest.

"Which way?" Lorcas asked as they came to a fork.

"That way." Terry sat forward and waved to the right. "Still a ways up."

"You really got back in here," Lorcas said.

"Looking for a good place to ride," Terry replied. "I didn't want to ride in this rutted track. I wanted to get up a little higher into a drier place. This direction looked like it was going uphill."

"It is," Lorcas said.

The two-track continued through deep forest, heading northeast. Eventually they came to the red Ford, slid off to the left with its left rear quarter-panel up against a tree.

Lorcas stepped on the brake and jumped out of the cab. The two walked around the truck for a minute, looking at its position.

"I think the best bet is to pull it uphill," Lorcas said. "That'll straighten it out without danger of it sliding sideways. Looks like it'll be drivable once it's back on the road."

He maneuvered the flatbed past the pickup to the right and parked it just uphill. The hill was not particularly muddy. He was a little surprised she'd gotten stuck there, rather than back in the flatter area, but perhaps she just hadn't been paying attention. He hooked a tow strap underneath the pickup and looped it through one of the rings on the body of the flatbed. To be on the safe side, he geared down to four-wheel-drive low, but it was an easy job. With Terry at the wheel, the pickup followed the flatbed up the hill and away from the tree. Lorcas kept towing until they got to a flatter spot, then stopped and unhooked.

"There you go," he said. He collected the tow strap and threw it back in the toolbox.

Terry inspected the dent in the quarter panel. "I really appreciate it," she said. "I'm sorry to put you out this way. Can I give you some cash?"

Lorcas raised his eyebrows. "Oh, no. No problem. I'm happy to help out." He looked around a bit uncomfortably, not sure where to go from there, conversationally. "I guess we should keep going up this hill until we find a better spot to turn around."

"I'll follow you," Terry said. "See you back at your house."

The forest opened up a few hundred yards further along, and Lorcas managed to maneuver the flatbed around in the woods. He waited, watching in his rear-view mirror until Terry got her pickup turned around and was behind him on the track.

Forty-five minutes later Lorcas punched in the code for the main gate and pulled up to the front of his house again. Terry parked outside the wall. Lorcas heaved the garage door up, took Terry's bike out to her, and lifted it up over the side of her truck bed for her.

"You want to come in for a soda or more coffee?" he asked as she climbed up and arranged the bike.

Terry grinned at him. "That's okay. Too much coffee and I'll have to find a place to stop between here and Lafayette."

"Well…" Lorcas hesitated. "You want to take a look around the castle?"

Terry hopped back over the side of the truck bed and stared at him seriously. "I thought you said it wasn't open for visitors."

"It's not." Lorcas shrugged. "But I can bring people up there if I want. It does belong to me."

"Really?" Terry squinted at him skeptically.

"I inherited the land from my Dad. I'm a partner in the venture, too, so I guess it doesn't one-hundred-percent belong to me, but I've got a controlling interest in it."

Terry glanced up the hill at the two buildings making up the above-ground part of the castle. "Sounds interesting. Let's go."

Lorcas led her off towards the ocean to where the staircase climbed from the neighborhood to the chapel. They hiked up the stone steps with the cliff on one side, lined by the low stone wall. The gated entry to the dungeon had disappeared after the collapse the year before, but Lorcas glanced at where it had been. He hadn't figured out how to get back down to that area yet, but the van should be there, parked next to the dungeon.

They followed the path around the side of the chapel to the back and entered through a large wooden door. The chapel was small, just one open room with stone benches lining the sides. The door to the steeple sat to the left of the front interior wall, accessed by several steps. The chapel was lit by a number of stained glass windows depicting various medieval scenes. The one farthest to the front on the left side was oddly made, with a series of interlocking gear shapes and astrological symbols and scenes of some type. Lorcas still wasn't sure what it meant.

A large door on the right side near the front led out to the King's Garden. Next to the door was a series of shelves containing the remnants of the Knight's armor. The helm, slightly dented, sat on the highest shelf. One gauntlet lay on another shelf; the second gauntlet had been crushed too flat to be repaired. The vest and foot and shin guards completed the salvaged parts. Near the armor was an iron stand in which the Knight's sword could be displayed, but lately Lorcas kept it in his house, since he'd been using it to chase the Bob-blob around on a regular basis. After all, the sword did not belong to the Knight. It belonged to the Fell Ken, an historical object that featured in several of Lorcas' books.

Terry wandered over to the armor and examined it, her hands clasped behind her back like a small child trying to keep herself from touching displays in a museum. Lorcas felt an unexplained tension rising within him. For some reason he didn't want her to examine the armor too closely or pick it up or touch it, but after a minute Terry turned and continued around the inside of the chapel, looking at the silver goblet in its niche at the front and glancing at the stained glass windows.

"Where's this go to?" she asked as she reached the steeple door.

"I'll show you. Go on in."

Terry went up the steps and pushed open the wooden door. The stone stairs beyond were steep and tall. Lorcas followed as she climbed upwards past the small landing at the first big, arched casement, past the second, slightly larger landing and casement, to the topmost real room of the steeple, below the final tiny attic or bell room. This was the largest room as well, taking up the whole of the interior of the steeple with just the single stair entering and none exiting to take up space, since only a ladder led to the bell room. Lorcas had placed several pieces of furniture within it, but the casement had no window; he didn't want things to get ruined by the rain that blew in, although he'd noticed that rain typically did not blow in, as though there was a pane of invisible and incorporeal glass in the frame.

Terry leaned out, one knee on the broad stone sill and a hand on the frame. "Wow! This is a great view!"

"Yes. It's a favorite spot of mine," Lorcas said. "Someday I'll probably have an office here," he added, remembering that this was supposed to be an exclusive hotel. He suddenly felt uncomfortable again. The third-floor study was his personal space, the window from which he launched to fly as his raven shadow, the Corax Lorecaster.

"Let me show you the Keep," he said hurriedly. "That's where the main part of the hotel will be."

He followed Terry back down and showed her out through the side door into the King's Garden, with its now well-marked well. The Keep was much larger than the chapel, with a second-story balcony running around the entire interior and two third-story balconies on the long sides. It was not really finished; Rook had lost interest after they'd rebuilt it following the collapse to its approximate former outline. Lorcas didn't care for it much, as it reminded him of death and destruction, the beginning of his true anger at the Koen. It was mostly empty, and for some reason the peaked shape, the emptiness, and the cold of the stone walls gave Lorcas the impression that he was in an attic rather than on ground level.

"Kind of cold and empty," Terry said, voicing his own thoughts. "I guess you're going to finish the interior?"

"Sure," Lorcas said. "We'll eventually add rooms, a banquet hall and conference room, that kind of thing."

"Is there any more? Anything up the hill?"

Lorcas shook his head. "Nope, you've about seen it all."

"Nothing underground? A wine cellar or something?" Terry grinned up at him. "Maybe a torture chamber?"

Lorcas smiled back uncomfortably. "Just a basement."

"Oh," Terry replied, glancing towards the back door of the Keep. "Interesting. Because I thought I saw something like a window when I was heading up towards the state forest. A window in the hillside. With bars."

"Well, there are some old ruins here and there," Lorcas lied as best he could on the spur of the moment. "There were some old miners' cabins up that way. You know, that explosion that nearly leveled this place was caused by unstable abandoned dynamite probably left here by miners a hundred years ago. They had dugouts, stone cabins, even underground storage crypts where they kept their explosives to keep them cool. I wouldn't go poking around up in there if I were you. You never know what you might run into."

Terry frowned. "Right. Wouldn't want to run into old unstable dynamite. But you'll have to take care of that at some point before you can open this place to the public. People will want to wander around, go hiking, and they'll naturally explore."

"Sure," Lorcas said. "We've got professionals looking at it. That's why we haven't expanded up that way. We don't want to run into anything unexpected ourselves. The last time was enough."

"I heard some people got killed," Terry said. "Anybody you know?"

"Besides my mother?" Lorcas said bitterly. "Yeah, several of my best friends."

Terry was silent for a minute. "I'm sorry. I didn't know. Your mother was killed?"

Lorcas nodded. "Standing close to the cliff when that slump happened. She went down, but they never found her body." He looked around the Keep. "Come on, let's get out of here. This isn't my favorite place in the world anymore."

Terry turned quickly and led the way out. Lorcas steered her away from the cemetery and down the hill towards his house. They contoured around the black pond at the foot of the hill. Terry stopped on the slope above it and frowned.

"Creepy reflection," she said. She glanced back over her shoulder at the actual castle. "It looks different somehow."

Lorcas stared down into the water. It did look different, but he supposed it was the distortion caused by the two-dimensional surface representing a three-dimensional object.

A few raindrops hit his face. He looked up at the darkening cloud moving in from just north of the castle. Something made him want to get inside and out of the weather, back to his drawings and his father's books. He urged Terry on past the tarn and down to the house.

He walked Terry out through the gate. She paused at the door of her muddy pickup. "I appreciate the personal tour. You must think I was being flippant up there, but I truly didn't know your mother and close friends were killed in the collapse. I'm sorry I brought it up."

Lorcas smiled briefly. "No problem. I know you didn't know."

Terry seemed to hesitate, but then she turned and climbed into the truck. She started the engine, then rolled down the window and waved Lorcas closer.

"Call me some time," she said, holding a slip of paper between her fingers. Lorcas took the paper, and Terry put the truck in gear and roared out onto the road.

Chapter Five

Lorcas woke in the middle of the night to rain splattering on the roof and a persistent drip somewhere in the house. He got up and wandered around for a few minutes, but he couldn't tell where it was coming from or where it was ending up. Finally he went back to bed, but the disruption of his sleep left him tossing and turning for the rest of the night.

He got up late and when he went downstairs there was a message on his answering machine. He usually used his cell phone, but he still had the old line in the house that had been there, with the same number, since his childhood. Few people used it anymore.

It was Carol. She'd decided to use his home phone for business, rather than his cell, for reasons known only to her. She had volunteered to help Lorcas with the disposal of his mother's belongings and the house itself. He'd accepted, since he had no idea how to go about such a thing and he didn't really want to deal with it. He'd been angry and incredulous at his mother's actions, but not enough to wish her demise. The horror of seeing her disappear over the edge during the slump remained, and he preferred not to have to comb through her personal stuff.

He dialed Carol's number on the old phone and she picked up right away.

"What is it?" Lorcas asked bluntly. He was grateful to her for helping with the house, but old feelings got in the way at times. Her sympathy and attention after Condra's death had had him swinging from nearly falling back into bed with her to grating his teeth in irritation.

"I've pulled aside a few pieces of furniture we didn't discuss," Carol said in a business-like tone. "There's a green-painted chest with glass inserts in the door, a kind of curio cabinet, which was in the living room by the door to the hall. You know which one I'm talking about?"

"Yes, that's been in my family since I can remember."

"Do you want me to sell it or do you want me to hang onto it for right now?"

Lorcas hesitated. "I guess hold onto it. I'll have to come get it at some point."

"A couple other things. There's a small wooden chest with metal straps and a box of books in a foreign language, both of which I found in one of the back bedroom closets."

"Hold onto both of those. I'll take a look and then deal with them myself."

"Alright, Lorcas, but I need to get them out of here pretty soon. I want to get the house professionally cleaned before we start showing it. When can you come get them?"

Lorcas hesitated. He didn't go to Lafayette any more than he could help. He usually picked up groceries in Seaside Heights or else Tondra had someone pick them up for him. As he stood trying to make a decision about when to take the drive, his eye fell on a slip of paper on the table near the phone. It was the phone number Terry Bell had given him.

"I'm not coming down to Lafayette any time soon, Carol, but I'll have a friend come over and grab that stuff and get it out of your way."

"Sounds good. I'll be there this morning at least, and maybe part of this afternoon. Your friend can call me and check that I'm here before coming over."

Lorcas hung up the phone and stood for a moment with his heart racing. It was a good excuse to call Terry. He wouldn't ask her to drive up today in the rain, but perhaps she could store the items until either he could get down there, or she could come up.

He pulled his cell phone out of his pocket and punched in the number written on the slip of paper, forsaking the house phone. Terry answered on the third ring.

"Hi, it's Lorcas Felken, the guy up at the castle," he told her.

"Of course! How are you doing?" she responded.

"Well, it's raining pretty hard up here. What's it like down there?"

"Huh. Not raining at all, just a little overcast. I can see clouds up to the north, though. Probably hanging over you and that castle."

"Listen, I was wondering if I could ask you a big favor."

"Sure," Terry said. "I owe you for pulling me out."

"No, you don't owe me, but this is something that would sure help me out. You remember I told you my mom was killed in that slump last year?"

"Yes." Terry's voice sounded more serious.

"Well, I'm in the process of clearing out her house and getting it ready to sell. The person who's taking care of it just called me and asked me about a couple of small things that I don't want to sell, that I'd like to keep. Family heirlooms. She needs them out of the house so she can show it, but I'm up here and the house is down in Lafayette. So I was wondering…"

"You want me to run over there and pick them up for you? I could store them at my parents' place."

"That would be great. I'll give you the address and Carol's phone number. Then I'll either get down there, or if you're coming up here again, maybe you could bring them up?"

"Well, I won't be biking up there if the weather stays like this, but we'll figure something out."

"Maybe if you come up I could show you a little more of the castle," Lorcas suggested. "If you're interested."

"I thought there wasn't any more of it," Terry said with the edge of a laugh in her voice.

"Not much," Lorcas said, "but there is a little I could probably show you."

"Deal, then," Terry said. "I'll go fetch the stuff and we'll set up a time for me to come up there. I have to work the next couple of days, though."

"No rush, maybe the weather will clear up," Lorcas said. "Thanks. This will help me out a lot."

"No problem," Terry replied.

Lorcas had begun pacing as he talked to Terry on the phone. Having told her he'd show her more of the castle, he now had to figure out some place safe to take her. They'd been entering the lower realms of the castle via a staircase that ran beneath the Keep, accessed from the interior of one of the walls which was built with a narrow hallway inside it, a kind of secret passageway. But that staircase led into the bowels of Rook's interior, haunted by the Bob-blob and who knew what else. As far as Lorcas could tell, there was no connection between that area and the old dungeon where the Knight had met his end and his mother had been briefly imprisoned. If so, it could be that the dungeon area was a kind of stand-alone cellar, a finite place he could show Terry that resembled a wine cellar or normal basement more than the miles of underground tunnels. But he needed to figure out how to get into it again.

As soon as he hit the 'end' button, Lorcas shoved the phone in his pocket and strode to the front door. He grabbed a jacket and pulled it on as he went out and around the side of the house.

He pounded on the door of Tomash's house but there was no answer. He peered through the high, thick glass windows to the side of the door, but couldn't see any movement. He gave up and followed the stone walkway down through the neighborhood, zipping his jacket as he went. The next most logical place to check was Tondra's and Alan's house, since Tomash's truck was still parked in his driveway.

The front part of Tondra's house had been converted to an office where she and Alan managed the affairs of the Fell Ken who were gathering around Rook. Lorcas walked in without knocking. Tomash was there, sitting next to Tondra and staring at a computer screen with a blank expression.

"Well, what brings you to this neck of the woods?" Alan joked, sitting back in his own chair behind another desk.

"Hey, Alan," Lorcas said. "I was looking for Tomash."

"Of course. Convenient," Tondra said with a glance at Tomash. "You set this up beforehand?"

"No, no, honest!" Tomash protested. "But hey, when the Lorecaster calls, ya gotta go!" He grinned and jumped up, leaving Tondra frowning at the computer, and grabbed a jacket from a hook by the door.

"What's up?" Tomash asked as they headed back towards Lorcas' house. "Not that I care. Anything to get me away from that office."

"I was thinking about the van."

Tomash glanced at him. "You want to go blob hunting? I'd have thought your last encounter would have put you off that for a while."

"I've recovered enough. The problem is, the van's parked down by the dungeon, or at least it was the last time I knew. But the door we brought it in through seems to be covered over now. That means the only way I know to get down there is through the well."

Tomash grimaced. "Yeah, that's not great. Plunging fifty feet through a muddy hole into a stone chamber is not my idea of fun, especially when we don't know how to get out again."

"So I figured we stick a ladder down in there," Lorcas said. "It'll be a tight fit, but it's better than nothing. We see if the van is down there and if it starts. If it does, we see if we can find another way into the dungeon that's attached to the rest of the underground."

"I'm game," Tomash said. "I've got a sectional ladder in my garage. I think it'll reach the bottom."

Tomash threw open the door of his garage and the two of them carried the ladder outside. Tomash shouldered it, sticking his arm between the rungs and balancing it front-to-back. Lorcas followed, taking care to avoid the end of the ladder. They paused at his house long enough for Lorcas to run inside and get a flashlight and the sword, in an old leather scabbard that had belonged to Tondra and been modified to fit. It had a long leather thong attached to it, and Lorcas swung it over his shoulder, positioning it out of the way across his back.

"Got your blob hunting gear?" he asked Tomash as they headed out.

"You bet," Tomash answered. He hooked a finger under his collar and pulled out a stout chain, upon which hung Lorcas' ring. Lorcas had given it to him after the collapse of the Keep, with the chain and an explanation, since it seemed a bit weird to be giving another guy a ring. It reminded Lorcas of his mother's fall into the dungeon, the beginning of her demise, and he'd never found it comfortable to wear anyway. But he knew it was an object of power, a connection to Rook, and it seemed logical to give it to his blob hunting buddy as protection. Tomash treated it as a good-luck token.

They took the stairs up to the chapel and the stone walkway around it to the King's Garden. Tomash set the ladder down next to the well.

After a few minutes of discussion about technique, Lorcas lifted the ladder and stuck the bottom in the well opening while Tomash slid the sections open. They lowered it section by section until the topmost rung of the top section was even with the lip of the well. At that point the bottom hit the floor of the dungeon, and the ladder stood supported by the stone.

"Well," Tomash said, standing back. "Who goes first?"

After a moment's hesitation, Lorcas shrugged and approached the well. He climbed over the stone rim and stood on a rung of the ladder. The ladder was slightly canted, rather than completely vertical. As Lorcas stepped down, he could feel the side of the well against his back. He squeezed closer to the ladder.

Six feet down, the stone ring of the well ended and the ladder stood in open space. Lorcas could feel it bend and bounce as he worked his way down in the dark. The impression of space around him and below him made the hairs stand up on the back of his neck.

Finally he stepped off the last rung and onto the stone floor. "I'm down," he shouted up. He flicked on the flashlight.

"No, turn that thing off," Tomash yelled down. "It's just in my eyes, and I don't really want to look at how much air I'm climbing through. I'll do it by feel."

Lorcas felt the ladder vibrate as Tomash stepped onto it and heard the ring of the metal rungs as he clambered down quickly.

Once they were both on the floor, Lorcas flicked on the flashlight again. He turned around, looking at the stone walls. When he'd first plunged into the dungeon the walls had been lumpy rock, but now they appeared finished and smooth. Oddly, on one wall was what appeared to be a window frame. The light bounced off glass in the back of the opening, but there was nothing but rock beyond.

The dungeon grate was in front of them, and beyond that the van, parked where Lorcas and Tomash had left it the year before. The door in the grate stood ajar, saving Lorcas from having to cough up the key to get it open.

Lorcas removed the scabbard from his shoulder. "Here, you take this," he said, offering it to Tomash. "I'll take the flashlight. And I'll drive."

Tomash took the sword. "Well, Tondra's the one who's good with a sword, not me," he said, pulling it from the scabbard. "I'm better with a bow."

"You're better than me with a sword," Lorcas admitted. He pulled the metal door all the way open and went through to the van. Although the passageway through which they'd driven the van had been tight, where the van was now parked allowed him to open the driver's side door. As he did so the interior lights came on in the cab, although the back of the van, behind a curtain, remained dark.

"Battery's good," Lorcas said.

Tomash squeezed past him, climbed into the cab, and clambered across to the passenger's seat, resting the sword between his legs. He settled in to the seat.

"Fire 'er up!" He grinned. "Let's see what we can do."

Lorcas stepped in and pulled the door shut. He fumbled for a minute and then found the key in the ignition. After a few sputters, the van started up.

"I wonder if we could die of carbon monoxide poisoning in here?" Tomash said, looking around.

"Doubt it," Lorcas said, putting the van in gear. "There's too much space. But we probably shouldn't sit here in our own exhaust for too long."

"Good idea," Tomash replied, "but where do we drive to?"

The headlights flickered and came on as Lorcas pulled the knob. There was a doorway ahead of them, but it was a person-sized door. To the right of that was a blank space of wall. He started forward slowly.

He was just about to hit the brakes when the wall wavered and disappeared, revealing a tunnel behind it. The van rolled through the narrow frame. As soon as they had passed through, the area behind them seemed to turn once again to stone.

The passageway widened a bit as they went. Lorcas was able to relax a little, without worrying about a minor moment of inattention resulting in the van bouncing off one of the walls.

"You know this area?" Tomash asked.

"Nope. Or I might, but it doesn't look familiar. But it keeps changing, so who knows? I'm figuring we should be under the Keep by now."

"Yep, check out this staircase to the left," Tomash said. "I think that's the one that branches off the stair we usually use. When we checked it out at first it seemed to dead end, you remember?"

"And we've ignored it ever since," Lorcas agreed. "Let's take a look."

Tomash followed him out of the van, and they climbed the staircase to where a second flight forked off to the left. A quick exploration showed that it led to the dungeon, through the door they'd seen. They returned and followed the stairs to a second intersection, where one could continue up or down along the flights of stairs they'd been accessing from the Keep.

"So we can get to the dungeon on foot from the Keep," Lorcas noted. They retraced their steps to the van and started off again. Lorcas tried to build a map in his mind to keep track of where they were at any given time, but it was difficult with no external reference points.

"These passageways are plenty wide enough," Tomash noted as they turned off into a downward-sloping corridor. "We're golden. The hunt is on!" He gripped the hilt of the sword and twisted it a bit, the tip biting into the floor.

"Do you think we'll be able to see the Bob-blob in the headlights?" he asked, turning to Lorcas. "I've never actually seen it, you know?"

Lorcas nodded. "Yeah, you were inside the Keep when me and Zumar were fighting it outside. I could see it. If it could be seen in daylight, I don't know why we wouldn't be able to see it with the headlights. It didn't seem to be afraid of light."

Tomash readjusted himself impatiently in the seat. "I guess when we see it we'll have to jump out and chase it down."

"Yeah, but we'll have a place to retreat if we need to," Lorcas said. "I feel better having the van."

"Wonder where it is?" Tomash muttered as Lorcas took turn after turn, working them down further and further into the depths of the castle. "Can you feel it when you're close to it?"

"Well, yeah," Lorcas admitted. "I feel kind of creepy when it's around."

"So how do you feel now?"

"Kind of creepy. But I've felt this way ever since we came down the ladder. I think this place is just sort of permeated with creepiness."

Tomash laughed. "So you can't do 'hot or cold' with it?"

"Guess not." Lorcas took another turn. The tunnel wound around a corner and suddenly became much narrower. Both of them rolled down their windows and pulled in the side-view mirrors. Lorcas continued slowly, but the passageway became skinnier. The walls closed in until they were inches from the doors on either side.

The van jerked and Lorcas lurched forward as it stalled. Tomash put a hand on the dashboard. "Damn!"

Lorcas cranked the key, but the ignition didn't catch. He hit the knob to turn off the headlights in case the battery was low, leaving them in an eerie glow from the dashboard illumination. The van still didn't start.

"Well, shit," Lorcas said, sitting back in his seat. He blew out his breath.

"Give it a few minutes. Maybe it's flooded," Tomash said. "Otherwise we'll have to hike out of here."

"I can't even get out my door," Lorcas said. "We'll have to go out through the back." He turned and yanked the curtain aside, squinting into the pitch-black interior of the utility van's back. He couldn't see a thing that way.

"And if we want to work on it, I don't know how we'll get to the engine," Tomash pointed out. "We won't be able to get past it to the front."

Lorcas shrugged. "We'll have to bring a ladder and crawl over the top or something. At least the tunnel's tall enough to do that."

Tomash sat still for a minute. "Too bad we didn't find it. I'm not sure driving around randomly is the way to do it. I wonder where it hangs out?"

"Yeah, it would be best to go get it where it lives, I agree. Maybe we can come up with some likely places for it to be. Zumar thinks it was created when Bob was buried in the cemetery, probably some accident of burial without Rook's direct involvement, which is why it's so distorted."

"That, and he was already dead by the time we got him up here," Tomash agreed. "There's a time limit on how long someone can be dead before their shadow can be rescued. That's why Perry and Delva couldn't be rescued even though they died right here in the Keep. We didn't get to their bodies for quite a while. But Bob was recently dead or maybe even just dying when Wyne and Marek brought him up here, and we got him in the ground pretty quick."

"Zumar thinks maybe the Knight's shadow was hanging around and merged with the Bob shadow, that they kind of gave each other something they each needed. After all, the Knight died here and was buried here pretty quick. His shadow might be more complete, but Korrin was kind of young. He might have needed some guidance or some purpose."

"Well, he seems to have gotten it," Tomash muttered.

"So if it is Bob who's controlling the thing, where would he hang out? Where would you hang out if you were a distorted dead Koen shadow?" Lorcas shuddered. A cold chill crept across his shoulders.

"Maybe in the graveyard," Tomash shrugged. "Or maybe somewhere else I felt comfortable. Or maybe somewhere my body was when it was living. The last place I knew as a living being."

"Yeah," Lorcas said stiffly, gripping the steering wheel. "And that place would be…"

"The back of the van!" Tomash hissed. He leapt up and swung around, wielding the sword, half-kneeling in the seat.

Lorcas threw his door open, but it slammed into the stone wall. He struggled to get out from under the steering wheel and turn around to face the back of the van.

A dark shape, darker than the gloom of the tunnels, came boiling out of the dark. It swarmed over Lorcas, enveloping him in pitch black. Blind and smothered, he crawled desperately without direction, falling between the seats. He felt like he was covered with a thick layer of foam or a giant marshmallow. His limbs moved slowly.

"Stab it, Tomash!" he screamed, and then coughed as black foam filled his mouth.

"I can't! I can't see you!" Tomash shouted. It sounded like he was a long way away. "I'm afraid I'll stab you!"

Lorcas felt his strength beginning to wane. He couldn't breathe. It was sucking his power out, his connection with Rook and the castle. He got his fingers into his mouth and pushed the foam aside desperately. "Stab me, then, for Christ's sake!" he screamed. "Just get the sword in it! Cut it! Do something!"

Suddenly the load of the black blob lifted a bit. Lorcas struggled forward into the open back of the van and managed to pull his face out from under the thing. He twisted and looked back just in time to see Tomash raise the sword over his head and bring it down. Lorcas closed his eyes and pulled himself into as small a ball as he could.

He opened his eyes a moment later. Tomash was rapidly slicing pieces off the blob. The pieces seemed to have lives of their own, scuttling around the van, crawling up the walls and seat backs. Lorcas reached down and shoved the rest of the blob off himself like a heavy quilt, then rolled forward and opened the van's back double door. Pieces of the blob spilled out and disappeared into the dark. The final, largest piece rolled off the back bumper.

Tomash stumbled over to Lorcas and knelt on the floor of the van, letting the sword down. "It's gone," he gasped.

"Yeah." Lorcas wiped his hands down his shirt sleeves, feeling for any part of it left behind. "But what about those pieces? Are they now going to be mini Bob-blobs running around?"

"Better than one big one, I guess," Tomash said.

"Unless they grow. Or merge back together or something," Lorcas said. "I figured the sword would just kill it. I didn't count on this."

"Maybe a word with Zumar would be wise," Tomash said. "What do you want to bet he knows more than he's let on?"

Lorcas grunted. "Even if he doesn't he's going to have to be warned. Let's get out of here. I'm done for today."

"I'm with you there," Tomash agreed. He stepped out of the back of the van and looked around cautiously. Lorcas found the flashlight between the seats and turned it on. He followed Tomash out and they walked rapidly and silently back up the tunnel to where it widened.

As they hiked higher in the castle, Lorcas began to relax a bit. The higher sections, those that had been under Rook's influence the longest, seemed safer and more controlled than the wild, barely co-opted lower levels. Finally they turned up the staircase to the Keep and emerged inside the north side wall. A small door led from there to the outside.

The rain felt good on Lorcas face as they retrieved the ladder from the well, slid the sections together, and made their way down the hill.

"I hope Rook doesn't mind a van stuck down in one of his pipes," Tomash said, "because I'm not thinking I'm going back in there any time soon to fix it."

Lorcas stopped suddenly. He could feel a rumbling under his feet. He turned and looked behind, back towards the castle. Tomash stopped as well.

The earth burst open off to the side of the Keep. A second later, the van was expelled. Lorcas and Tomash gaped as it flew out of the earth a good twenty feet into the air, and then described a steep arc to the ground. It crashed on the side of the hill, parts flying here and there. The two of them stood silently for a long moment, staring as the van settled into its new location and the rip in the earth rapidly resealed itself.

"Well, I guess Rook doesn't want the van stuck in one of his tunnels," Lorcas said finally.

"Like spitting out the shell of a sunflower seed," Tomash said in an awed tone.

"I hope no one's still looking for that thing," Lorcas noted.

"Probably are," Tomash said. "We'd better find some way to drag it off. It'll probably be okay there until we figure out what to do with it."

"What the hell?"

Tomash and Lorcas turned to find Zumar behind them, staring at the gently rocking wreck of the van.

"The van had a little accident," Tomash said.

"No kidding. I guess using it to run around the castle is out of the question now."

"Uh, yeah," Lorcas said. "About that. You'll be happy to know that we had a successful encounter with our friend the Bob-blob."

Zumar perked up. "Really? Is it dead, or gone, or whatever happens when you stab it?"

Tomash and Lorcas looked at each other. "Not exactly," Lorcas admitted. "But Tomash was able to chop it into little pieces."

"Little dead pieces?" Zumar asked suspiciously.

"Well, no. Just little pieces."

"You mean now there are hundreds of little Bob-blobs running around down there?" Zumar fumed.

"More like fifteen or twenty," Tomash admitted.

"I thought when one of us stabbed the Bob-blob with the sword, it would die or go away or something," Lorcas said accusingly.

Zumar shrugged. "So did I. But Korrin wielded the sword before you bled on it. Maybe it has some memory of him or something. Or maybe your blood isn't strong enough to make the sword deadly yet."

"Is it going to merge back together into one, or are all those little blobs going to keep running around now?" Lorcas asked.

"I have no idea. All I know is I want it gone completely so I don't have to look over my shoulder all the time and I can hunt for Raine and see if I can get her to come back. She won't with that thing running around." Zumar sighed.

"It's not very deadly the way it is," Lorcas assured him. "Unless it merges back into one big thing, I don't think we have to worry about the pieces. The most they could get hold of is a rat."

Zumar nodded. "Don't have to worry about the van, either."

Lorcas and Tomash turned again. Behind them, the van was slowly sinking into the earth as though it sat on quicksand.

"Damn," Tomash said as he watched. "This whole day calls for a beer."

"I agree," Lorcas said. "You got any?"

"Whole case," Tomash said. "Guess we should ask Tondra and Alan to come over to make up for me skating out of the paperwork again. They'll want to know what's going on in the castle, anyway, what with vans flying around in the air."

Lorcas looked towards the neighborhood, where a small knot of people had gathered, pointing towards the spot where the van had appeared. At least they were all Fell Ken, Lorcas thought. It would be hard to explain things to anyone who was not.

Chapter Six

Low clouds in the western sky gave the sunset an orange tint outside the big picture window. The light suffused the office with a warm glow.

"I don't want you to come here again," Jack said firmly as he turned away from the sunset. He leaned back in his chair and interlaced his fingers. "It's too dangerous. We'll meet in Lafayette or we'll meet at the marina and go out in the boat, but not here. Somebody could see you."

"Okay, boss," Terry said. "Whatever you say." She smiled and swiveled from side to side in her chair. "So you're planning on meeting me again in the future. Does this mean I pass your initiation?"

Jack raised his eyebrows. "What initiation is that?"

"Oh, come on. I've accomplished the first part of my mission! Surely I rate an apprenticeship in your secret society." She leaned forward suddenly and squinted one eye in fake suspicion.

"There is a secret society, isn't there? Like the Freemasons or the Knights Templar?"

"Neither of which are secret, since you're talking about them. But I guess you could consider the Knights of Earth Natural to be a secret society. One of the most secret on the face of the planet, in fact."

"Though of course you wouldn't know if there were societies more secret than yours," Terry pointed out. "What I don't understand is, if you truly believe this Rook thing is so dangerous to the entire Earth, why be all secret-squirrel and underground? Why haven't you enlisted the military or the CIA or something? Some powerful organization with the know-how and technology to really go after this thing?"

Jack sighed. "Because they think we're kooks. I don't blame them. Frankly, I think people who chase Bigfoot around and imagine alien spacecraft hovering over wheat fields leaving crop circles are kooky, so I understand. Even worse, it's been four hundred and fifty years since we had any evidence of Rook's existence at all. It's a bit hard to approach the CIA and tell them that four hundred and fifty years ago in eastern Europe, our distant ancestors believed there was some mysterious entity that was plotting to destroy the Earth, and we've only just found it again living in a rock on the Pacific Coast."

"Okay, I get your point," Terry mused. "But as far as alien spacecraft being kooky, Rook must have gotten here somehow, at some point in the past, if you don't think he's native to the Earth."

"Right," Jack said, "but we don't think he arrived in a spacecraft. He probably arrived inside a meteorite or fell out of a comet or something very similar. At some point he moved out of whatever that object was, probably because it was damaged, and got into the block of stone that was eventually chiseled down to become the cornerstone."

"So six hundred years ago he splashed down in Europe, crawled out of his meteorite into a chunk of granite, and conveniently got made into the cornerstone of a castle, under which a body was coincidentally buried to create his first Shadow, or Messenger, or whatever you call it?"

Jack spread his hands impatiently. "No. I mean, you've got the general gist of it, but if you think the castle under which Zumar was interred was the first, you're off by probably thousands of years. It was the last, now the second-to-last, in a long line of constructions. And there's plenty of evidence that Rook was much more developed at certain times in the past than he was in Zumar's castle. That one was a failure, in general. Paracel, the Lorecaster, or Sorcerer, or Wizard, whatever you want to call him, wasn't very smart. He didn't have the imagination to figure out what Rook was, or could be, and he didn't make a lot of progress. Though he did come up with some interesting symbols of power, some tools," Jack mused.

He got back on topic. "At other times in history Rook was almost certainly much, much more powerful, and only defeated by concerted efforts coupled with luck. Now, for the first time in thousands of years, he's got a good, solid entourage and a pliable Lorecaster, and he's on track to regain a great deal of that lost power."

Terry studied him seriously for a moment. "Well, I'd be very interested in learning about some of those past incarnations. Did the Knights leave any records of what he looked like or what he did? Most importantly, how did they defeat him then?"

"All in good time," Jack said with a quick smile. "This is history I'm not sure even the Lorecaster knows. Rook has a habit of only telling the Fell Ken what they need to know to function at the current time. He doesn't really get how humans understand their world. Of course there were keepers of this information among the Fell Ken just as there were among the Knights, but they are dead

75

now, at least the ones in this country: Lorcas' father, Perry, and Delva. I'm not sure how much was passed on to Tondra and Tomash. Their parents are in Europe, and I doubt they'll make the journey here, even if called. Certainly very little has been imparted to Lorcas, and I don't want him getting hold of any information we can continue to control. It might give us a little edge in the future if he's taken by surprise."

"And you don't trust me?" Terry asked. "You think I'll tell him, what, in the throes of passion?"

Jack re-crossed his legs uncomfortably. "Of course not. But things could happen. Let's just be on the safe side, here."

"Need-to-know basis and all that, huh?"

"For the time being. Now, do you have any more questions?"

"Yeah," Terry said. "I do have a couple. You didn't tell me that when you tried to blow up the castle thirteen people inside it died."

"I figured you read about it in the paper," Jack said casually. "It's not like the deaths weren't reported."

"No," Terry agreed, looking down for a minute. "But the news said it was the result of the explosion of old dynamite from mining days, too. They didn't report things like, oh, you know, how all those people were personal friends of Lorcas."

Jack studied her, but said nothing.

Terry sat forward in her chair. "Or how that slump was caused by the explosion and all the people who went over the cliff with those houses were members of the Knights of Earth Natural, your own organization."

"That was an accident, pure and simple," Jack said. "I had no idea the slump would happen. My goal was to collapse the Keep and stop the castle from being rebuilt. I realized that some people might die, but…"

"Some people might die?" Terry laughed shortly. "You could have blown it up in the middle of the night when no one was there! You did it during the coronation to create the maximum number of casualties you could!"

"Alright," Jack said resignedly. "I did it to scare the piss out of the Fell Ken, okay? To prove to them that we're serious and we're not going to let Rook get rebuilt, and to take out Perry and Delva. I was hoping we could end it all right there, that we could knock it back to a point where Rook wouldn't want to pick things up again, or couldn't, at least not for a while. I knew the entourage would be in there and I was hoping that if they were dead or injured, Rook wouldn't be able to continue. I killed them, and I did it on purpose."

Terry sat back slowly in her chair and stared at Jack for a long moment. "Well, okay then," she said calmly. "I want to know where things stand. I want to know who I'm working with and why things have to be the way they do. You told me things could get dangerous. Now I know how dangerous they could get."

"I told you, you can back out at any time," Jack reminded her.

Terry laughed again. "I'm not backing out. I don't want to end up like Lorcas' mother, either. But I have to admit, I'm curious. I want to see this thing, encounter this thing, whatever it is."

"I have no intention of you ever encountering Rook," Jack corrected. "I'm just looking for information. At some point you'll have done all you can do for us, and you'll bow out of this operation. I also don't want you to be complicit in whatever happens next."

"What if I want to be more involved?" Terry asked slowly. "You've been telling me how this thing is an alien presence bent on using our world for its own purposes. I'm not sure I believe you. Frankly, it sounds like a lot of bizarre superstitious garbage. Kooky, like you said. But let's say somewhere along the line I get convinced. At that point I'd believe that this thing has to be stopped in order to save the world, right?"

Jack shrugged. "That's what we believe."

"Then I'd be obligated to try and do something to stop it if I could, wouldn't I? I mean, once I believe, I've got two choices: fight it or join it. Assuming I wanted to fight it, I'd want to do anything I could, even if it was dangerous, to protect the future of the Earth."

"We'll cross that bridge when, and if, we get to it," Jack said. "Right now I just want a mole, someone inside, someone to tell me what things look like and what's going on."

Terry sat back and was silent. She studied her fingers, drumming on the arm of the chair. Jack wasn't sure if she was going to continue the harangue and inquisition, or if she was simply absorbing what he'd told her.

After a minute she looked up again. "So, I told you on the phone about my bike trip and that he took me into the top part of the castle afterward," she said in a calmer tone of voice.

"Yes," Jack said. "What's your initial impression?"

Terry considered. "The castle? It looks like a normal building with Gothic or medieval architecture. There are a few weird pieces of decor. But I got a feeling there's more to it than he showed me. We went into the little chapel with the stained glass and he took me up into the tower, but then he seemed to get nervous and we left pretty quick. The Keep, the bigger building, is pretty empty at this point."

"The tower's the Lorecaster's personal space," Jack nodded. "I'm surprised he took you up there at all. That means he trusts you at least a bit. What did he seem like, himself? You know none of the Knights can get close to him anymore, so it's hard to tell."

"Well, he seemed normal. He didn't seem nervous except when we went up in the tower. He helped me get the truck unstuck, flirted a little, showed me his drawings. He didn't seem dark or brooding or even all that depressed over the death of his friends and his mother, just kind of bitter but accepting."

"Rook is probably protecting him from being overwhelmed. That's one of the advantages of being in close contact with Rook: the ability to do things without having to suffer the consequences. How about any of the items I mentioned?"

Terry nodded. "I saw what I think is the staff you were looking for. It's leaning up against the wall just inside his door. I didn't get a chance to look at it closely to see if it comes apart. I didn't see the sword, the key, although I suppose that's small enough to be hidden anywhere, or the ring. He's definitely not wearing the ring like you thought he might be. I saw a silver goblet in the chapel and a few items on a desk in his house, but none of them were things you'd mentioned. I did see parts of a suit of armor, too, probably the one Korrin was wearing. There was a stand that could hold a sword next to them, but no sword."

"No ring, huh?" Jack mused. "Wonder what he did with it? He was seen wearing it last year. As for the key, there's some evidence that the Lorecaster keeps it on his person. It might be the most difficult to obtain, at least while the Lorecaster is alive. Did you see anybody else around the area? Anybody strange looking?"

"Some people around the houses but nobody up close. You wondering about anybody in particular?"

"Well, the Messenger. I guess you'd know if you'd seen him. I'm curious about how corporeal he is and what he looks like."

"You mean you don't know?"

Jack shook his head. "No, I've never seen Zumar. I know about him only through history and through what Condra told me. But it's not important at this point. See if you can't get back up there and just keep an eye out. Don't do anything that might tip anyone off or cause suspicion."

Terry stood up and fixed Jack with a strange expression. "How far do you want me to go to gain Lorcas' trust?"

Jack looked up sharply. "That's up to you. But be careful. I'm telling you, he's not to be underestimated. He's the perfect storm: malleable, depressive, introverted, isolated, and willing to let Rook use him as he needs to. And that means Rook's power can flow through him with very little interference. You don't want to be in the way when that happens."

"Right," Terry said, flipping her keys in her hand. "But I might want to be standing off to the side watching. Just one more question."

"Shoot," Jack said.

"You said a minute ago that it might be difficult to get the key, at least while the Lorecaster is alive. Are you currently, at this moment, making plans to kill him? I want the truth, and if I don't think it's the truth, I'm out of here."

Jack looked her in the eyes. "At this time, we are not making specific plans to kill the Lorecaster."

Terry searched his eyes with hers for a long minute, the keys dangling from one finger. Then she turned abruptly. "I'll be in touch. I'll let you know when I've got an appointment to get the truck fixed, too. You're still paying for it, right?"

"Of course. I said I would pay, and I will."

Jack watched as Terry strode out of the office and disappeared into the foyer. She was definitely a wild card, but he had no other brilliant ideas at the moment, and he needed information.

A moment after she left, Don slid quietly into the office.

"You hear everything?" Jack asked.

"Yeah. It sounds like she's off to a good start. But she already knows things about us, particularly you, that she shouldn't."

"If worse comes to worse, I'm sure you'll make the right decision," Jack said.

"I'm sure I will," Don replied. "Nice equivocation about the Lorecaster. What do you think about the key and the ring?"

"I suspect Lorcas has them on him at all times, visible or not. Leave that to Terry to discover. We'll figure out what to do about it when we know. The staff shouldn't be too hard to get, and the sword is large enough that there are only certain places it could be hidden."

"It's possible one of the other members of the entourage is holding some of the objects for safety's sake."

"I thought about that," Jack said. "Most likely it would be Tomash or Tondra. But once again, there's nothing we can do at this point but wait."

"It might be a good idea to set up some more formal watches," Don said. "We've been relying on reports from Knights when they happen to see one of the Fell Ken in town. I've got a few people who'd be willing to spend more time keeping an eye on things."

"Sounds like a good idea," Jack agreed. "I'd like to know where Tomash, Tondra, and Alan are at all times and what they're doing in and around the castle. And I'd like to know if anything's happening with Delva's house, which is still for sale, and with Perry's shop. There's no sale sign there and no sign of occupation, but it still feels creepy."

Don nodded. "I'll set it up, then."

"One more thing," Jack said. "There's an estate sale happening at Lorcas' mother's place this evening. I'm going to try to get there and see if there's anything important I can pick up. It's being run by Lorcas' old girlfriend. I'm going to try and talk to her a little bit as well, see if she can give us some insight into Lorcas."

"She doesn't know anything about us?"

"I doubt it. She's not Fell Ken, and she and Lorcas broke up just prior to him starting to build the castle. In fact, their break-up might have precipitated his openness to contact."

"She won't be of a lot of use if she's not seeing him regularly now."

"Probably not, but it will be interesting anyway. I'll close up the office. See you tomorrow."

Jack remained at his desk for a few minutes after Don left, gazing out the window, deep in thought. Finally he turned back to his desk and located his truck keys under a pile of paper. He needed to pick up something to eat before heading to Lafayette and the evening estate sale.

He shifted uncomfortably. He'd been feeling the odd prickling he got when one of the Fell Ken was around or when he was close to Rook. At first he thought that Terry's close contact with Lorcas might have caused it, but now she was gone and he still felt it. Probably Tomash or someone else from Rook's entourage eating dinner in some restaurant nearby or filling up with gasoline, he thought with a shrug.

The sun slid behind the curve of the ocean, leaving a lingering orange twilight. Jack closed the office and turned off the lights behind him. No one else was left, and he checked the front door to make sure it latched behind him. Then he headed for his truck in the lot.

As he walked, he squinted at the row of trees lining the office parking lot. There were several boulders there, and it seemed to him he could see a figure standing on one of the rocks in the deepening twilight. He took a few steps closer. The figure shifted a bit and Jack thought he heard someone clear his throat gently. Senses on high alert, he walked closer to the rock.

A young man stood on top of the boulder, clad in jeans, a white T-shirt, and leather shoes. He was grinning widely, his arms crossed, his hair tousled and yet not moving with the breeze. Jack stared at him, puzzled. It almost seemed that he could see the dark outline of the trees behind the young man, through his body. He felt a bolt of adrenalin.

"Who are you?" he hissed.

The young man laughed. "My name is Andelko Zumargaston Stolar," he announced with a slight accent, taking an exaggerated bow. "Pleased to meet you, Jack Bright."

"Zumar!" Jack took a step closer and stood at the base of the rock, studying the shadow with a mixture of curiosity and dread. Zumar was more corporeal than he had imagined. He had always thought of the Shadow as just that, a shadow. But this was an individual, almost solid in appearance, three-dimensional and able to converse as would anyone.

"But wait!" Jack frowned. "You can't be here! Everything I've been taught says the Messenger can't exist outside Rook's influence!"

"That's right!" Zumar replied. "I can't. What do you think of that?"

Jack paused. There was only one explanation, but he didn't want to admit it. It couldn't be true!

"Step off the rock," he growled, moving forward again, this time to the very base.

"Afraid not," Zumar said. "I see you've figured things out. Rook's extended his influence, alright. All the way to your doorstep. So I can sit here and stare at you, but I can't get off this rock yet. What do you think's next? I'll bet there's a good layer of bedrock under this cliff, probably runs right under your office, there. Maybe I'll pop up in your basement. Maybe Rook'll take your nice concrete building from right under your chair!"

Jack felt a wave of rage sweep through him. This swaggering little braggart, unreachable and yet so close, was torturing him with his failure to stop Rook's inexorable expansion.

"I wonder how you live with yourself, if it's living you do?" Jack snarled, leaning in. "You're an abomination, the risen dead, a zombie. Don't you realize what you are? Don't you ever think about all those people you left behind? Everyone you ever knew, dead long before you. Don't you ever think about your parents, your father and mother, your sisters and your older brother? How they never knew what happened to you, how they suffered and wondered all through their lives, never knowing you were stripped naked and tossed in a hole under a cornerstone after having been caught swindling the people your father had sent you to trade with? Must be hell, all that guilt you must feel."

Zumar flinched, but a moment later he smiled resolutely. "You're a nasty fellow, Jack Bright," he said. "I see you know quite a bit about my past. But you must feel a bit guilty yourself. After all, you're the one who dumped tons of rock on a bunch of innocent people, killed Condra, sent Bob and Korrin to their deaths, sent all those people who were doing your bidding sliding down to the bottom of the cliff, buried under tons of mud. I can't say I'll be sorry to see you go, when you do. And you will."

Jack put a foot up on the boulder and waved a hand through Zumar. He felt a strange sensation, but there was nothing to grab. "You can't touch me, you evil little bastard," he snorted.

"Not yet," Zumar agreed. "Soon, Jack Bright. Soon." As Jack watched, Zumar slowly sank out of sight and disappeared into the boulder.

Jack turned and strode to his truck angrily. He jumped in and slammed the door, and as he turned the key, he thought to wonder how long Zumar had been there and what he had seen. Terry's truck had been parked there for at least an hour, and she'd left only fifteen minutes before. That could, perhaps, be explained as a legal clerk delivering papers to his company office. Jack had dealt with her firm before, and indeed Kyle had first met her that way. But harder to explain was the fact that he had been at her truck himself in the parking lot, pawing through the items she had picked up to store for Lorcas. He'd been up in the truck bed, skimming through the books, opening the trunk, examining the curio cabinet for hidden compartments.

But the shadow had given no indication that he'd noticed anything or anyone else. Surely he would have flung that in Jack's face as well. Don had left minutes before, and he certainly would have called Jack if he'd seen Zumar. Jack had to assume that Zumar had arrived just minutes prior to their encounter. And it was likely that Zumar had no idea who Terry was anyway. He probably hadn't seen her during her brief encounter with Lorcas. Nevertheless, it increased his estimation of the danger Terry might be in. They could definitely not be seen together, and she'd have to stay completely away from Kyle as well.

He punched in the address of Lorcas' mother's house in Lafayette. He doubted there would be anything useful at the estate sale, but it was worth a good look. It would give him some kind of idea about how Lorcas might have grown up, some insight, perhaps, into his psyche. And a discussion with Carol, if he could broach the subject, would give him insight into Lorcas more recently. The only issue would be whether or not others of the Fell Ken were present at the sale, either to pick up items or to provide security. But he doubted they would be; Lorcas would have given away to the Fell Ken anything they wanted, and would have given special access to early buyers. And Terry had managed to confirm that Lorcas himself would not be there when she'd picked up the items earlier. So it would likely be safe enough, and it would take his mind off his encounter with Zumar.

Chapter Seven

Lorcas awoke with a start and lay for a moment in his bed, his heart pounding. A familiar, but lately uncommon, feeling pervaded his brain. He was being summoned by Rook, and urgently.

"I'm coming, I'm coming," he muttered as he swung his legs off the side of the bed. He sat for a moment, then headed for the bathroom where he splashed water on his face quickly. He pulled on a pair of jeans and a long-sleeved T-shirt and pulled his hair back into a ponytail as he jogged down the stairs. He wondered if he had time to make a cup of coffee.

As he came into the living room he saw Zumar plastered against the door to the spare bedroom. He was backed against the door as if holding it up, hands spread wide. Lorcas frowned when he noticed that Zumar appeared to be panting.

"Did you feel that?" Zumar hissed, eyes wide.

"You mean Rook? Yeah, that's why I got up," Lorcas said. "You alright?"

"What do you mean, am I alright? That summons nearly slammed my brain right out of my head! It still feels like someone's pounding on the inside of my skull!"

"I didn't notice anything that extreme," Lorcas said. "It's just been a while since he called us, maybe you forgot."

"I didn't forget," Zumar snapped. He cautiously left the safety of the door to follow Lorcas into the kitchen. "I've been in communication with Rook for hundreds of years, remember? You're acting like it always feels like this to you."

Lorcas shrugged as he slipped a coffee capsule into the machine. "You mean it doesn't to you?"

"No," Zumar admitted. "I've never felt Rook this way before. Never, not even back in the days of Paracel."

"Well, that's weird." Lorcas wasn't particularly alarmed, though. The summons didn't feel any stronger to him than Rook's presence had when he first flew his raven-shadow. Then, it had made him nauseated. Now it was old hat.

The coffee began pouring into the mug he'd placed under the spout. Just as he removed the mug, someone pounded on the front door. Not knocked: pounded. Lorcas jumped and sloshed some of the hot coffee on his hand. He slammed the mug down on the counter in irritation and slapped the lever to turn on the cold water in the sink. He ran his hand under the cold water for a moment then wiped it on his pants, picked up the mug, and started towards the entryway.

The door, which he usually didn't lock, burst open before he could reach it. Tomash rushed in, a fine mist from the low clouds outside settled on his hair and shirt.

"Did you feel that?" he demanded.

"Yes, I felt it," Lorcas replied, puzzled.

Tomash looked to be in the same state as Zumar: almost panicked, his eyes wide. His blond hair stuck out in all directions, as though he'd jumped out of bed and not bothered to clean up.

"Jesus, it nearly knocked me out of bed!" Tomash exclaimed.

Lorcas looked at the coffee mug in his hand, then handed it to Tomash. Tomash took it with shaking hands.

"Lorcas isn't feeling it," Zumar explained as Tomash sipped the remaining coffee and Lorcas added another capsule to the machine.

"No?" Tomash studied Lorcas. "Well, I've never felt anything like that in my life. You mean that's normal for you?"

"I guess," Lorcas said.

"Well, can you answer him? Tell him we're coming!" Tomash pleaded. "Then maybe he'll stop yammering."

"I already told him," Lorcas replied. The pressure in the back of his mind was obvious, but not serious. He wondered if Rook was sparing him somehow, or if he was used to it, or if, perhaps, he just dealt with it better than Tomash and Zumar.

"Rook, let off a bit," he muttered. "We'll be there."

"That's a little better." Tomash took a larger gulp of coffee.

"Better finish up," Lorcas said. "He's not known for patience. He woke us up because he wants us now."

"I don't think I really need to go," Zumar said with a note of panic. "There's no reason I can think of that I would need to..." He grimaced and doubled over, clawing futilely at the back of the couch for support. "Okay, okay! I'll be there!" He straightened cautiously and looked around as though he expected Rook himself to materialize in the living room.

Lorcas put his mug down on the counter, still a quarter full. "Come on, then. Let's go see what he wants."

Tomash and Zumar trailed behind him as he left the house and turned towards the castle in the morning fog. He wasn't used to either of them lagging behind; it seemed strange and uncomfortable. But Rook's summons wasn't unnerving him the way it seemed to be bothering the two of them. He chose the stairs near the oceanside wall and climbed quickly to the chapel.

It seemed obvious that they needed to get inside and probably down into the underground part of the castle, so Lorcas skirted the chapel and pulled open the side door to the Keep. The three of them crossed the echoing flagstone floor to the opposite side and Lorcas opened another door that looked as though it should lead to the outside, towards the cemetery. Instead, it led into the interior of the wall. To their left a set of stairs rose to the upper floors of the Keep. To their right was another door, currently unlocked but with a suspiciously-sized keyhole in its metal doorknob plate. Lorcas imagined that when the building was being used more regularly, he'd be able to lock and unlock it with his unpleasantly-stored key.

The door opened inward and revealed a short landing and another staircase, this one leading down. It was dark, but as they entered, the passageway became suffused with a gray light. Lorcas had no idea where the light came from. It always happened when he entered, and he assumed it was some favor of Rook's to allow the humans to navigate in the castle's gloomy underground.

Lorcas trotted down the stairs to the next landing. When he glanced over his shoulder, he saw that both Tomash and Zumar lingered near the top.

"Maybe I should go back and get the sword," Tomash said.

"Maybe not," Lorcas said impatiently. "We don't need it right now. Rook will protect us."

"He hasn't been," Zumar pointed out.

"Well, he hasn't been paying attention. He is now. Come on."

Lorcas turned to the next flight of stairs. He heard Tomash clattering down after him into the cool, damp interior.

Several flights down, the stairs ended at a hallway. The hall led generally south, as far as Lorcas could figure. To the right would be the passageway that led to the dungeon where Korrin Bright had died. Down another flight they would encounter the spiral stairs that would take them into the large, vaulted interior space. Many other passageways and staircases, from spiral steps to tunnels big enough for a van, branched off from there. Lorcas led them confidently down. He had no question which way to go. It was like a game of hot-and-cold: he could tell which way led him closer to Rook, or at least to where Rook wanted him to be.

Tomash and Zumar were now bunched up behind him. "I don't like this at all," Tomash muttered as they clattered down another tunnel. "It's making me nervous."

"Why? It's just Rook," Lorcas said. "I mean, yeah, he makes us all nervous, but there's nothing different about this."

"Oh, yes, there is," Tomash disputed. "I've never felt Rook this strong. He feels… malevolent."

"I agree," Zumar panted.

"I can't believe you've never felt anything like this," Lorcas said to Zumar. "Rook talks through you. You're the Messenger!"

"Maybe it's because I'm getting more solid," Zumar mused. "Maybe I couldn't feel him as strong when I was barely more than a shadow. Or maybe you're right. He hasn't called me lately and I might have forgot," Zumar admitted. "I'm really only necessary during the first part of things. Now that Rook has a Lorecaster and an entourage, why would he need a messenger?"

Lorcas glanced at him. "Well, I'm sure he has some purpose in mind for you."

"Yeah, that's what worries me," Zumar muttered.

Lorcas concentrated on where he was going, occasionally pausing at one intersection or another to make a choice. They were going deeper into the earth, gradually winding down. The tunnels were now rough-hewn rather than smooth-walled like the ones closer to the surface. The air was cool, damp, and earthy-smelling. Every once in a while they heard skittering sounds and stray bumps and bangs down one passage or another. There was just enough light for them to see their way, the gray illumination emanating from some mysterious source, perhaps the walls themselves. Sometimes they passed large, Gothic-arched openings with the glitter of glass in the back, like the one Lorcas had fallen into.

He became aware, slowly, that there was another sound besides the hard nails of small creatures on stone. It was like a distant wind or the surge of the tide. At first he assumed it was just that: the waves rushing in to the base of the cliff and receding. They certainly must be far enough down into the earth to be level with the ocean by now.

But as they continued he became less sure. The air stirred around them as though a breeze moved through the tunnels, one way and then another. The surging sound became louder, and Lorcas remembered, uncomfortably, the terrifying sounds he'd heard before escaping through the barred window. This time, though, he swallowed his fear and continued, urged on by Rook's call.

Eventually they entered what appeared to be a large chamber, with a number of doors leading out one way and another and a ceiling that receded into the dark recesses above. The back corner was darker than anywhere else in the room, and Lorcas squinted, trying to determine if there was, in fact, an alcove of some type there. The surging wind was the loudest it had been. As Lorcas stared across the chamber, with Zumar and Tomash crushed up behind him, a dim light seemed to ignite and grow brighter. It was oblong and yellow, with a dark slit in the center. There was nothing else to be seen.

A sudden rumble of rock made Lorcas jump. He spun around to see all the passages leading out of the chamber slammed shut with stone doors. They, or at least he and Tomash, were trapped in the chamber.

Lorcas turned back to the glowing eye, his heart pounding in his chest.

"Are you prepared?" Rook hissed, his voice overpowering the chamber and echoing off the rock. Lorcas took an involuntary step backwards: Rook was speaking aloud, not whispering in his brain.

"Prepared for what?" he managed to ask.

His mouth felt dry; whatever fear Tomash and Zumar had felt earlier seemed to be catching up with him. He glanced behind. Tomash and Zumar were plastered against the wall of the chamber.

"For that which is next," Rook replied. "It is time. Congratulations. It has been long since any came this far, Lorecaster."

"Um, thanks," Lorcas stammered. "What happens now?"

"Choices must be made. Some will rise, and some will fall. For some, the time has not yet come. For others, it is past."

"Okay," Lorcas said resolutely. Rook had a tendency to speak in riddles, and he was used to it by now. "What does this mean for us?"

Rook paused, and the wind blew through Lorcas' hair. "Your kind wish concrete explanations for everything. This I cannot give. I do not think that way, nor do I experience the world as you do. In this stage, let us say, my connection to your physical world will increase and change. This must be, in order for me to continue my mission and fulfill my purpose."

"Well, that makes sense," Lorcas agreed. "I may not be totally clear on what your mission actually is, but I can see advantages to being more physical."

"Yes. And in order to proceed, my connection to you must also increase. It is through you I now learn about the world and manipulate it as I desire. You will allow me to flow through you. You are ready. You are open to me, as you have always been. You have been faithful and done as I asked. But our connection must become even stronger. Even now, it moves in that direction. And it will mean many changes for you and for those around you."

"What kind of changes?" Lorcas glanced again at Zumar and Tomash, who were now flanking him on either side, staring curiously at the yellow eye.

Without warning, a dark mist, insubstantial but darker than the darkest corners of the chamber, curled out of the alcove, shot forward, and halted a foot from Zumar's face. Zumar pressed back against the wall. He did not seem to be able to move through the stone, otherwise he certainly would have fled.

The mist, like a tentacle, slid slowly around Zumar's neck. Zumar clawed at it, choking, but his hands could not connect with it.

"This one!" Rook hissed like a broken steam main. "His time is over. As you become more important to me, Lorecaster, he becomes less so. I have preserved his form for many times the normal life of your kind, and he has served me well. But soon he will dissipate, like the smoke of your fires. I will use his life force, such as there is left, to strengthen my connection with your world. He will go to the nothing into which your kind dissolves."

"No!" Lorcas shouted in shock, his voice echoing off the walls. "You can't do that! It's not fair! Zumar's been trapped in here for hundreds of years. He was young when he died. He never had a chance to live a normal life. You've used him for years to do your bidding. Now you'd simply abandon him, or worse?"

The black tentacle loosened and uncurled from Zumar's neck. It withdrew a short distance, leaving Zumar on his knees on the rocky floor. "You wish to spare the Messenger, Lorecaster? Such can be done, if you will it. I can grant him more, even, than I have given him as of yet. But this is a great sacrifice on my part. Without his final life force, I cannot take the next step. If you wish to spare him, I will require a sacrifice of equal value from you."

"Alright! Alright, then! What kind of sacrifice?" Lorcas demanded suspiciously.

"The sacrifice your people have always made, and the one I require," Rook replied. "The sacrifice of binding, of supplication, of acknowledgment, of surrender to the universal power. The sacrifice of a life, to be given to me freely and of your own will, Lorecaster."

"What, you mean like a goat or something?" Tomash asked with a nervous laugh.

"No," Rook whispered, drawing the response out long. "I mean a human life."

Tomash blanched and shrank back as though he regretted having drawn attention to himself. Zumar attempted unsuccessfully to exit through a crack between one of the stone doors and the wall.

Rook continued. "Is it not traditional in your culture? The sacrifice proves unquestioning commitment to the cause and cements the bond between the members of the group. It decreases the chances of betrayal. And it is necessary to allow me to move beyond my confines, without which I cannot continue. So, Lorecaster, who will it be?"

"What do you mean?" Lorcas whispered.

"Which will it be? You have refused the Messenger to me. But what a sacrifice to give me the King!" The mist darted forward again and caressed Tomash's face. "This one, then, is your choice? You are right: he doesn't seem to do much. Although he was cultivated to take the role of the King, to lead your people through the changing times, and it would be a shame to waste that, his sister could take the lead. So be it."

The mist curled around Tomash's neck, and he fell to one knee. Lorcas jumped forward, grasping at the tentacle, but it was insubstantial in his hands.

"What are you doing? Stop!"

Once again, the tentacle relaxed. "You have refused me the Messenger. Yet you must provide me with an equal sacrifice. You must give it to me freely and of your own choice, and it must be a life meaningful to you. Therefore, I allow you to choose. Which will it be?"

"Are you suggesting that I choose whether or not to sacrifice Tomash or Zumar to you?" Lorcas asked incredulously.

"This is your choice, and the reason I called you here today," Rook said. "I intended to take the Messenger, but you have refused me. I have identified a suitable substitute, yet you refuse me him as well. Yet I must have one. You alone have the power of choice, Lorecaster, as you have the power I have given you since childhood, a power that will eventually change your world. Remember what is promised to you!"

Lorcas stared into the eye. "What if I change my mind? What if I decide I don't really want this power? I'm not that big on power, anyway," he said desperately.

Rook hissed low under his breath. "Think. You, as we change this world, will have the ability to do what you want to do with humanity. If you desire it, hunger will be eradicated. If you desire it, war will be forgotten. If you desire it, inequality will disappear. This we can do as we move through the Earth. Would it not be selfish to refuse this? Would it not be selfish to retreat from your responsibility to the rest of your kind? It is only you who can save them in the future. Otherwise they will die in droves. What is one life in comparison?"

The pupil of the eye narrowed for a second, then expanded again. "Do you find it difficult to choose, Lorecaster?" Rook continued. "One life for the rest of your kind?"

"What about all those people we've given you before?" Lorcas demanded. "Korrin, the Knight, and Bob, who we buried in the cemetery? What about Raine? What about my mother? What about Perry and Delva?"

The black mist hovered before Lorcas. "None are sufficient. None were sacrificed to me. None were given willingly to me, to allow me to use them to move into your world. Nor was it the right time. They will not do."

"Well, neither of these guys will do either," Lorcas said decisively. "Much as I like the idea of being responsible for creating world peace, I can't give you either of my friends. If that makes me unsuitable, then I'll go. You can find another Lorecaster."

"Is that what you think?" Rook hissed. "Without me you are nothing. You have been nothing all of your life. Your only true purpose is as a conduit for me. This you must accept; it is your life, your duty, to save the rest of humanity by helping to guide them through the times to come. Without you, my power will tear the Earth apart, and I will pay no heed to those who fall before me. With you, I temper my strength. Do you think it is so easy to forsake this life? Without me, what will you be?"

Lorcas gasped. He felt as if something had been ripped from his mind. The pain, both physical and mental, was like the pain of grief. He blinked as Zumar faded from his sight and disappeared. The mist that was Rook and the yellow eye were both gone. He stood in some dank cellar with dirty floors. Tomash, with the sweat of panic on his upper lip, stared at him through the gloom. An empty feeling suffused Lorcas' brain, as though everything and everyone he'd ever known had suddenly disappeared from the world. It was almost intolerable. His mind flashed to the picture of his mother standing on the seaside cliff, the earth opening beneath her, plunging to the bottom amid tons of mud, trees, and boulders. The grief of his loss speared him like a knife, a grief he had never truly felt. Perry and Delva's faces flashed in front of him and he felt the pain of their deaths as well. The horror of finding Raine dead in the mist, the loss of his father, all of these seemed fresh and sharp. He realized that Rook had been protecting him, dulling the edge of his pain.

A moment later Rook came rushing back into his brain. Lorcas sucked in a deep breath. Zumar reappeared, the black mist hovered before him.

"Do you think you would prefer to live without knowing all that you know now? Without ever seeing or interacting with those you've come to call your family?" Rook demanded. "You would never see Zumar again, nor be aware of his presence. The deaths of those you have known and cared for would seem without reason. You see how it would be. I will grant it if you desire it."

Lorcas shook his head. "That's not what I want. But I can't sacrifice either of my friends either," he whispered. He wondered if he had the strength to deny Rook this request. Confusion and panic welled up within him.

The black mist sucked back into the dark alcove, and the eye slowly faded from view. Only Rook's voice remained. "You refuse to sacrifice these members of the Fell Ken? You would suffer for the sake of those of the entourage?"

Lorcas looked up. "Yes, if that's what it means."

There was a long pause. "That is well," Rook said finally. "Your loyalty is noted. Is it not better to protect your friends and family than to throw them to the fire?"

Lorcas nodded, unsure.

"So be it. But you must bring me some other. It must be someone who is meaningful to you. Bring this one to me and I will spare these two and the others of the entourage. It should not be difficult. As you have noted, several others lie buried within my influence. You have done it before."

"Okay," Lorcas said uncertainly. His agreement with this request could at least buy time to get them out of there. "I'll do it, if you'll promise not to touch Zumar or Tomash."

"You must do it, one way or another. Do not think you wield the power to force my hand. Nevertheless, I will make you this promise and bind you to yours. And I will give you a sign of my promise, a sign that I give life as well as take it."

Rook paused for a long moment, the wind of his breath rushing in and out slowly. "I give you this gift," he said. "The being you call Raine exists. Her spirit has not departed. I will grant her

98

increased substance, as I will grant it to the Messenger. Is this well with you, Lorecaster?"

Lorcas nodded. "Yes."

"Go now, and return with your chosen sacrifice. Do not take too much time."

The stone doors shot open, and Lorcas, Tomash, and Zumar scrambled into the passageway and up through the tunnels towards the light and air above. None of them spoke until they had gained the relative safety of the Keep. There all three of them paused, gasping for air.

Zumar leaned over, hands on knees. "I'm not used to being out of breath," he said with an abrupt laugh. Lorcas laughed too, more a release of stress than an expression of humor.

"Are you feeling more corporeal?" he asked.

Zumar nodded and glanced up at him. "Down there I couldn't go through the walls. I was just as trapped as you were. I thought that was it for me. The ungrateful wretch, after all I've done for him!"

"You're not kidding!" Tomash chimed in. "What the heck was going on down there? He'd kill off members of his entourage because he thinks he's some kind of god requiring sacrifice?"

"Some might call him a god," Zumar noted grimly. "In ages past he would certainly have been identified as one, or as a demon. And he does hold the power of life and death and the fate of the world in his hands, or whatever he's got in place of hands."

Lorcas studied the flagstone floor. "He wanted to make a few things clear to me, I think. He wanted me to know what my life would be like without him. He wanted me to know what I could expect to accomplish with him: the end of war, world peace, no starvation, no inequality, etcetera. He wanted me to understand that he holds the reins, that he grants these powers and he can take them away. And he wanted me to know that if I don't cooperate with him, I'll be responsible for whatever happens to the people of the Earth when he rises to his full power, whatever and whenever that is. And if I do cooperate with him, I'll be the hero."

He looked from Tomash to Zumar. "Something else, too. He allowed me to play the hero in front of you, to step in and save your lives. He wanted to build me up, to show both of you the kind of power I'm going to hold. I'm not sure why he chose this time to make this little demonstration, but maybe it's true that he's ready to move to a new stage. What do you think, Zumar?"

"This is all new to me," Zumar said, straightening. "If he didn't mean to eat me alive, to turn me into the smoke of our fires, as he said, he was making a convincing show of it down there. Although he might have been feeding some terror into my mind. I'm not sure. Remember I've only been around since the castle in which Paracel was Lorecaster, and Paracel really wasn't that powerful. He didn't understand what was going on like you do. That was maybe my mistake or Rook's mistake. But we never made it this far."

"So you don't know what the next stage is going to be?" Lorcas asked.

"No."

Tomash frowned. "Do you know if he really needs a sacrifice or if this is all just some elaborate test?"

"I don't know that either," Zumar said. "It's possible he really does need a human life, the way you might need food or a supplement to your food once in a while. Like a vitamin. I wouldn't blow this off, Lorcas. You've got to find him someone."

"And it's got to be someone I care about in some way," Lorcas said thoughtfully. He thought about Carol, but he doubted she'd fit the bill, and besides, he didn't think he could really offer her up as a sacrifice, however cynical he felt about their past relationship. It was too gruesome to contemplate: purposefully choosing a human being to die, or whatever would happen if it was not death, and leading that person to it. He wasn't sure what he was going to do.

"Did Rook withdraw from you down there?" Tomash asked, cutting into his thoughts.

"Yeah," Lorcas said. "I never really realized how much a part of my mind he is and how much he's protecting me from stuff I'd otherwise have to deal with. He's right, though: what would I do if I wasn't part of this? This is the most connected I've ever felt to any group of people, any cause, any purpose. Without it, without him, I'd feel pretty alone. I don't know that I could deal with it. After all, this is what I was made for, so to speak. This is the thing in life I'm really good at, you know? And drawing fish."

"If Rook withdrew from me, I'd die," Zumar said with a shudder. "I can't imagine what it would be like not to be connected to him. It's not just him, it's all of you, like a network. I can feel everyone here at least a little bit. Not having that would drive me crazy."

The crazy thing, Lorcas thought, was that he had been led to this: that slowly he'd become so intertwined with the Fell Ken and with Rook that he'd actually consider sacrificing a human being as some sort of 'vitamin', as Zumar put it. But he couldn't think about it now; the relief of temporary reprieve was still uppermost in his mind.

Outside the Keep it was still misty, almost coalescing into rain. They hurried down the slope to Lorcas' house.

"I think it's time for some wine," Lorcas said, pulling one of Marek's bottles across the counter.

Zumar shuddered. "You really want to be more connected to Rook right now?"

"Uh, no." Lorcas shoved the bottle back. "How about some more coffee?"

Tomash nodded and collapsed onto the couch. "I wonder what Rook meant about Raine?" he mused.

"I dunno," Zumar said, "but I'm going to go check once I can get myself to go back in the castle. Maybe she'll show up here."

"I wonder if I should tell Tondra about all this," Tomash sighed.

Both Lorcas and Zumar shook their heads. "Leave it be," Lorcas said. "If he'd wanted Tondra, he'd have called for her. There's no need for anyone but us three to know what Rook's requested. It would be pretty hard to explain to anyone else, actually."

Tomash raised his coffee mug in Lorcas' direction. "Here's to world peace, equality, and an end to hunger," he said. "You could get started on that any time, now."

"About the only hunger I can end is my own," Lorcas said. "I guess that'll have to do for now."

Chapter Eight

The next day Terry called to set up a time to bring the items from Condra's house by. Lorcas suggested she bring it up in the morning the following day, when she was off work, so they'd have time to look around the area if she wanted.

She arrived about eight-thirty. Lorcas had been up for a couple hours, waiting nervously for her. He unloaded the cabinet from her truck carefully, noting that Carol had wrapped it in a mover's blanket to protect it. He'd have to thank her for that. The smaller objects he placed in the library where he could examine them later. The books might be valuable, if he could read them.

He pulled the door of the library shut and went back outside. Terry was unloading a few personal items. He'd been thinking about the upcoming day. One thing he really didn't want to do was go back into the castle after the events of the previous week. He wasn't in any mood to discuss his progress on the sacrifice front with Rook, and he wasn't sure that Rook wouldn't jump to conclusions if he brought Terry inside.

"Hey, it's a nice day for once," he said. "Why don't we skip the castle and take my UTV up into the state forest? There are a bunch of other roads up there that you didn't get to see on your bike. One goes right along the coast and there's usually not anyone there."

"That sounds interesting," Terry said. "It's okay to take the UTV up in there?"

"On the roads and on certain designated routes," Lorcas replied. "Don't worry, I won't go crashing off into the forest. I have a lot of respect for these woods. I grew up around here same as you did."

Terry gave him a sidelong glance, and Lorcas wondered if he'd said something wrong, but he couldn't figure out what. But she only said, "Come on, then, let's go," and turned towards the garage.

Lorcas pulled up the garage door. He'd slotted the UTV in there after a little reorganization. It was pretty tight, with the building materials and various larger pieces his dad had collected stowed in there.

"Nice forklift," Terry said.

"You saw it before when you stuck your bike in here, didn't you?" Lorcas asked. He climbed into the UTV and turned the key.

"I did." She took a few steps to the side to let Lorcas pull the UTV out. She bent slightly sideways, squinting into the interior of the garage. "What are you planning to do with the God-awful statue back in the corner?"

"That's a family heirloom, very important. Going to mount it right outside my front door someday," Lorcas said seriously.

Terry eyed him. "Sorry."

Lorcas grinned. "Joking. I bought it to get the stone block it was mounted on. I wanted to add it to the castle's foundation layer. Gives it some authenticity, you know?"

"And now you're stuck with the statue," Terry noted. "You might be able to sell it. People go for stuff like that."

"Moldy fake Greek half-naked woman? No accounting for taste." Lorcas pulled the UTV close to the front door and ducked inside to grab a day pack he'd stashed in the entryway. "Got water and some snacks."

He slung it into the back and slid in behind the wheel. Terry put her sweatshirt underneath the back seat, in the storage container.

They trundled down the road to the main gate. Once through the gate, they retraced their path along the outside of the wall, turned out of the neighborhood, and turned left at the T intersection, taking the same route Terry had taken in her truck.

"It's funny," Terry said as they bumped up the two-track past the barred window in the hillside, the view of which Lorcas tried to block with his body. "It's like we've gone out of one micro-climate and into another. It seems to be raining all the time where you live, but now we're in an area where it's pretty dry."

"There's been a statewide drought," Lorcas pointed out. He looked around at the forest and the litter beneath the trees. It did, indeed, look quite dry. He'd heard that the fire danger was high, and the news featured wildfires throughout the west on a nightly basis.

"Except at your place," Terry mused. "I wonder what feature of the landscape causes it to be wetter there? Maybe it's the castle itself."

"I doubt it," Lorcas said quickly, although the idea had occurred to him. "It was wetter there when I was a kid, and we just started building the castle two years ago. You can tell it's been that way for years: the vegetation's different there."

Terry hopped out to open the wire gate at the boundary of the state park. Beyond that, Lorcas took the left-hand fork in the road, rather than the one that led to where Terry had gotten stuck. The two-track soon narrowed, and they encountered another fence and a narrower gate, with a series of signs indicating which activities could take place behind it. Full-sized vehicles were prohibited but all-terrain and off-road vehicles were allowed, as long as they stayed on the track.

The route, narrower and steeper now, wound through the forest, in and out of patches of sunlight. Lorcas slowed to negotiate a rocky step. A minute later they came out of the forest and onto the ledge of the coastal cliff. The bright sun reflected off the ocean hundreds of feet below. The route continued to the right, but Lorcas stopped and shut down the UTV.

They climbed out and took a short walk to the rim. A solitary fir clung to the rock, gnarled and bent by exposure to wind and weather. The roar of the ocean sounded distant and muffled.

"Nice," Terry said. She spent a long minute staring down at the sea. "Did you used to come here as a kid?"

Lorcas laughed. "Well, my dad did drag me up here a few times, but unwillingly. I didn't really appreciate it. I wanted to play video games and draw and I resented being taken away from my friends every summer. Now, though, I see it real differently. I'm very lucky to have this in my back yard."

Terry nodded. "I see it as a national treasure, this fantastic coastline, the way the ocean has created the cliffs over hundreds of thousands of years. I like thinking about the deep history of this place, how erosion worked on the landscape over time, how it still works the same way today, and how it'll keep working the same way far into the future. It's a kind of consistency that's comforting to me, the march of time, the progression of the natural world, the feeling that things will continue the same even after I'm gone." She paused, then turned suddenly to Lorcas. "How about you?"

"Well, I don't think I could have said it better myself," Lorcas replied. "I kind of feel like a guardian, with my own property right on the southern boundary." In fact, he realized, while he might appreciate the consistency of erosion and the deep time evident on the coastline, he was working to change the Earth forever in a drastic way. He felt a touch of guilt, but then, things always changed, nothing stayed the same, and perhaps Rook could be seen as another step in the evolution of the Earth. He certainly wasn't going to gainsay Terry, or even begin to describe Rook and Rook's plans. He knew how bizarre and unbelievable it would sound. He, himself, had been introduced to it slowly, in fits and starts, even after having been groomed to understand it throughout his life.

"Come on," he said, "this trail runs up the coast for a long way. There are lots of good viewpoints and they get better as we head north."

Terry followed him back to the UTV and they resumed their journey, winding slowly in and out of the edge of the forest. The trail was rocky, often no more than a cleared area between the trees. He had to concentrate on what he was doing, where he was putting the tires. He was proud of how well he'd learned to drive the thing during the last year. He was feeling pretty confident.

There were several more undeveloped overlooks, and then they intersected an improved road leading to a fenced cliff with several seats at strategic locations in the shade of the trees. Lorcas turned off the UTV and grabbed his pack from the back.

"Lunch time," he said. He chose a secluded bench to the south of the overlook, set down the pack as a place-holder, and followed Terry out to the edge, where the fence allowed them to lean over and look down at the waves crashing against the rocks. Lorcas looked south along the coastline, but the castle was not visible from that point. To the north the cliffs broke up and it was possible to access the coast itself from elsewhere in the forest. He could see small figures on the sand in a sheltered cove.

He glanced over at Terry. She didn't seem to have a fear of heights: she was leaning over the metal barricade, which hit her a little above waist height, her hands on the top rail, studying the tide below. Lorcas studied her instead. She was wearing a ball cap that pinned down her dark-blonde hair, but the strands below the hat blew around in the breeze, whipping into her face. She was wearing a pair of sport shades rather than the big ones he'd seen her wear before, and a long-sleeved rash-guard style shirt. He had a feeling she could probably hike him into the ground.

"You up for a hike after we eat?" Terry asked, echoing his thoughts. "I'd like to go a little further up the coast, but we can't bring the UTV any further, right?"

"Correct. We can hike if you want." Lorcas returned to the bench and unpacked what he'd brought: several different types of cheese, salami, breads, and crackers, not the grocery store kind but stuff he'd bought with Marek's help at the Wyne Shoppe, where they stocked top-of-the-line wine-related snacks. He'd also brought some sparkling juice to wash it down.

"Nice!" Terry said appreciatively as he spread things out on the bench between them, together with a small cutting board and knife, some napkins, and a couple of plastic cups. "This is the good stuff."

"Yeah, I'm kind of picky." Lorcas shrugged. He wasn't, really, but he'd learned to appreciate some of the higher-end brands while he was dating Carol, so he had some background knowledge. It couldn't hurt to offer good food.

The silence was nice after the chop of the UTV engine, and they ate with few words exchanged. A jay showed up and hopped around on the forest floor, angling for crumbs.

"Stellar's Jay," Lorcas identified. "Pests, but pretty."

"You know your birds?" Terry asked as the black-crested jay bounced around, cocking its head.

"Not so much, just the ones around my house," Lorcas admitted. "I'm better with fish and reptiles. Kind of partial to ravens, though," he added thoughtfully.

"Right, *Corvus corax*, the common raven," Terry said, startling Lorcas with her use of the scientific name. "Strong fliers, intelligent, curious, can survive in pretty much any habitat. I'm surprised more people don't like them. They're one of my favorites as well. People just think of Edgar Allen Poe when they hear 'raven', but there's much more to them."

"Absolutely!" Lorcas said enthusiastically, happy to find something they agreed on. "I've thought about trying to draw one."

Terry turned to look at him quickly. "Would you draw me one? Maybe flying or sitting with a backdrop of the cliffs and the forest?"

"I can try," Lorcas said. "I have some experience drawing rocks, anyway."

He packed up the lunch and stuck the pack under the back seat of the UTV to conceal it from passers-by while they hiked. They followed a well-developed trail north from the overlook along the cliff's edge to the point where it branched to go into a campground or down to the beach they'd seen. There was another overlook there that allowed them to scramble down a short way on the rocks to a secluded spot. Lorcas led the way. They paused in the shade of the cliff and Terry leaned back against the rock.

"This has been really nice, Lorcas. I've enjoyed every minute," she said.

"Yeah?" Lorcas had been thinking it was pretty nice, himself. He propped himself on one elbow just next to her. He could feel his heart beating in his chest, against the key. He took a step and turned in to her, leaning in for their first kiss.

A few minutes later they heard kids climbing down towards them. They scrambled back up to the overlook and retraced their steps to the UTV. It was late afternoon by the time they rounded Rook's hill and entered the neighborhood.

"Is there a name for this hill?" Terry asked. "What are you going to call the castle when everything's finished? You have to call it something, right?"

"We haven't decided yet. Maybe we'll hold a contest or something. You got any ideas?"

"I'll think about it. Maybe something to do with a raven, Raven Ridge or Corax Castle or something."

Lorcas glanced at her, thinking how appropriate that would be. He pulled in through the main gate and stopped the UTV in front of the garage. He turned off the engine and sat for a minute, waiting for Terry to gather her things.

"Can I take you out for dinner?" he asked.

Terry grinned. "I'd rather just stay here. Have you got anything we could cook up?"

Lorcas raised his eyebrows. "I'm sure we could stick something together. I've got wine."

"Heck, we could just eat more of that cheese you brought for lunch," Terry said as she got out of the UTV. "You could start drawing that raven for me, sketch it out, maybe."

"I could do that." Lorcas opened the door for her and followed her in. She hung her jacket up on one of the hooks in the entryway before heading for the living room. There, she plopped on the couch and unlaced her shoes.

"You mind if I take my shoes off? They're kind of new and they're hurting my feet."

"Go ahead. I've got extra towels and stuff if you'd like to jump in the shower. You want a drink?"

"A shower would be great," Terry said, jumping up. "Then I'll be ready for a glass of wine."

Lorcas was glad that things were fairly clean and organized upstairs. While Terry was in the shower he tidied his bedroom, just in case. He took a shower and changed clothes after she was out, and came downstairs to find her relaxing with a glass of Marek's wine. He wondered briefly how it would affect someone who wasn't Fell Ken, but he doubted it would do her harm. He poured a glass for himself, brought in the leftovers from lunch, and sat down next to her on the couch.

110

"What will people think, seeing my truck parked here all day?" Terry grinned.

"None of their business," Lorcas said. "It certainly isn't any concern to me."

"Well, that's good. It might be here for a while. After all, I won't be able to drive home after drinking, will I?"

"That certainly wouldn't be safe," Lorcas agreed. "Can I get you some more?"

After several glasses of wine, Lorcas set up his tilt-top table, taped a fresh sheet of paper to it, and with Terry leaning over his shoulder, sketched out the basic plan of a raven flying over the coastal cliffs. He had enough experience drawing the castle's stones now, which he often hid within his drawings, that the rocks didn't concern him. He'd also drawn some vegetation as background for his fish, although not firs and spruces. The raven concerned him a bit more, but he quickly came up with an outline he liked. It seemed to come naturally. Terry chose some music and played DJ while he sketched and began filling in a few details, and brought him more wine.

Things that evening moved along more quickly than Lorcas had anticipated. Maybe it was the wine, he wasn't sure, nor did he care. He was glad he'd tidied up his bedroom, though.

The next morning he trotted down the stairs, pulling a T-shirt on, to get coffee going while Terry was still upstairs. As he walked into the living room, Zumar popped out of the library. He was looking a lot more solid, but still too obviously inhuman to pass off as a neighbor.

"Hey, Lorcas," he whispered, gesturing for him to step closer.

"Not now, Zumar!" Lorcas hissed. He could hear Terry moving around near the top of the stairs.

"It's important!" Zumar insisted, spreading his hands.

"It's not that important! Wait until later." It couldn't be that important. Rook wasn't calling and none of the Fell Ken had come for him. It was obviously some Zumar thing, and it could wait.

Zumar slid back into the library with a scowl as Terry descended the stairs.

"Coffee?" Lorcas asked.

"Please. Then I have to get out of here. I have to work and I'll be pushing it to get there on time. Fortunately it's the bike shop so I don't have to change clothes. Can I call you later?"

"Of course! Or I'll call you, if you don't mind." Lorcas handed her the first cup of coffee and stuck another pod in the machine for himself. Terry took it and sank into the couch. Lorcas turned on the TV. "News?"

"Yeah, I like to see what's happened overnight."

He was just about to sit down next to her when someone knocked on the door. It was still quite early, before eight. They'd gotten up early since Terry had to leave.

It was Tomash. He craned to look over Lorcas' shoulder into the house. "Step out for a minute, Lorcas," he said in a low voice.

Lorcas stepped out, pulling the door not quite closed behind him. Zumar stood off to the side, eying Terry's big red truck. Lorcas noticed that the quarter-panel had already been replaced.

"Well?" Tomash asked with a grin and a raised eyebrow.

Lorcas turned immediately and headed back for the house, but Tomash grabbed him by the shirt.

"I was joking! We didn't call you out here to discuss your love-life. We can talk about that later. Zumar's got something important to tell you," Tomash said. "We didn't want your guest to overhear."

"Well, I'd like to spend all the time I can get with my 'guest' before she leaves for work," Lorcas said, "so make it snappy, Zumar. I assume it's really important, since you obviously woke up the King to get my attention. Hurry up and tell me, or I'm going back in."

"I found Raine," Zumar responded, uncrossing his arms. He grinned and bounced on his toes.

"What?" Lorcas glanced back towards the house; he'd raised his voice in his surprise. "Where? Is she okay?"

"You'll never believe where! She's in Perry's shop!"

Lorcas took a moment. He frowned. "Perry's shop -- in Seaside Heights? How did she get there? How did *you* get there?"

"I followed Bishop the cat. It's a long story."

Lorcas raised his hand. "Okay then, wait for me at Tomash's until Terry leaves. She has to go soon anyway. I'll come by and hear the whole story in a few minutes."

He pushed open the door and joined Terry in the living room. "Sorry, business. That was one of the co-owners of the castle. He wants me to help with some decisions today."

"I'm not keeping you, am I?" Terry asked.

"Not at all. It's early. They can wait."

"Alright. I've been thinking. Once you finish that drawing of the raven, I might be able to use it as a pattern for a stained glass piece. I've been taking classes for a while now and I'm good enough to make big pieces with some complexity. It might be something you could hang in your castle, if you like it. But I'd need to get back in there, in those two buildings, to look at the sizes and shapes of things and the color scheme. I mean, it could go in what you call the Keep, but maybe in your tower. It needs windows."

"That would be great," Lorcas agreed. "Next time you come up we'll walk back through the Keep and the chapel." The upper stories surely wouldn't be dangerous, he thought. Besides, she'd been in there before.

She studied him intently for a moment. "If you want, I could make it kind of a memorial to your mom," she said softly. "Unless

113

you prefer not. We could add some elements that were special to her, something subtle. But only if you want."

For a minute, Lorcas did not know how to answer. A range of emotions washed through him, reminiscent of his time in the dungeon with Rook. No one had suggested anything of the sort before. On one hand, it was a thoughtful gesture, more thoughtful than any of his friends in the Fell Ken had been. But he wasn't sure how appropriate it would be. Others might think the site where she'd gone down over the cliff was a good place for a memorial, but given her feelings about the castle, he wasn't so sure himself.

"I'll have to think about it," he finally said. "It's a really nice idea, and I appreciate you suggesting it."

"You let me know," Terry said. "I'm sure it's hard, her going like that. And I'll think about it, too, and look at some other memorial windows to get some ideas."

Lorcas stood outside his house until Terry had successfully navigated the main gate and her truck passed by outside the wall. He watched as she turned out of the neighborhood. Then he strode quickly to Tomash's house.

"So? Tell me what's going on," he demanded.

Tomash was brewing coffee, and Zumar paced in the cramped living room, between stacks of paperbacks and workout equipment.

"I haven't been seeing Bishop much lately," Zumar began. "I figured he was doing cat things down inside the castle, you know, getting his fill of shadow-rats and the like. But one afternoon I saw him taking off from one of the interior hallways to the south, down a really narrow passageway. I hadn't even noticed it before. I followed him to see where it would go. I knew he wouldn't be able to cross out of Rook's influence so I figured I was safe if I followed him."

"So this tunnel went all the way to Seaside Heights?" Lorcas jumped ahead impatiently.

Zumar nodded. "It took me a long time. I just kept going and going. I could tell there wasn't anything outside the tunnel that was under Rook's influence. It was like a long feeler snaking down towards town. But finally I came to a place where I could tell the influence was spread out more. Bishop led me out to the surface between some rocks next to the ocean. I followed him and found out I was on the seawall that runs along the marina."

"The one where Jack Bright's boat is parked," Tomash put in. "The *Natural Seize*. Zumar could see it."

"Couldn't get to it," Zumar shrugged. "Anyway, I went back down and followed another path that branched away from the marina, uphill. This one brought me out to a big rock on the edge of a parking lot. I stood out there for a few minutes. Was getting a little claustrophobic with that narrow channel and everything, and I was a little worried about the mini-blobs, even though I didn't see any of them. There was a big, low building right on top of the hill, looking out over the ocean. What do you know, I see this guy walk out and head for his truck. It was evening by then and I couldn't see him that well, but boy could I feel him! I knew right away it was one of the Koen, and I guessed it had to be someone powerful, probably their leader. So I made sure he noticed me."

"You did what?" Lorcas asked.

"I talked to him. He saw me and came over. I figured it was Jack Bright. Boy, he wasn't happy that Rook's influence had landed right outside his office!" Zumar laughed.

"Zumar, that wasn't smart," Lorcas sighed. "Now he knows. It would have been better to just keep that secret for a while, don't you think?"

Zumar shrugged. "I kind of thought it was more fun to tease him a little. Anyway, that's all I did that day. It took me most of the night to get back here. But today I decided to go back and see if Rook had extended any further. I kind of felt pulled that way, you know? So I hiked down there yesterday. This time there was a new tunnel leading off towards town. I followed that one until it popped me up into a basement. I went upstairs, the whole thing was strongly under Rook's influence. And it was Perry's shop!"

"And Raine was there?" Lorcas asked, fascinated.

"Yep! Normal as anything, not as solid as me but she could shuffle papers around and move small objects. She was tidying up, just like she was going to open the door and start selling things. She was kind of, well, confused, I guess. She's not sure what all has happened, but she was real happy. She said she was home. She has full use of the house behind the shop, too."

"Good thing we didn't sell that place," Tomash said.

"No kidding," Lorcas agreed. "You said she's confused. What does she know and what doesn't she know? About Delva?"

Zumar looked off uncomfortably. "I don't think she knows that. I didn't tell her, but I will. I guess someone has to."

"Yes, and you're probably the best one," Lorcas admitted. "Delva's house is technically Raine's now, although how we'd transfer the lease over to a shadow I don't know."

Zumar bounced impatiently on his toes. "There's more! I didn't even tell you this, yet, Tomash," he said smugly. "I told you I came up through the basement. You ever been down there?"

"I didn't even know there was a basement," Tomash admitted.

"It's kind of dark and Rook-like," Zumar said. "It comes out under one of the cabinets in the shop."

"You came out through a cabinet?" Lorcas asked.

"Didn't have to. There's a trigger that causes the floor of the cabinet to rise up and also unlocks the cabinet door," Zumar said. "It was set up so it could be triggered by the touch of a shadow. Perry's doing, I'm sure. He knew a few tricks. But that's not the interesting thing. That basement is full of boxes."

"Sure, a lot of people store stuff they're not using in the basement," Tomash said with a shrug. "Although not many store them in a basement that's only accessible through the floor of a cabinet."

"Exactly," Zumar said. "They aren't just boxes. They look like shipping containers of some type, and I couldn't get in them. I think they're shielded somehow, maybe with a heavy sheet of metal inside the wooden exterior. They're all the same size, too, not just stray boxes."

"Well, that is curious," Lorcas agreed. "I'd like to have a look and see if we can get into them. Perry did leave everything to Cliffview Estates, so whatever's in them ought to belong to us."

"Technically Tondra and Alan are the executors," Tomash said.

"We should definitely tell them about Raine, too," Lorcas said. "Then all of us could go down together, just like old times. Visit Raine and see what's in the boxes."

"Sounds like a plan," Tomash said. "I'll tell Tondra if you want, and we'll set up a time when all of us can meet there."

"I wonder if that will raise any eyebrows in Seaside Heights," Lorcas mused. "You know the Koen have got to be watching that place."

"We could put out a rumor that we're going to re-open it," Tomash joked. "We've got somebody to run it now, we could make a little extra money!"

"That would go over well: ghost runs antique shop in Seaside Heights. I can see the paranormal investigators swarming all over the place right now."

"Well, eventually people probably won't be able to tell, especially in dim light, if Rook keeps his promise. Some day we really could re-open it," Zumar said.

"Right up your alley," Tomash noted. "You were a merchant once, weren't you?"

Zumar sighed. "Well, I would have been one if I hadn't died. My father was a dealer in small objects like glass vials and boxes, wooden utensils, the kind of stuff that what you'd call the middle class nowadays, the new merchant class, was beginning to want. My older brother had his own business and my older sister married the man who partnered with my brother. My sister was educated, particularly good at math. She kept their books. My younger sister would probably have been married off to someone similar, but I never found out. Me, my father apprenticed to a wood-crafter so I could see the production side of the business for a couple of miserable years. Afterward he sent me traveling to make deals with suppliers inland from our coastal shop. That's where I ran into trouble."

He paused for a minute and looked off into the distance. "They're all dead now, of course. Never knew what happened to me and I never knew what happened to them." He turned back to Tomash and Lorcas. "Raine's pretty much all I have, the only one I can touch and interact with, except for Bishop. And the Bob-blob, which doesn't count. And I'm really not feeling so good about Rook right now. I'm thinking I might go down to the shop permanently and live there with Raine. Work around the shop, keep things clean and ready for whatever we end up doing with it."

Lorcas nodded. "Wish I could give you a ride down there, but I don't think that will work. I guess you'll have to hike."

"Yes. Maybe later I'll be able to ride a bike or something. That would help. But I don't plan on coming up this way real often, anyway."

"We need some spies down in Seaside Heights, and if Zumar and Raine can keep an eye on Jack Bright's office and even his boat, that's good news," Tomash pointed out.

At home Lorcas thoughtfully did the dishes, then took a look at the drawing he had started the night before. It now had a deeper meaning, the possible start of a memorial to his mother. What elements would he add that would be meaningful? He realized he didn't know any more about his mother and her motivations than he had his father. There were few now who did.

Instead of working on it, he unpacked the trunk and box of books Terry had brought and took a quick look through them. They were probably the last ones his father had been working on translating before his death. The slips of thin paper were stuck in between the leaves, with his father's scrawl across them. The spines had small labels near the bottom, which Lorcas recognized as his father's filing system. There were spaces in the library for them, he saw, but he left them out for the time being. Evening reading material -- at least, for evenings when he wasn't otherwise occupied. He hoped those would now be rare.

Cornerstone: The Delving

Chapter Nine

Lorcas waited impatiently for the following afternoon, which was the soonest Tondra had decided she and Alan could break away from managing Cliffview Estates and the Fell Ken's business to go to Perry's shop. He had spent nearly an hour on the phone with Terry in the evening, chatting about the trip up the coast and other little things, and it had felt easy and natural. She'd called briefly that morning to tell him she'd be working all day at her paralegal job, and that she probably wouldn't be able to get up to Cliffview for a couple of days, but they'd talk and keep in touch. Lorcas distracted himself by working on the drawing of the raven, the cliff, and the forest.

He had planned to ride down to Seaside Heights with Tomash, but Tondra sent her brother down to Lafayette early to pick up some building supplies to help shore up a couple of the summerhouses and the skirting around Perry's shop, which was in bad repair, along with the steps. Rather than jump in with Tondra and Alan, Lorcas decided to drive down by himself in his Subaru.

Marek and Wyne were already there when he arrived, standing impatiently at the back near the entrance to the attached house. Tomash's truck with a flatbed trailer was there as well, taking up most of the rest of the alley parking. Lorcas parked on the gravel driveway that ran alongside the shop and house and divided the property from the neighbors.

"You remember where the spare key is?" Tomash asked. He was fishing around under the back stairs, coming up with nothing but cobwebs.

"Not under there. Perry didn't like the idea of spiders. I think it was behind one of the loose siding slats. But I think Tondra moved it anyway."

They didn't have long to wait. Tondra and Alan showed up a few minutes later. Tondra had the key on her key chain. She brushed past Lorcas and Tomash, stepped up the spongy stairs, and let them all in. They gathered in the living room, which was slightly musty-smelling but otherwise much like when Lorcas had first been introduced to the Fell Ken. As they scooted furniture around, Zumar appeared, grinning, and Raine rushed into the room a moment later.

"Hi everybody!" she announced happily. She looked diaphanous, like fine lace, Lorcas thought. But her voice was strong and she was grinning from ear to ear.

She slid over to Lorcas and leaned on him, wrapping her arms around his waist. Lorcas realized that he could actually feel her, the way he'd felt Zumar grab his ankle. He responded with a careful hug. Raine smiled up at him.

Everyone else was smiling too. "How've you been?" Tondra asked.

Raine released Lorcas and put her hands on her hips. "Hard to say. I don't remember a lot. I just suddenly kind of jerked awake, and I was here in Perry's shop. Of course, I spent a lot of time here when I was… alive, so it's a logical place for me to end up. And I feel better than I felt before all this happened! I feel stronger somehow, like I have more energy."

"I wonder what caused it?" Tondra mused. "I'm glad you're back, it's just so weird."

Lorcas glanced at Zumar and then to Tomash. Both met his eyes briefly. He was sure they were all remembering Rook's promise in the depths. Rook was as good as his word, apparently.

"I'm sorry about your grandmother," Alan offered. "I know it's new to you."

Raine looked down. "It's alright. I kind of knew it, somehow. But I'll tell you one thing." She looked up, her eyes burning and dark within her pale face. "It makes me realize how dangerous the Koen are, and how intensely I dislike them. If they thought they were going to discourage me, they've got another think coming. They've just made me more determined than ever to get this show on the road and start a new and better world where things like that can't ever happen again. Delva would want that."

The group settled into the various chairs and sofas. Raine perched on the arm of the large couch. Lorcas took one of Marek's wine glasses and sipped the now-familiar concoction. The wine was cold from the ice in the chest, and it made him realize how stuffy it was in the house. Living up at Cliffview, he was used to moving air and the coolness of the perpetual rainclouds that hovered over the area. He got up and propped the back door open with a boot-scraper. There was no screen, but the flies were minimal outside anyway. He returned to sit on the couch next to Raine.

"I'm ready to go," Raine was saying. "I'm sure I can do something to help from right here. I love it here, it feels so familiar. It's way, way better than trying to live in the castle! And I feel like it's mine, so it's better than Lorcas' place, too, no offense, Lorcas. But I'm not going to be happy just drifting around an antiques shop. I want to do something! I think we could turn this into Fell Ken headquarters or something."

"Most of us are up at Cliffview now," Tondra said. "But we definitely need eyes and ears on the ground in Seaside Heights, and we're making plans to move some more of the Fell Ken into the area. Eventually we'll move into Lafayette, too. We want to control the triangle between Cliffview, Seaside Heights, and Lafayette. You are going to be valuable to us, Raine, as this moves on. We'll figure out some way to keep you busy and get you back and forth to the castle easily."

"I feel like we're on the verge of something new, something important," Raine said, looking around at the group. "It's just a feeling I have. I've been watching the news, and all the environmental issues around the globe, they're terrible. Rook can fix it. He can stop all the wars and the terrorism. We just need to support him and help him move forward as fast as possible."

"I think that's a little over-optimistic, Raine!" Tondra said with a laugh. "We've got a long, long way to go!"

Lorcas glanced at Tomash again. Raine was more right than Tondra or any of the others knew. But it also made him feel better about Rook: he had kept his promise to help Raine, she felt better than ever, Zumar was happy and Rook's view that he could improve the world was echoed by Raine. He suppressed the thought of the sacrifice he would somehow have to provide.

"Besides discussing what Raine and Zumar can do for us here and welcoming Raine back, there are a few other things we need to talk about," Tondra continued. "Let's get the quick stuff out of the way. Zumar, can you tell us about your new discoveries?"

"You mean besides Raine and this place? Well, I can get to Jack Bright's parking lot and see his office any time I want now, and I think Raine will be able to do it, too. And I can get to the marina and see his boat. That means we'll be able to keep an eye on him whenever he's working."

"It's almost like Rook is attracted to places the Koen frequent and extends tunnels in those directions," Tondra mused.

"Of course he can feel the Koen just like he can feel us," Tomash put in. "After all, we're distantly related."

"Sure," Tondra said. "Anyway, that'll be very useful. I'd like you to keep an eye on what Jack's doing on a regular basis, if everyone else feels the same way."

The motion was agreed to, and Tondra went on. "What else, Zumar?"

Zumar grinned. "Shall I show you?"

"No, just tell us. We'll explore when we're done with the meeting," Tondra replied.

"I found a secret passage to the basement, and there are a bunch of packing boxes down there with who-knows-what in them," Zumar said.

"Perry didn't mention them in his will," Alan told the group. "He did say that everything in his house was to be left to Cliffview Estates Incorporated, including the property, so I think we're safe there, whatever is in them."

"I expect it's something Rook needs at this point in time," Tondra said. "Rook has a way of leading people to and pointing out what it is he wants exactly when he wants it. He's not one for just telling folks where and when to look."

"It's just the way he is," Raine put in. "He's all feeling, not so much talking. That's what's great about him, so pure!"

"Pure or not, it probably means he's taking another step or entering a new phase," Tondra said.

"So what do you think that next phase is?" Lorcas asked casually.

Tondra gave him the look that usually meant he should know the answer himself, but he was used to it by now.

"Other than expansion, I'd guess Rook is getting prepared to begin to move outside the stones of the castle himself," Tondra said. "Our historical information says that at some point when his influence is strong enough, he'll be able to become corporeal, something like Zumar, and that as things continue he'll become more and more independent."

"You don't say," Lorcas commented.

"But that's stuff Perry knew, and he didn't leave the details with us, unfortunately. I'm hoping there's some clue in the boxes downstairs."

"Well, let's go see," Tomash said impatiently. "It seems like we're going to need whatever it is soon."

They followed Zumar and Raine out through the door that connected the house to the back side of the shop. Zumar stopped short inside and gestured to a large curio cabinet with a glass front. When everyone was gathered around, he reached up under the overhanging lip of the top, and there was a 'snick' as the front of the cabinet popped open.

Lorcas pulled the doors further open and watched as Zumar reached down and pressed a small wooden clip just behind the door-sill. The floor of the cabinet rose slowly, taking the objects resting upon it and the cabinet top with it. Beneath it was a dark, narrow hole.

When the floor of the cabinet was high enough, Zumar scrambled down a ladder inside. Lorcas followed him, and Raine simply appeared in the dim basement. The others made their way down one by one.

The small room contained a number of packing boxes, each about four feet wide by two feet high. They were wooden crates, solidly built.

"I wonder how they got them in here?" Lorcas said, turning around to look at the room. There didn't seem to be another exit, except for the very narrow slot-like tunnel through which Zumar had originally entered.

"Built the house over them?" Tomash suggested. He reached up for the toolkit Alan was handing down to him.

Alan followed the toolkit down, bringing a big flashlight. He shone the beam around the walls, found an electrical conduit, and followed that to a switch behind the ladder. He flipped it, and a single dim overhead light came on.

"Wonder which one we should go for first?" Tomash asked. He flipped open the toolkit and pulled out the tray. After a moment of digging, he brought out a small pry-bar.

"How about this one that says 'Number One' on it?" Zumar grinned and patted the lid of one of the boxes. Tomash leaned over, read the large stenciled print, and laughed. He stuck the little bar under the lid of the crate. He pried it up a bit, then worked his way around, loosening it.

"Give me a hand here," he said. Alan and Wyne stepped forward and grabbed the front edge. They yanked a few times, then tilted it up. The bottom of the lid was lined with what looked like a lead sheet. Underneath was packing material.

Tondra leaned in and carefully pulled out some of the material. The first thing revealed was a smaller crate, about eighteen inches on a side. It was tied shut with thick twine. Tondra worked at it for a minute and loosened the knot with the help of a fid from Tomash's toolkit. She untied it, lifted the lid, and pulled out still more packing material.

"I was wondering what ever happened to that," Zumar said as the contents were revealed.

"You know about this?" Tondra asked. She lifted the object out with a skeptical expression.

The item was a fat, crucifix-shaped object, metallic on the back and deep red, glassy stone on the front, with ornate metal decorations along the edges. It was about a foot tall and a foot wide, and from the way Tondra held it, Lorcas could tell it was heavy.

"Yeah," Zumar said. "If you look, there's a hollow on the dais in the Keep, just in front of the King's chair. This used to fit there."

"Looks religious," Tondra said.

Zumar shrugged. "The Fell Ken were religious, back when this was created. They believed the power of the castle was associated with their devotion. Others believed it was a place of the devil. Thus the split between those who became the Fell Ken and those who became the Koen. They didn't call us 'fell' for nothing."

Tondra passed the object to Alan, who examined it and then passed it on.

"I've seen the depression in the floor," Tomash said as he received it. "I just thought it was a niche like any of the others. There are a bunch of them scattered here and there, different shapes. Do all of them have inserts?"

Zumar nodded. "They do. If we're lucky they'll all be here."

"Do they do anything?" Lorcas asked.

"Not sure. They didn't used to, as far as I know, but you know how Rook is. Maybe he imbued these objects with some symbolic power."

Tondra turned back to the packing case. "Is there anything else in there?"

Alan dug in the packing material and found several smaller boxes. Lorcas helped him remove them one by one. They were quite heavy. Tomash went to work on them.

When the first lid came off, the group leaned forward. No one spoke a word for a moment.

"Wow," said Tomash finally.

"Wow, indeed," Alan agreed.

The box was full of what appeared to be gold coins. The other three boxes pulled out of the crate were similarly filled.

"Okay," Tondra said when the fourth box had been opened. "I think maybe we should pause here. I think maybe we should put the lid back on these four boxes, put them back in the crate, and leave them here for the time being while we try to figure out what to do."

"I agree," Alan said. "This is a huge amount of gold. I think we should take one coin and see if we can figure out online where it came from and what it is. But what we can't do is start dumping a huge amount of gold coin onto the market. That will bring some eyes upon us for sure, eyes we probably don't want due to how we've managed the building and inspection and all the financing of Cliffview. We need to be really careful."

"Well, we were wondering how we were going to keep financing the Fell Ken with Perry gone," Lorcas said. "I guess we know, now."

Alan flipped one coin in his hand as Tomash carefully closed up the boxes and replaced them in the crate. "I think this calls for a little celebration!"

"Good thing I brought some more wine," Marek said. He made for the ladder.

Tondra handed Lorcas the cross-shaped object, and he handed it up to Marek, then retrieved it after he climbed up through the cabinet himself. He assumed he'd be the one to place it in the depression in the floor. He put it on the counter in the kitchen as everyone gathered in the living room again and Marek started busily opening more bottles. Though they couldn't drink, Zumar and Raine joined them. In the late afternoon sun, Raine looked, Lorcas thought, like one of those curtains people sometimes had in back of the heavier drapes, just to cut down on the sunlight a little. Objects behind her had a peculiar wavy appearance.

Too excited to sit, the group milled in the area between the kitchen and the living room. They passed the gold coin from hand to hand, joking about treasure. Lorcas glanced towards the open back door, then did a double-take. He froze with his wine in hand. Alan, to whom he'd been talking, noticed his expression and looked that way as well. The gold coin lay still upon his open palm. The silence spread to the others quickly as they all stared at the door.

Terry Bell stood just inside the door in the living room, staring directly at Zumar and Raine. "I, uh, saw your car outside, Lorcas, and I thought I'd drop in and say 'hi'."

Tondra moved swiftly behind Terry and kicked the boot-scraper out of the way. The door slammed shut. She turned the deadbolt quickly. Terry glanced at her, then around at the rest of the people standing still and silent in the room.

"Well," she said lightly, putting her hands on her hips. "This is an interesting little group. Most interesting are you two." She nodded at Zumar and Raine.

Zumar looked at the floor, then at Tondra. Raine stood fluttering by the window.

"I'm not real sure what to say," Terry said. "Looks like I've crashed a party of holograms."

"That's as good an explanation as any. Just let us turn off the projector," Marek said, moving towards the kitchen with a glance at Zumar.

"Oh, please," Terry said with a forced laugh.

"You don't really believe they're holograms, do you?" Tondra asked curtly.

"I'm not sure what to believe at the moment. Would you like to provide me with an explanation I can accept?"

No one answered. After a minute Lorcas stepped forward. His mouth felt dry. He wasn't sure what Tondra was planning.

"Terry, let me introduce you to everyone," he said. "Marek and Wyne, Tondra, Tomash, Alan, and Zumar and Raine. Everyone, Terry Bell, mountain-biker and paralegal. And a friend of mine."

Terry stuck her hands in her back pockets and rotated to view Tondra, behind her near the door, then back to the others. "Hey, I don't mean to be rude, but this looks a little sinister, folks. I, uh, could just go right back out this door and pretend none of this happened."

Alan glanced at Tondra and took a step forward, blowing out his breath audibly. "We didn't mean to make you feel threatened, Miss Bell. You just took us by surprise. I don't know if you know what we've been planning up at Cliffview Estates, but once the castle opens to the public we'll be holding mystery weekends…"

Terry interrupted with a short laugh. "Oh, come on, that's not going to go over with me any better than the hologram stuff. I've known since I showed up there the first time that something weird was going on. I still don't know exactly what, but I've been putting two and two together. That explosion that happened last year that killed Lorcas' mother and all those other people? My bet is it was intentional and that someone was trying to get rid of that castle. And I'll bet it wasn't because they thought it would compete with other hotels in the area, of which there aren't very many. My bet is that someone freaked out because they thought something sinister was going on up there, and they couldn't get the authorities to believe them so they decided to take things into their own hands. How am I doing so far?"

Everybody glanced at one another, but it was Alan who spoke up once again. "Pretty good. You can understand why we're a little concerned about strangers."

"Sure," Terry replied. "I would be too. But look at it this way. What I've seen here today, these two --" she gestured at Zumar and Raine, "what am I going to tell anyone about this? I mean, I can't even explain it. No one is going to believe me anymore than they believed whoever it is that tried to blow you up last year. The difference is, I'm not freaked out. I'm curious. And there's something else, too. I'd never hurt Lorcas. In case you didn't know, we're intimate, to be formal about it."

"Lorcas?" Tondra asked, crossing her arms. Alan grinned.

Lorcas slid an arm around Terry protectively, feeling the heat from her admission not only to the group, but also to him. "It's true."

Tondra gaped at him. "Lorcas! We should be vetting anybody you have anything to do with!"

"You don't 'vet' Tomash's girlfriends, God knows he has plenty of them," Lorcas snapped.

"Tomash only dates Fell Ken!" Tondra responded. Tomash reddened.

"Well, he knows about Terry," Lorcas went on, turning to Tomash. "I think he can vet people just as well as you can!"

"Tomash?" Tondra scowled, turning to her brother. Tomash shrugged helplessly.

"And Zumar didn't feel anything strange about her, did you, Zumar? He was in the house part of the time Terry was there," Lorcas continued.

"He was?" Tondra swiveled to Zumar.

"He was?" Terry turned to Lorcas.

"Not the whole time," Lorcas said uncomfortably. "He was in the den downstairs."

Zumar hesitated. "She doesn't feel like Koen," he agreed grudgingly. "She's just some normal human being."

"Which is exactly who Lorcas shouldn't be hanging around with!" Tondra began, but Alan raised a hand.

"Has she been in the castle?" he asked.

"Only in the top part."

"And Rook didn't react?"

"No. I listened pretty carefully. No objection from him."

"Well, there you go. There's your vetting," Alan said.

Terry looked from him to Lorcas and back.

Tondra spread her hands. "Alright. I agree, that's better than what I could do. But I still think we need to come to some sort of agreement here, and make a few decisions."

"I think one decision's already been made," Alan said. "Seems like Lorcas has decided to spend some time with Ms. Bell. If I can put in my two cents, I'd say that next time she's up there,

Lorcas takes her back into the castle and very specifically asks Rook to take notice. If all goes as well as the first time, then there's no problem. Remember, I'm neither Fell Ken nor Koen myself. I'm just a 'normal human being', as you put it, Zumar. And Tondra had to make the same decisions and introduce me to the ideas of the Fell Ken at one point, too."

Tondra studied Alan. "But things were a lot less far along at that point. Nothing this freaky. You were exposed to those ideas slowly, not all at once."

"Nobody's going to believe her, like she said," Alan argued. "All we need from you, Terry, is a guarantee that you won't talk about our activities and movements. We'll make more decisions as things move along."

"You've got it," Terry said. "I appreciate your reasonableness." She looked around, eying Raine and Zumar once again. "Now, if it's okay with you, I have to go back to work."

Tondra opened the door and propped it open with the boot scraper again. She stepped aside to allow Terry free access to the outside.

"I'll call you later," Lorcas said, letting go of Terry.

"If you don't mind, I think I'll take a little time to digest all this," Terry said dryly. "I'll call you."

Lorcas nodded glumly, cursing internally. "Okay."

Terry smiled. "Walk me out to my car?"

Lorcas glanced at Tondra, who nodded. "I think we're going to close this meeting down now anyway. We can talk later, Lorcas."

"Hey, don't everybody split just yet," Tomash said. "I need help unloading some of that lumber from the trailer. I picked up stuff to redo the stairs and porch."

Lorcas removed the cross from the kitchen counter. He followed Terry out, noting that her truck was parked between the house and the neighboring property, in front of his. She'd come in from the street, not the alley, and he realized his car was easily visible from the front of the store. She must have seen it while driving by.

Tomash scrambled up on the flatbed. "I'll hand stuff down, you guys just stack it behind the house. I'll come down and sort it out later," he said. He paused and stripped his shirt off and tossed it down, already sweaty from loading the flatbed before the meeting.

Terry paused and Lorcas noticed her eyes flick up and down Tomash's body. He felt a twinge of jealousy. Tomash worked out on a regular basis and he was fit and trim. But Terry's vision seemed to settle for just a moment on the chain around Tomash's neck, bearing the ring Lorcas had given him. Then she turned abruptly back to Lorcas.

"I didn't mean to cause a scene."

"I know," Lorcas said. "I think things will be alright. You've already been in the castle."

"What difference does it make?"

"I'll explain later, or at some point, anyway," Lorcas said. "I'm not sure you know what you've gotten into, hanging out with me."

Terry smiled. "Not sure I care."

She took a step closer and slid an arm around his waist. Gratefully, Lorcas pulled her closer and kissed her.

"I'm glad this happened," Terry said. "Now you don't have to hide anything from me. I felt like you weren't telling me everything when we were together before, like you were concealing something. Now we can be more open and honest with each other. I like that."

"I like it too," Lorcas said. "Will you call me when you've thought things over? I don't want to bug you, but I would like to hear from you."

"I'll call you tomorrow," Terry said. "I really want to start learning about what I saw here today, and I want to spend more time with you. Your creepy friends, not so much, although the dark-haired guy seems okay."

Lorcas laughed. "That's Alan, the non-Fell Ken. I'll be waiting to hear from you, then."

Terry climbed into her truck. Lorcas watched her back out and waved as she took off. He knew Tondra was going to want to talk to him about Terry, but he didn't feel like there was going to be a problem.

He stowed the stone cross in his car, then helped move the rest of the lumber off the flatbed.

"I'll see everyone back at Cliffview, I guess," he told Tondra, Alan, and Tomash.

Tondra frowned. "Wait just a minute, Lorcas."

Lorcas halted unwillingly as he pulled open the door of his car. Tondra crossed her arms and nodded, looking out of the corner of her eyes. He followed her gaze to a car parked up the street on the opposite side of the road.

"That car's been there since before we arrived," she noted. "I think we're being watched. Lorcas, I want us to drive back in a group, and I want you in the middle. Alan and I will go first and Tomash will bring up the rear. Just for safety's sake."

Lorcas glanced at the car, trying not to be too obvious. He wasn't really surprised, but on the other hand, he wouldn't have noticed if Tondra hadn't pointed it out. But there wasn't much the spy could have learned. Zumar and Raine had remained inside, and the rest of them hadn't been flaunting their finds out in the open. The stone cross was wrapped up. And now that they knew they were being watched, Zumar and Raine could spy on the spies and short-circuit any nefarious plans for Perry's shop.

Back at Cliffview, Lorcas brought the stone relic up to the chapel. He waited until Tomash, Tondra, Alan, Wyne, and Marek were all there. Then he took the few steps up the dais towards the big chair he'd bought at the flea market in Lafayette. It had survived the explosion intact, sheltering several people from falling stones. Sure enough, directly in front of it was a depression in the floor

135

matching the shape of the cross. He held the heavy stone and metal object over the depression for a minute, turning it from side to side, trying to decide which way to put it in. It didn't seem to matter. Finally he set it down. It rotated a quarter-turn by itself, then dropped into the hole.

The others gathered around. They watched as the cross seemed to meld with the floor, creating a smooth patch of red stone with ornate metal edging around it. Lorcas ran a hand over it, impressed by how snugly it fit. He wondered briefly how it had been removed from the original castle in the past.

"Well, that's interesting," Tondra said.

Lorcas glanced up and saw that she was not looking at the stone like the rest of them, but rather at the northern wall of the Keep.

"What's interesting?" Tomash asked, following her gaze.

"That," Tondra said, pointing. "Can't you see it?"

Lorcas stood up and stared where Tondra pointed. Indeed, he could see something: big, slanted letters, glowing faintly red, beginning to appear on the wall. He scanned up and down and side to side. They seemed to cover the wall, each letter as large as his hand, but he couldn't read what they said. It appeared to be the language many of his books were written in, but he couldn't translate yet without the help of his father's notes or his computer vocabulary.

Tondra took a few steps closer to the wall and ran a hand up over the letters. "Warm," she said, "but not burning hot. Feels like it's engraving itself into the wall."

"Can you read it?" Tomash asked, turning to Lorcas.

"Not me," Lorcas said. "We'll have to see if Zumar can translate it for us."

"I wonder if it's going to stay, or if we need to write it down?" Marek asked. He pulled a small pad out of his back pocket without waiting for an answer and began copying the script quickly.

It didn't seem to be fading, though, and Lorcas had a feeling it would remain.

Tomash walked around the Keep, examining the floor. "Here are the other holes," he said. He pointed out three others, each corresponding to a specific wall. "We'll have to see if the other stones are in the packing crates and put them in. Maybe we'll get more writing."

"I don't want any of the entourage going back there alone," Tondra said. "Buddy system. We'll work out a time to go get more of the items. For now, let's just concentrate on getting this piece translated."

Chapter Ten

"I know where the ring is," Terry said as soon as Jack picked up the phone.

"Already?" Jack replied in surprise. "I mean, that's great! It's just that things have been moving along faster than I expected."

Terry laughed. "Well, I saw a meeting of the Fell Ken at that old antiques shop and I ran the gate, so to speak. Zumar and another shadow were there, a girl. You should have seen their faces when I walked in!"

Jack took a moment to compose himself. "I'm not sure that was wise. They could have reacted badly."

"Right, but they didn't. I decided to take the chance and move myself a little further into their confidence. Besides, I want to know more about what Lorcas is doing, for my own curiosity if for no other reason. There's no way we could get any closer with him concealing major parts of his life from me."

"You don't necessarily need to get any closer," Jack warned. "I want what information you can get easily and safely. You've already done far more than I expected. I don't want you in danger."

"This is what I want to do. You can't control my relationships in life. I rather like Lorcas, to tell you the truth. He's unusual, mysterious. I want to get to know him better for my own sake if not for yours."

Jack kept his opinion about that to himself. Terry was headstrong and independent, and he hoped he'd made the right choice bringing her in. The last thing he needed was her going over to the Fell Ken with the knowledge she had of the Knights and their activities.

"Okay. I understand," he said. "Tell me about the ring. How hard is it going to be to get hold of it?"

"Well, that's the problem, alright. I'd say it's going to be really difficult. It's hanging around Tomash's neck."

Jack grimaced. "Are you sure it's the correct ring?"

"No. You didn't give me a good description, and I only got a few seconds' look at it. But it was dark metal, fairly large, ornate, and I can't figure out why else Tomash would be wearing a ring on a chain around his neck, can you? It has to be something he wants to keep with him, something special, but something that maybe doesn't fit him or he doesn't want to wear in public."

"Sounds likely," Jack admitted. "Don't worry about trying to obtain it. We'll figure something out. I'm not even sure yet exactly what items we need."

"Maybe I could get a little closer to Tomash," Terry said with a tone that Jack interpreted as teasing. "He's pretty good looking."

"We need to concentrate on Lorcas," Jack said. "Leave Tomash alone. At least for now."

"Well, if you say so," Terry laughed. "Apparently he prefers Fell Ken ladies anyway!"

"I have to go now, I've got a meeting," Jack said. "Keep me informed and for God's sake don't put yourself in any more danger!"

Jack shook his head as he replaced the phone in the charger. He realized he'd forgotten to ask more about the girl she'd implied was a shadow like Zumar. He didn't have much time to consider what she'd said, though. Jason Japert, the lead detective on several intersecting cases in which Jack was involved, had made an appointment to talk to him. Jack wasn't looking forward to it, but he felt the need to present an appearance of cooperation to allay suspicion. So far Japert seem to be wavering on the edge of putting two and two together, to the detriment of the Knights and Jack in particular.

There was a quick knock and Don opened the office door without waiting for acknowledgment. He threw himself down on the couch in his usual spot. Jack briefed him quickly on Terry's latest report.

"I'm not sure what to do about it yet, but we'll eventually have to figure out some way to get that ring," Jack said.

"I've got an idea or two," Don replied darkly.

"Don't do anything rash, at least not yet. Do you want to stay for Japert's meeting and support me?"

"You bet," Don said. "I want to know what he knows or suspects as much as you do."

Japert arrived precisely on time. Jack and Don both stood and offered a hand.

"Hey, Jack! Long time no see," Japert greeted them enthusiastically.

He always sounded a bit naive, almost childish. It was, Jack suspected, an act calculated to put people off their guard.

"I hope you don't mind Don sitting in."

Japert shook Don's hand as well and then flopped onto the couch in Don's usual spot, leaving Don standing a bit uncomfortably off to the side. Jack relaxed into an armchair offset from the couch, in front of the desk, to seem more informal. Don quickly grabbed one of the leather chairs that sat off to the side and pulled it over.

"You were so helpful last year with all that stuff that was going on, you're so good with the area and all, I was hoping you could help me with a few more questions. Observations, really. Like to hear your take on them, maybe you can tell me how you think things fit together."

"Anything I can do to help. Does this have something to do with Bob?"

"Yes and no," Japert said. "We haven't found him."

"That's too bad," Jack said. "It's harder in some ways for someone to be missing than known dead."

"Mm-hmm, that's true," Japert agreed. "You know, I didn't grow up here, like you guys did, which is why I have to rely on you and folks like you at times. But I've been here about twelve years now. This is a pretty quiet area. I don't even merit the title 'Homicide Detective' because there aren't enough homicides in this county to keep me busy. Usually. I'm a 'Major Crimes Detective'. So I get involved whenever one of the Big Eleven comes up."

Jack raised an eyebrow, and Japert held up a hand, counting off on his fingers. "Murder, Manslaughter, Mayhem, Rape, Assault, Burglary, Theft, Larceny, Robbery, Arson…" He frowned. "What am I forgetting? Oh, yeah, Battery. There are others, of course, but those are the traditional state felony crimes."

"What the hell is Mayhem, anyway?" Jack asked.

"Technically it means cutting off a body part. We don't usually use it anymore, we charge something else." Japert shrugged. "Anyway, it seems that in the last year and a half, I've gotten involved in more major crimes than in the previous eleven years altogether."

He readjusted himself on the couch. "It started with your nephew's disappearance. Me and my partner, Lon, investigated that. We determined he was probably suicidal, based on your statement and the statements of others who knew him. We found evidence he might have jumped off one of the cliffs up there to the north." He jerked his chin towards Jack's bay window. "That was the first time Lon and I went up there, to Cliffview Estates. I didn't even know that neighborhood existed before that."

"It's been a summer home neighborhood for years," Jack said. "Very few permanent residents, and with the economic downturn there were a lot of people who wanted to sell. It was a good time for someone to come in and buy the area out. Smart move, providing the hotel eventually makes money."

"Right," Japert mused. "Then, of course, your friend Robert Dover, Bob, disappeared without a trace. The owners of that wine shop in Lafayette were found with his car. But there's no evidence of foul play. Their story checks out, the car seems to have been abandoned with the keys in it behind their shop and they moved it to get delivery trucks in there. Okay. But what do you know, turns out they're connected to Cliffview Estates as well."

"Coincidence," Jack said with a shrug. Ironically, he realized, he was protecting the Fell Ken. "This is a pretty small area. Everybody knows everybody in this triangle between Lafayette, Seaside Heights, and Cliffview Estates."

Japert nodded. "That's what I thought. But did you know there was another disappearance around that time? Didn't make as big a stir. Teenage girl disappeared. Her grandmother didn't seem too worried about it. In fact, it was reported by the girl's friends, not the grandmother, who she actually lived with. And what do you know? The grandmother turns out to be an investor in Cliffview Estates."

"And then there was the explosion," Jack offered. "Delva, that's who you're talking about, was killed up there along with a bunch of other people."

Although he knew, or suspected, what had happened to both Korrin and Bob, he didn't know what had happened to Raine. He had heard about it and been suspicious, given that he knew Delva was Fell Ken, but he couldn't quite figure it out. Now, however, Terry's mention of a girl shadow with Zumar seemed to fit.

"Yep. So I've got three disappearances, not counting the explosion, all in a short period of time, all with connections to Cliffview Estates. Now, you're right that this is a small area, but I hate coincidences. They pay me to have a suspicious mind, and stuff like this makes me suspicious."

"I don't know what I can add," Jack said, glancing at Don.

Japert sat silent for a minute. "How well do you know this young man whose property the hotel is being built on, this Lorcas Felken?"

Jack shrugged. "Can't say I know him at all personally."

"You knew his father?" Japert squinted at him. "His father would be more in your age group."

"Uh, a few years older, I think. We weren't in the same classes in school. I didn't really know the guy," Jack replied. "I knew who he was, that's all. We didn't run in the same circles. Lafayette's not *that* small."

"Small but not that small," Japert mused.

Jack winced. Japert was making a point of recalling his own words. "Otus Felken died under mysterious circumstances about twelve years ago, right after I moved here, did you know that? Possible poisoning, though they never were able to identify what kind of poison or a suspect. Now that's bugging me."

Japert blew out his breath and put his hands behind his head, studying the ceiling. "Otus Felken, father of the owner of Cliffview Estates property, dies under mysterious circumstances. No suspects. Korrin Bright possibly commits suicide, no body, at Cliffview Estates. No suspects, case is open. Bob Dover disappears without a trace; his car is tied to people tied to Cliffview Estates. No suspects. Raine disappears; her grandmother's not worried, connected to Cliffview Estates. No suspects, grandmother later dies in the explosion at Cliffview Estates. You seeing a pattern here?"

"Sure," Jack agreed. "I don't know what it means, if anything. That's your job."

"Uh-huh." Japert studied him. "There are a few other odd things going on around here lately. Since I'm part of the investigative team in charge of the explosion case, I get wind of all sorts of rumors. A lot of those rumors lately involve Cliffview Estates and the properties that belonged to some of the folks who died up there."

Jack shrugged. "I haven't heard anything."

"Well," Japert said, pushing himself off the couch, "some of those rumors involve you, too. I wanted to let you know that I'm still looking into the cases of your nephew and your friend Bob. Those cases aren't closed, and they're not forgotten, at least not by me."

Jack rose and extended a hand. "I appreciate you keeping me updated. I don't know what those rumors could be, but I'm sure you'll tell me when you can."

"Of course," Japert said. He nodded to Don. "I'll let myself out. You take care now."

After he left, Jack turned to Don. "Great. Another thing to worry about."

"He could be of some use if we can point him in the right direction," Don offered. "If we can get him concentrating on the Fell Ken instead of us."

Jack shook his head. "I don't want him around at all. There's too much to lose. If he pokes into the Fell Ken too deeply, he'll be bound to find out there's a closer relationship between us than we've been letting on, and that will definitely bring him down on us like a pit-bull. Don't let him fool you; he's sharp as a tack under that innocent face. Let's not forget what we did last year, Don. Other people are not going to understand."

"No," Don agreed. "They never do."

After Don left, Jack closed up the office, last out as usual. He had no one to go home to besides his cat, and he could enjoy the view from his office while he worked on his computer, one of the best views in Seaside Heights. His house was tucked down in the trees, inland from the ocean without much of a view. A typical evening might include a couple of hours out on the *Natural Seize*, time at the gym, dinner out with Don or one of the other Knights, a hike along the seaside trail system, or quiet time at home reading. But if none of those appealed, he preferred to spend time at the office after everyone else had left.

As he headed towards his truck he scanned the boulders and the forest edge south of the parking lot for any shadowy figures, but he saw none. Squinting through the evening gloom, he failed to pay attention to where he was walking, and it wasn't until the last moment that he realized how soft the asphalt felt underfoot. It was too late, and he plunged through, grasping futilely as he slipped past the pavement.

The landing fifteen feet below was not soft. He landed on his feet and took most of the force through his knees, then rolled sideways and backwards. He stopped himself by throwing out his arms. He sprang up almost immediately, his heart pounding. He knew without a doubt that he had fallen, by accident or by design, directly into one of Rook's spidery tunnels.

He scanned the ceiling and walls quickly, but the small chamber in which he'd landed was formed like an igloo with a rounded top leading to the hole through which he'd fallen. There was no way to climb out: even if he could scale the walls, he couldn't cling to the overhanging roof. He pulled out his cell phone, fortunately undamaged, and blew some dust off the face. But he got no reception at all, unsurprising given that he was fifteen feet below ground and within Rook's influence.

"Damn." Jack turned around in the chamber, trying to orient himself by the angle of the weakening sunlight falling through the hole. With the light of his cell phone he could see two passageways leading out: one to the north, or what he thought was north, and another generally leading south. North would take him closer to Rook and thus into areas more strongly controlled by the Fell Ken, and if Rook wasn't aware of his presence yet, walking towards him would surely draw unwanted attention. He started off to the south, aware that his choice to move away from Rook might in fact be no choice at all, but further design.

The passageway was completely dark once he left the chamber, and so narrow that his shoulders brushed the walls if he didn't walk down the exact middle. Fearing pits or other traps, he kept his cell phone screen illuminated for a little light, swiping the screen every time it went dark. The channel led on, generally straight, slightly downhill, for a considerable distance. Jack followed it unwillingly. Claustrophobia tickled at the back of his mind, but he ignored it as best he could.

It was hard to judge distance. He could tell he was walking slower than usual, with short, careful steps. The minutes slipped by on the display on his phone. The darkness was unrelenting, the tunnel seemingly unchanging. He could have been walking around in circles for all he knew, and he wouldn't put it past Rook to design something of that nature. It could even have been a spiral. He put his hand on one wall uncertainly. The passage seemed straight to him, but he wasn't sure he'd be able to tell if curved slightly.

Finally he came to a fork in the tunnel. He paused, studying each direction carefully. It seemed that the air was fresher, less stagnant by a small margin, down the right-hand tunnel. Hoping for some outlet he turned that way.

In a few minutes he could tell that a small amount of light was filtering in from up ahead. The dark was now a diffuse gray and he could just barely discern the walls on either side. He hurried down the tunnel, forsaking his cell phone, to a dead end. Up above, daylight showed through small chinks between large, dark rocks. He turned underneath, examining them. They were ten feet over his head. The smell of seawater came along with the diminishing daylight of late afternoon. He was fairly sure he now stood under a section of the seawall that passed the marina where the *Natural Seize* was stored, but the spaces between the rocks could admit nothing larger than a cat, and the rocks were too large and heavy for him to move on his own.

He stood contemplating his options for a minute. He still had no cell phone reception. He could start yelling for help and hope someone heard him, but it was past closing time for the marina, unlikely that anyone would be there except a security guard pacing the perimeter fence, perhaps too far away to hear. He didn't relish the thought of standing for hours, trapped within Rook's influence, waiting for help. Perhaps the best idea was to at least try the other fork in the tunnel.

He turned back the way he'd come, resolutely holding the cell phone ahead of him again. Almost immediately he felt a change come over the environment. His claustrophobia increased. The air felt stifling, and the walls felt closer. He reached out to one side. The walls *were* closer! Slowly, the sides of the tunnel seemed to be closing in. Jack began to move faster, almost running. He glanced over his shoulder. Behind him, in the gloom, he could tell that the tunnel had already closed too far for him to retreat. His shoulders were now rubbing along either side of the passageway. He staggered along in the dark, tripping over the uneven floor, his face whipped by small roots sticking out of the sides.

Finally he stumbled into the wider area at the fork. A quick glance showed him that the way back to the parking lot was nothing but a jumble of rock and oozing stone. The only way passable was the unexplored fork. He turned down it, cursing Rook, his choices gone.

His panic lifted a bit as this channel didn't seem to be suffering the narrowing of the other two. He slowed a little and took more care. The tunnel veered to the left, but no other passageways forked off the main route. He had a feeling he was moving slightly inland, away from the coast.

Suddenly the tunnel began to slope upward steeply. Jack climbed along the stone chute, through a small doorway, and into what appeared to be a dead-end chamber. He waved the phone around. It had the look of a basement, with smooth, concrete walls and piles of packing crates around the sides. There was a ladder on the far side, but the top appeared to end at a solid ceiling.

Behind the ladder Jack saw what might be electrical conduit. He made his way to it and followed it to a switch box. He flicked the switch, and dim light filled the room from overhead, brighter by far than the cell phone's face light. He switched the phone off after checking for reception once again, and stowed it in his back pocket.

Jack turned to the ladder. It had to indicate a way out, since there didn't seem to be any other. He climbed it rung by rung and put his hand on the ceiling above. He slid his hand around carefully, trying to cover every inch of surface. There was definitely a seam, circular and large enough to admit a person. Against the back wall he felt a slight bump, shaped like a bar. He pressed it and ducked back down the ladder as a disk cut out of the ceiling began to rise.

Jack pressed himself against one of the walls and watched, wondering who he'd alerted to his presence. However, when no one appeared and he heard no sound from above, he carefully stepped up the ladder again. He poked his head through the void and looked around.

He knew immediately where he was. It was Perry's shop, now closed and dusty. He'd been in there on a few occasions before, mainly just to let Perry know he was still around, watching, and that he had his eye on the Fell Ken. Jack took a few more steps up. He was inside a large, glass-fronted curio cabinet. He quickly discovered the latch that would open the front from inside, and let himself out into the shop.

He knew from Terry's report that the Fell Ken had been there recently, but there didn't seem to be anyone inside at the moment. There was a front door leading out to the street and a back door that led to the residential part of the building, plus a door that led into a little kitchen behind the register.

He was tempted to flee the house immediately, but now that he knew where he was and Rook didn't seem to be chasing him anymore, he was very curious about the packing crates in the basement. He worked his way back down the ladder and looked around. There was a small crowbar lying on one of the crates, and a quick look showed him that the top of that crate had been forced recently, leaving little splinters of wood lying around and denting the underside of the lid. The other crates looked undisturbed.

He considered for a moment. If he opened any of the undisturbed crates, someone would certainly notice that they'd been tampered with. He certainly couldn't carry away whatever was in them at the moment, and if someone noticed they'd been disturbed they'd move or empty them. While it was possible he'd never be able to get back there, he decided it was to his advantage to keep his visit as secret as possible and simply gather information.

However, no one would know if he re-opened the crate that was already damaged. He could at least take a look. He grabbed the crowbar and easily loosened the lid, which had been laid on top of the crate but not tacked firmly down. It was heavy, but he managed to get it far enough up that he could prop it open with the crowbar. Then he carefully stuck a hand in and began to explore.

He had noticed an empty, smaller box on the floor, which he assumed had been removed from the crate. Sure enough, there was a space inside where the box would have been sitting. There were a couple other boxes that had been opened but otherwise didn't appear to have been moved, or had been replaced in the spots they'd come out of. Jack stuck a hand in one of them and came out with what appeared to be a gold coin, which he pocketed. No one would miss a single one, he hoped, since there appeared to be a lot of them.

He dug around in the packing material carefully until he located, in the back and under the material that would have cushioned the removed box, a package that felt smaller than the rest. He pulled it out to get a better look. It was wrapped carefully in a thick, canvas-like fabric, but from the size and feel of it, Jack guessed it was a book. He peeled back a bit of the fabric, enough to confirm his suspicion. He hesitated. It was tempting, but something that size would likely be missed. Reluctantly, he re-wrapped it and carefully replaced it where it had been.

Jack pulled his cell phone out once again and waved it around inside the crate, trying to get a better look. Packing material, small boxes, nothing he could take that wouldn't be missed. Just as he withdrew his hand he saw it: a tiny point sticking out of the packing material up against the back wall of the crate. He reached in, straining to get his fingertips to the back of the crate. He balanced the cell phone in the packing material and gingerly grabbed the point.

He pulled up a small envelope, made of something other than paper. He gently lifted the uppermost flap and slid out one of several objects within. He felt his heart miss a beat.

What he was looking at was a small scrap of stiff material with several square openings cut out of it. He knew immediately what it was: a code card, a device that, when laid over an encoded block of text, showed you which letters to pick out to create a coherent sentence. He quickly looked at the rest of the objects. There were five such cards, and a folded piece of vellum with a series of words written on it. Probably a check sheet to show you examples of words you should be able to locate, or show you how to use the cards, he guessed.

Jack glanced around quickly, as if someone might be sneaking up behind him in the basement. He set the envelope down carefully and replaced the lid on the crate. Then he scrambled up the ladder with the envelope, returning once to switch off the light.

Jack ducked out of the curio cabinet, located and pressed the inside lever that allowed the interior of the cabinet to slide back into place, and closed the glass front. Then he made his way around the register display shelves and into the kitchen area. There was a side door leading to the outside, preferable to simply walking out the front or through the house. He opened it an inch, peered out, then let himself out onto the little side landing above a few perilous old wooden stairs. He walked quickly away from the house down the sidewalk before pausing to pull out his phone again.

This time he had plenty of reception. "Don!" he exclaimed when his cousin came on the line. "You'll never guess where I've been. I need a lift back to my truck. I'll give you the address. I'll explain it all when you get here."

He stuck the phone back in his pocket, a feeling of elation replacing the panic and frustration he'd been experiencing. He'd escaped Rook's clutches, and he'd gotten something that might be valuable. He brushed dirt and bits of root out of his hair and off his shirt and pants as best he could. His stomach growled; Don could take him to dinner to celebrate and they'd take a look at the envelope's contents later.

Forty-five minutes later he and Don sat relaxed in a back booth in a cozy back-alley restaurant on the south side of Lafayette. Jack was still wearing his dirty clothes, but he knew the proprietor wouldn't mind; besides the owner being a Knight, the restaurant catered to local farmers and bike-touring groups.

Jack put the envelope on the table between them. "Shall we see what we've got?" He carefully slid the five cards and the vellum sheet out of the envelope and spread them on the table.

Don laid a hand on the envelope. "Feels like Fell Ken," he said quietly.

Jack nodded. "I think we've got something important here. Whether Rook meant for me to fall through into his tunnels or not, I came out the winner."

Jack explained how using the cards on a coded block of text would reveal the correct order for the letters to be in. "Usually spaces or marks indicating the ends of words are included. It's a first step, although once we've got real words, we still don't know the language. But it will make it easier to guess and to associate certain collections of characters with pictures. I'm hoping this set of cards will work on the book I've got in my office."

"But how will you know which card to use when?" Don frowned.

"Hopefully the check sheet will tell me or show me. If I can find the words, or the sets of characters, on the check sheet, I'll know I'm using the correct one. It will take some work. But if I'm lucky, I'll eventually be able to identify the procedures and verify the items that allow the failsafe device to be activated."

He slid the cards back into the envelope. Don drove him back to the parking lot at the office after dinner. They looked carefully at the lot in the dark and walked around the perimeter and across the area where Jack must have been walking when he plunged through, but there was no sign of any hole or disturbance to the asphalt. Eventually Jack got in his truck and followed Don out of the lot. It did not make him feel any safer not being able to see the hole and knowing that there was a Rook-created channel running under the parking lot of his office.

Cornerstone: The Delving

Chapter Eleven

Terry did not call. She did, however, send Lorcas a long, rambling email full of her thoughts about what she'd seen and her attempts to reconcile that with reality. Lorcas replied, assuring her that she wasn't crazy and that she'd understand more about how things worked in time.

"Maybe I'll come by and see you after work," Terry replied. "Just a quick visit. I never did get the measurements I wanted for the window."

"Any time," Lorcas replied quickly. "I'll keep an eye out for you."

As he was finishing up his reply, Zumar and Raine arrived. Zumar let them in through the front door without knocking, rather than just coming in through it. The door opened slowly but steadily for him.

"Tondra told me about the writing on the wall," he said. "She wanted me to come take a look."

"Did you walk the whole way?" Lorcas asked. It was still only mid-morning.

"Sort of. We can both move faster than a walk and we don't get tired like people with body weight do," Raine told him. "Andelko's slowing down, though." She elbowed him in the ribs.

Zumar said, "I took Raine down to Jack Bright's place yesterday evening to show her how to get there and we went through all the tunnels that Rook's made so far. It looks like he's pushing on towards Delva's place. We found a new tunnel going in that direction and explored it. We popped up a few times on top to see where we were."

"Jeez, Zumar, don't let anybody see you," Lorcas said. "You don't know what you're coming up into when you do that."

Zumar grinned at Lorcas' chiding, as usual. "We just poked our heads up. We got all the way to Delva's yard before we felt things beginning to fade. Hung out and looked at the house for a while. It was nice being someplace new." He paused and shook his head thoughtfully. "There's been someone else down in the tunnels. I could feel it."

"Plus there were footprints in the dust," Raine said. "And some of the tunnels had little pieces of gravel all over the place, like stuff had fallen off the ceiling. It wasn't there when we left to go to Delva's, but it was when we came back."

"Did you follow the footprints?" Lorcas asked. "Where did they come from? Did they go both directions?"

Zumar scratched his head. "Yes, dunno, no. The footprints dead-end at one of the intersections. The person was coming from that way, but Rook's been moving the tunnels around and destroyed the rest of them. In the other direction, they dead end at the basement under Perry's."

"Has anyone been in the shop?" Lorcas asked, concerned.

"After you folks were all over the place, who could tell?" Zumar asked. "There wasn't anyone there when we got back. It's possible we missed someone when we were at Delva's."

"Odd, though," Lorcas mused. "Who else would be walking around down there?"

"Maybe your weird girlfriend? She seems to pop up unexpectedly."

"Excuse you?" Lorcas protested. "I thought you said you liked her fine."

"I said she *felt* fine, as in, not a Koen. I didn't say I liked her."

"Well, it's none of your business," Lorcas snapped. "I like her, and that's what counts."

Zumar raised his eyebrows. "I don't know. What Tondra said about keeping you safe makes sense to me. But if it's not your girlfriend sneaking around down there, it's got to be one of us. We should probably find out who. Ready to go up to the Keep?"

Lorcas put his laptop on the couch and followed Zumar and Raine up to the Keep. Tondra, Tomash, and Alan were already there, studying the script. It had turned a charcoal gray, as though it was burned into the stone.

"Can you read it, Zumar?" Lorcas asked.

Zumar tilted his head and squinted. "I can translate it roughly. I'm surprised Rook didn't just write it in English. It's not like he doesn't know it at this point."

"Maybe he just thought it would look more impressive in fiery red script in a foreign language," Tomash said. "What does it say?"

Zumar cleared his throat and read aloud in a theatrical tone. Lorcas smiled to himself; Zumar's Slavic accent added auditory import in the way the fiery letters had added visual weight.

""You who would reject change, recall: those things that do not change, die. But change requires bravery beyond that of most men: for to change, one must leave this life behind and embrace another. Along this way lies the road to the future." And there's a separate line at the bottom: "Here is the seat of death and life.""

There was a long moment of silence. "So what's that supposed to mean?" Lorcas finally asked.

"I'd say it's either meant as encouragement or a warning. Could be either one, or both at the same time," Tondra replied.

"Most likely encouragement, since it's meant for the Fell Ken," Tomash said.

"But it could be a warning for the Koen," Zumar noted. "I'm sure some of them could read this, too."

"But Rook wouldn't let a Koen walk around in the Keep," Lorcas noted, "so it would be an odd place to put a warning for them."

"I'm not sure Rook can tell the difference between the Fell Ken and the Koen," Zumar said, crossing his arms.

"What? What about Korrin Bright? The Knight?"

"What about him? Rook let him walk right in, Knight-suit, sword, and all, and chase you around the chapel. The only reason you got away was because you harnessed Passage Power by running through the doors a bunch of times. You stopped him, not Rook. Once you dumped him in the dungeon, Rook decided to finish things off for you, since you obviously weren't pleased with the guy."

"And there was Condra," Tondra said. "I know she was a married-in Fell Ken, but she was working with the Koen. Rook didn't seem to care about her, either, until it became obvious you needed his help. I think Zumar's right: I'm not sure Rook can tell the difference between the Fell Ken and the Koen. Our families split apart in fairly recent times, from Rook's point of view. Either that, or he doesn't care."

"But the Koen don't know that, do they?" Lorcas demanded.

"I doubt it," Tondra said. "From their point of view, every time they've gotten too close to Rook, a disaster has happened."

"Let's keep it that way," Alan said. "And I have to agree with Lorcas: since it's unlikely the Koen know that Rook can't tell the difference between them and the Fell Ken, they wouldn't risk sending one of their own into Rook's domain."

"Relieved, Lorcas?" Tomash teased. "Your girlfriend can be indoctrinated into the secrets of the Fell Ken without issue."

Lorcas shrugged. "My mother and Alan got in. It does make things easier, though."

Zumar had been silent for a few minutes, staring at the wall.

"What are you thinking, Zumar?" Lorcas asked.

"Just trying to figure out exactly what Rook means," Zumar said thoughtfully. "Obviously he's reminding us that the Fell Ken are those on the side of change, Rook's change, and that those who can accept change, like us, survive. He's saying that this is the way of the future. But that last part worries me a little, the part about "one must leave this life behind and embrace another", and "here is the seat of death and life." I hope he's being figurative about that."

Lorcas caught Zumar's eye for a moment, remembering the sacrifice Rook had demanded and the suggestion he'd made that either Zumar or Tomash be that sacrifice. If Rook was referring to that, though, he was being too obscure.

"Well, you keep thinking," Tondra said. "We brought the other floor stones. Alan was considering getting safe-deposit boxes for the coins, so we needed to see how big of one we would need for each box. We pried the lids on the other crates to see how many boxes of coins there actually are, and unpacked everything from the first crate completely. It had the other three stones in it, plus a book and a couple other things."

"What's the book?" Lorcas asked.

"I've got it down in the office," Tondra said. "You can have it, since you're the resident expert at translating them." She glanced at the wall. "Or filing them, anyway."

She picked up an object wrapped in fabric from the front of the dais. Alan and Tomash each picked up another.

"Do you want to do the honors, Lorcas?"

Tondra turned back the flaps of cloth to reveal a dark-blue, glassy stone of about the same size as the cross, but in the shape of a diamond. Lorcas took it and looked around for the spot in which to put it. He found the indentation on the north side of the Keep, just west of the door to the tunnels, underneath the inscription.

He slid the stone in place and stood back, not sure what if anything to look for. After a few moments, there was a grinding sound from the front of the Keep. A smooth, blank area of stone behind the throne on the western wall split into pieces, which rotated out to form a six-pointed star. Markings made it resemble two triangles laid over the top of one another in opposing directions. The center sank in to form a depression, and within that area an embossed drawing consisting of several rectangles, triangles, and circles appeared.

"What the heck is that?" Tomash wondered.

Since the panel appeared to be done rearranging itself, everyone pressed up closer to it. But no one seemed to have an answer.

"Well, maybe the book we grabbed says something about it," Tondra said. "Or maybe you could do some research in your father's library, Lorcas."

"I'll see what I can find," Lorcas agreed. He hesitated. "Let's put off placing the other stones for right now. Stow them under the throne, and we'll do it after I have some time to figure out what this one means."

"Agreed," Tondra said. "No need to rush when we don't really know what we're doing." Alan and Tomash placed the other two wrapped packages on the dais, and Lorcas followed them down to the office to retrieve the book.

The day was bright and sunny, for once. The castle stood in sharp relief against the skyline, with a deep, clear blue as its background. Lorcas studied his shadow on the ground as he left the office. A strange shadow it was, certainly. He didn't see it that often, at least not clearly, due to the overcast weather. That was probably a good thing, he considered: Terry might know something about the true nature of the Fell Ken, but she didn't necessarily need to know that her boyfriend could separate his shadow at will and fly around in the body of a raven. He brought his arms out to the sides. His shadow responded, but with oddly distorted features. His shadow-arms looked more like wings. He flexed the feathers in his mind and the wing-shadows fluttered in response. Lorcas cocked his head. There was something slightly different about the wing-shadows, but he wasn't sure quite what.

He felt a swell of strength within him. He hadn't been flying much lately. Today would be a fantastic day to do it, with a brisk breeze off the ocean spilling over the cliff, the sparkling sea below and the brilliant sky above.

Lorcas strode quickly back to his house and made a second cup of coffee, which he poured into a metal mug with a lid. Near the door he paused long enough to grab his staff, which he always took along when he intended to fly. It seemed to ground him and make it easier for him to return to his body. Then he headed up the hill towards the chapel.

He pushed the back door open and paused in the dim interior, lit only by the light through the stained glass windows. Usually Zumar would be in the area, able to help and guide him if necessary and able to raise the alarm if there was a problem, but Zumar had disappeared along with Raine. He could run back down to the neighborhood and let Tomash know, or Alan or Tondra, but really, it wasn't necessary. He had flown by himself before without a problem, even rescuing Zumar from the Bob-blob during the assault on the castle.

His shoes echoed on the stone stairs as he trotted up to the third story. He took a few swigs of his coffee, grimacing because it was still very hot, then set the mug down and settled himself in an armchair he'd moved up there. It was far more comfortable than the stone seat near the window, and he could readjust the armchair as necessary for safety and efficiency. He leaned the staff carefully against the sill of the big open casement.

Then he relaxed into the chair and moved his shadow away from his body. He felt himself shrink to the vantage point of a raven. A big raven, he thought fleetingly, as he hopped up onto the sill. He raised his wings, feeling the wind gathering beneath them. The lift was intense and immediate. He rose a few inches, then tilted forward and down, spiraling around to catch the updraft in a location where he wouldn't be borne into the side of the castle.

He was feeling very strong. He had felt good the day he'd seen Jack Bright and his boat near the base of the slump, but he felt even more powerful now. Every beat of his wings bore him farther than ever before. When he stretched them to glide, he could feel the resistance beneath them as if he lay on a mattress.

He drew further away from the castle, over the edge of the cliff and above the sea. As usual, he worked his way down along the edge of the neighborhood, over the slump where the remnants of houses still protruded here and there. He followed the shoreline down through the neighborhood to the trees on the south side.

He often turned around there and headed back towards the castle, afraid to move too far beyond Rook's influence. But he was bored with flying over the neighborhood, and he didn't feel any diminishing of his strength like he usually did. Of course, he considered, Rook had extended his influence lately, all the way down to Seaside Heights. He wondered if he could find and follow the tunnels, and how far he could get. He would have to be careful, but he felt fine so far.

Lorcas swooped down closer to the ground. He swung back and forth across the southern edge of the neighborhood, where he could just begin to feel Rook's influence waning. Then he felt it: a strong uplift, similar to the feel of the castle itself. He turned and began to follow it. It was almost as if he could see it, rolling out ahead of him like a faint stripe of color. He rose a bit higher to avoid trees and found he was still able to track the route. He flew confidently on.

As he got closer to Seaside Heights he passed over some small rural neighborhoods. Several people looked up and pointed as he flew overhead. He was a bit surprised that a raven would attract any attention; they weren't uncommon in the area. But then, he felt larger than he had in the past; perhaps they were just pointing out a larger-than-normal raven.

He was elated to find that he could fly right past Jack Bright's office on the hill, where Zumar had accosted the Koen leader. Near there the route branched, and he took the right-hand route and followed it to the marina. He could feel the influence end there. He landed on top of the sea wall for a moment and took a quick look around. Jack's boat was there, parked under the canopy, with a shiny new propeller on the right-hand engine.

A dog trotting through the marina caught sight of him and started away, then came back barking. Lorcas flapped a few times and rose into the air, catching the breeze from the sea. He followed the route back the way he'd come, then took the second branch. This one led him down into Seaside Heights itself. Soon he was circling Perry's shop. He thought about trying to follow the route to Delva's, but he'd never flown that far before, and he had miles to go before he got back to Cliffview.

Lorcas flew strongly along the route back to the north. His confidence was increasing by leaps and bounds. Flying was actually fun again; he might do it more often if he could explore the countryside like this.

Suddenly he felt a powerful thump in his chest. It was as though someone had punched him with full force. He dropped out of the air and struck the ground, where he struggled to gain his feet, his wings spread and useless in a situation where he needed hands. A moment later he felt another strike. He crumpled on his side, gasping for air. He couldn't breathe. The pain in his chest came again.

Had he flown outside Rook's influence? Lorcas struggled to look around and to feel what was going on. It seemed to him he could still sense the route; in fact, he seemed to be right in the middle of it. It wasn't that he was outside the route; something else was going on.

Encouraged by the fact that he was still in contact with Rook, Lorcas forced himself to his feet, ignoring the ongoing pain. He hopped a few feet to a boulder and clambered awkwardly and painfully up it. At the top, he spread his wings. The breeze was there. Painfully, he flapped a few times and managed to gain some altitude. He nearly fell from the air again when another powerful shock struck his chest, but he managed to maintain his altitude and orientation.

He closed his eyes for a moment and willed himself to feel the staff leaning on the sill of the study. It was like a beacon in his mind, and he fixed his awareness upon it. Determinedly, he flew onward as fast as he could manage. He felt a great urgency to return to the castle.

As he got closer, he began to consider whether or not something could be happening to his physical body. That thought sent a bolt of adrenalin through him: if his body died, would he die as well? Could the Bob-blob have reached the tower, or a group of blobs? Were they swarming all over him, smothering him with no resistance?

He flew over Cliffview Estates and forced himself to flap enough times to rise to the window in the tower. The pain was incredible; he didn't think he could last a moment longer in his raven form.

As soon as he entered the casement he was sucked back into his human form. The mental shock was tremendous. He struggled to open his eyes. He felt huge confusion, as well as pain and disorientation.

When he managed to open his eyes a slit, he was even more disoriented. He'd expected to see the view out the window, but instead he saw nothing but stone. It occurred to him that he'd fallen out of his chair somehow, and was lying on his back on the floor. There was a loud buzzing in his ears, and his limbs felt paralyzed. In addition, there was a terrific pain in his chest and the taste of blood in his mouth.

Slowly his hearing began to clear, and he could hear a voice, although he could not respond.

"Lorcas? Lorcas?" asked the voice, with a hint of panic. "Can you hear me?"

Lorcas rolled his head a bit, feeling the stone on the back of his skull. He still couldn't speak. He tried to lift a hand. His vision was clearing quickly, and he felt that his hearing and ability to move would too, given a few minutes.

"Lorcas! Thank God," the voice continued. "I was so worried!"

Terry, Lorcas realized. She was kneeling next to him on the stone floor. He rolled his head to the side and looked at her, then down at himself. His chest was bare, his shirt lying open to the sides.

After another minute, he was able to push himself up on one elbow. He flipped one flap of his shirt closed and blinked in confusion. His chest was still terribly sore, as was his throat.

"What's going on?" he croaked.

"Lorcas, you weren't breathing!" Terry exclaimed, grabbing his arm. "I couldn't find you at your house, so I came up here to measure the casement for the stained glass. And I found you sitting here in your chair, and you weren't breathing."

Lorcas frowned, trying to make sense of the situation. He rubbed his chest, feeling for the key-shaped scar. "I wasn't?"

"No! And I got you on the floor and I couldn't find a heartbeat either! And you know there's no cell phone coverage up here, so I... I did CPR."

Now things were beginning to make sense. His chest was swollen and sore because Terry had been doing CPR on him. Had he actually not been breathing, or had he simply been so deep in his flying trance that Terry had mistaken his state for unconsciousness? He wasn't sure.

"Lorcas, we have to get you to a hospital," Terry insisted.

"No! No," Lorcas replied. "I don't need a hospital."

"But you were unconscious. You weren't breathing and you didn't have a heartbeat. That's not normal! We have to figure out what's going on."

"No!" Lorcas said again. He pushed himself up and struggled to get himself into his armchair. Terry supported him. "Sometimes I just go into a kind of trance, Terry. It's happened before. It's not a big deal."

"Not a big deal?" Terry laughed sharply. "Oh, okay, Lorcas, whatever. But I was doing CPR on you. Pumping on your chest, you know? I could have broken ribs, damaged cartilage, whatever. If nothing else, you need to go to the hospital for that."

Lorcas raised a hand. "Okay, Terry. I will consider it. Really. Right now I just really want to go home and lie down. If you can help me down the hill, we'll see what I feel like in a half-hour or so, okay?"

Terry pursed her lips, but she nodded. "Okay. I'm going to stay with you until I'm sure everything is okay, though."

"That's fine," Lorcas said. Terry slipped an arm around him and helped him to his feet. In reality, he thought, she'd actually caused his problem, not fixed it. But she meant well, and he did appreciate it. She must have been frantic, he thought, finding her boyfriend apparently unconscious in an area where she couldn't reach emergency services.

166

They made their way slowly down the steep stairs. Lorcas put out a hand to steady himself against the wall. He jerked it back immediately: the wall felt spongy beneath his palm, and it almost seemed as though his hand had sunk into the structure of the wall itself. He glanced at the stone, but there was no mark or hand-print there. Terry didn't seem to have noticed his reaction. He wiped his hand on his pants reflexively.

He trudged stiffly down the stairs with Terry supporting him. He had to admit, his ribs felt like they could be cracked. But he also knew there wasn't a lot to be done for damaged ribs, although if they continued to feel like this he might want some pain pills.

By the time they reached his house, he was feeling a lot better. His mind was clear, his hearing and vision were fine, and he was beginning to feel stronger. At least he hadn't vomited on Terry, something that had occurred more than once in the past when he was returning from flying.

"Should I go get your friends?" Terry asked after depositing him on the couch.

Lorcas shook his head. "No, that's okay." He started up suddenly, but the pain in his chest brought him back down. "Damn! You didn't by any chance grab my staff, did you?"

"You mean that walking stick that was leaning up against the wall? No, I didn't figure it was important."

"It is kind of important, but that's okay. I can go get it later."

"No, I'll run up there and get it. It'll only take a minute. I don't want you hiking back up that hill."

Lorcas waited until Terry was gone before carefully examining his chest. The area around the key scar was too swollen for him to tell what was going on there, but it almost felt as though the key had been displaced. It would probably find its way back to the proper location, he considered. He buttoned his shirt, noting that it was undamaged. Terry had carefully unbuttoned it rather than ripping it when she had started CPR. That was nice of her, although a bit unusual, he thought.

A few minutes later Terry returned. "Where do you want this?" she asked, holding out the staff.

"Just lean it in the corner there by the door," Lorcas said. "Thank you for getting it."

"I need to make a phone call," Terry said. "I'm supposed to be at work soon, but I'm going to call in sick."

"No, no," Lorcas said. "I'm probably just going to go to sleep, anyway. Don't miss work because of me."

"But I don't feel good leaving you alone," Terry insisted. "Let me get your friend Tomash."

Lorcas was about to protest again, but the door of the library swung open. Zumar stepped out and stood, hands in pockets, observing the two of them.

"I'll keep an eye on him," he said nonchalantly.

Terry scrambled up from the couch. "Did you hear us talking? Do you know what happened?"

"Lorcas can tell me," Zumar said. "I'm perfectly capable of getting help if he needs it. You can go on to work."

"Well…" Terry hesitated. "I suppose, if you promise to check on him regularly."

"Oh, I will," Zumar said. "I don't have to sleep much."

Lorcas struggled to his feet and took Terry's hands. "I really need to thank you. I'm sorry you were so scared and I really appreciate what you did for me."

Terry nodded. "I'm sorry I hurt you. I was really worried, but you're okay now. Just don't put off going to the hospital if you need to. And I'll call you later, or tomorrow. Okay?"

"Okay," Lorcas smiled. "I'm feeling better already. I'll be fine."

Terry collected her things and headed out towards her truck. When he heard the truck's engine start, Lorcas turned to Zumar.

Zumar walked slowly across the room, maintaining eye contact. He did not stop until he was inches away. Lorcas, half a head taller, looked down with some discomfort into Zumar's gray eyes. His stare could be disconcerting, and Lorcas had always chalked it up to him being several hundred years old, but sometimes he wondered what it was Zumar thought he was seeing and what was going through his mind.

"You look a little ragged around the edges," Zumar finally said.

"Yeah, somebody just thumped on my chest and nearly disassociated me from my shadow," Lorcas said with an uncomfortable laugh. He turned away from Zumar and made some room by lowering himself onto the couch.

"Not just that," Zumar said. "You look like you're becoming less corporeal."

Lorcas stared at him. He thought of the feeling of his hand sinking into the stone wall. But he felt plenty solid right now. His hand crept down to the couch cushion, testing its solidity.

Zumar narrowed his eyes. "You're becoming more like Rook."

"You mean more like you," Lorcas said uncertainly.

"No. I'm dead, technically. Only my shadow still exists. You still have your body and your shadow. You can move from one into the other. But it's becoming so each one is a little bit more of the other. That's more like Rook."

Lorcas swallowed. He tasted blood in his mouth. "I don't want to talk about it right now."

"Uh-huh." Zumar turned away abruptly. "What happened up there? What did she do to you?"

"She thought she was saving my life," Lorcas said dismissively. "It wasn't her fault."

"Really. How do you feel?"

Lorcas considered. "Weird. I feel a little weird. But that's to be expected." He rubbed his chest again.

Zumar went over to the staff where Terry had propped it in the corner. He ran a hand gently along it. Lorcas watched, wondering what the heck he was doing. Zumar, however, said nothing.

"Look," Lorcas said, feeling the need to defend Terry, "I know you don't like her. She's an outsider, I grant you that. But I haven't seen anything that would make me suspicious. There's no reason for you to be so stand-offish with her."

"Isn't there? Our fates are bound together, Lorecaster, like it or not. If anything happens to you, I'm screwed. It's my job to be suspicious for you, and it's in my best interest as well. You could have disposed of me for good down there in the cellar the other day, but you stood up for me instead. Maybe it wasn't ever Rook's intention to do anything to me, maybe it was a test like you say. But I owe you for it anyway. I'm going to make sure you're safe whether you like it or not."

Lorcas rolled his eyes in exasperation. "Whatever, Zumar."

"You should have some wine," Zumar said decisively. "You need strength, and Rook can give that to you."

He walked into the kitchen and scooted a glass across the kitchen counter. Then he wrapped a hand around the wine bottle and slowly inched it across to the glass. Lorcas watched over the back of the couch with interest. Zumar tilted the bottle without lifting it, and a narrow stream poured into the glass. When it was about half full, he grabbed it with both hands and brought it to Lorcas.

"Thanks," Lorcas said as Zumar carefully lowered the glass into his hands. "Have some yourself."

"I'll do that," Zumar said. "I'll stay until I'm sure you're okay. Then I've got to head out. I have a few things to do."

Lorcas drank the half glass, then got up to get himself some more. Zumar was right; it made him feel a lot better, almost normal, except for the sore chest and the weird taste in his mouth. A sudden inspiration hit him.

"Don't go anywhere yet, Zumar. I want to try something, now that I can see you a little better than I was able to in the past."

He flipped a new sheet of paper onto his drawing table and taped it down, then adjusted the table so he could stand facing the living room and the chair where Zumar sat. Quickly, he sketched an outline. He'd never drawn a person before, at least not since he was a kid, before he was serious about his art. But a couple glasses of wine later, he had a passable beginning sketch of Zumar's young, rounded face, large eyes, and tousled, wavy hair. He was pleased with it by the time he decided to quit for the night.

Zumar grinned when he saw it and tipped his wine glass in mock salute. "The immortal immortalized," he joked. "I'm off, now. Don't try any solo flying again anytime soon."

Cornerstone: The Delving

Chapter Twelve

The day following the incident in the tower, Lorcas woke up restless and uneasy. He felt empty, lost, and unsure. It was as though something was missing, but he wasn't sure what. He rubbed the scar on his chest; the pain from Terry's CPR was abating, but the scar bothered him as it had when he'd first gotten it. He hadn't used the key in a year or more and rarely thought about it, so it was odd to have his attention drawn to it. The scar felt flatter than usual, and he contemplated bringing the key out, but that was unpleasant, and he convinced himself that he should just try to ignore it.

He went into the bathroom and looked in the mirror. He examined his reflection, especially around the edges. Was what Zumar had said true? Did he seem less corporeal, more shadowy? He couldn't tell for sure. The thought of his hand sinking into the stone of the chapel gave him the shudders. He had awakened multiple times during the night with a shock, having dreamed of it. He was getting tired, stressed. He dug out the medication he'd been prescribed for depression before Rook, but it was well expired and he threw it back in the bathroom drawer, unwilling to chance taking any.

Downstairs he flipped through his drawings. He examined the one he'd started of Zumar. It was pretty good, he thought, but it needed a lot of work. His model was missing, as Zumar was nowhere to be seen.

He looked at the one he was doing for Terry's design. Terry was at work, he knew, and he figured there was little chance of seeing her for at least a couple of days. It would be a good opportunity to get some work done on the design so he could pass it off to her next time they got together. The more he thought about it, the more he wanted to make it into a memorial. His mood was right to put that kind of inspiration into the piece.

Strange thoughts moved through his mind once again. The radio was playing in the background and his attention was taken for a few moments by an old song. He looked back again at his drawings. They had been his life before Rook: technical, but still art, his personal connection to culture. There was no specific Fell Ken culture of which he was aware, although his father's books seemed to indicate a kind of shared history. Who knew what culture, if any, Rook and his kind possessed?

What had Rook promised him? The opportunity to create peace, a world with no terrible wars or disease. But, Lorcas realized, people had to have something to inspire them, to motivate them to move forward. It seemed to him that inspiration often came from hardship. He didn't want human beings to lose that creative power, to lose art, music, and culture. It would be, he considered, the loss of that which makes us human.

Rook mainly operated through fear and motivated with mystery and secrets. That wasn't sufficient anymore. He needed to have more detail, to know more fully where they were going and why he should stick with it. He didn't know what he wanted anymore or why he should want it.

He shook his head to clear his mind. He had felt this way before. He had to stop himself from descending into that pattern of thinking. In reality his life had been much more complete and satisfying since he'd begun his association with the Fell Ken. He needed to continue to focus on that. It seemed to be his fate to be connected to this next stage that the world was entering. Things could be worse; he could be totally unaware of what was coming and completely unprepared. As it was, he was on the front lines. Or he was the front line himself, he considered.

His phone rang and he set his pencils down to pick up the phone from the coffee table.

It was Terry. "Just thought I'd check on you," she said. "I'm glad you're up and around. Did you go to the hospital?"

"No, I'm fine. Just a little tired. I heal fast. It's part of the power of this place. Don't worry about it."

"Did Zumar do what he said? Did he keep an eye on you?"

"Of course," Lorcas said. "He was here for a long time. I even did a drawing of him. I'll show you next time you're up here."

"Well, I need to come up later today or tomorrow after work and take some measurements so I can finish designing your stained glass window. I planned to take the measurements yesterday, but…"

"Yeah, come up any time," Lorcas said. He felt his mood lift a little. "I'll take you back into the tower. You said you wanted to look at the Keep, too."

"If I remember correctly, there are some small upper windows in there, and I thought they might make good spots for sun-catcher style stained glass, if you want them."

"Sure," Lorcas agreed. "See you when you get here."

With renewed vigor Lorcas returned to his drawing. By late afternoon he had a pretty good design, featuring the raven, just the edge of a castle turret on one side, forest on the other side, and a viewpoint that allowed a distant glimpse of the edge of the cliff, with a small, lone figure standing upon it. He added the finishing touches just as Terry pulled up outside the wall. He heard her truck, then a minute later the latch on the gate, and met her at the door.

"It's not too complex, is it?" he asked as Terry perused the drawing.

"No. It'll be a challenge, but I'm not a beginner anymore. I just need to get the dimensions. I might have to expand or contract certain parts to fit the shape."

Lorcas noticed she was looking beyond the drawing table towards the library. He had left the door ajar after putting the book Tondra had brought him on the desk a few days before. He hadn't shown the room to Terry; it felt a bit too private.

But before he could distract her, Terry walked quickly over to the door and peered in. "What's this? It looks like a den."

"My dad's library," Lorcas said, hastily meeting her there. He swung the door a bit further but didn't step in, hoping that would discourage her from entering herself. "Kind of musty and dark. I don't use it much."

Terry scanned the room. "This is where Zumar was. What was he doing in here?"

"Probably looking at books," Lorcas said. It hadn't occurred to him to wonder, himself, although Zumar didn't live there anymore and really had no business snooping around his house. He'd have to have a talk about privacy with the shadow, especially if Terry was going to be there on a regular basis.

"Lots of books, alright. Odd kind of color pattern on the shelves. It looks like scales," Terry observed.

"A filing system of my dad's," Lorcas said. "He had some interesting ideas about organization."

"Your family seems to have a thing for scales," she said. "Your father used them as organizational tools, you draw fish and reptiles."

"Hmm. I never really realized that," Lorcas admitted. In fact, scales or scale-like structures seemed to be a recurring theme with Rook, now that he thought about it.

"What's that?" Terry asked, pointing at the sword. It was leaning up against the wall in the corner where Lorcas usually left it when he wasn't blob hunting.

"Eh, some old artifact," he said with what he hoped was a disinterested shrug. "Come on, let's go to the chapel."

"Don't make me sing that old song about going to the chapel," Terry joked. "I don't think we're at that stage yet!"

Lorcas led her up the hill and through the chapel to the tower, although he knew she knew how to get there herself. He patted the wall tentatively, pleased to find it solid. He helped Terry position the tape measure she'd brought and waited while she added the dimensions to a quick sketch she made. Then they headed for the Keep.

"I don't remember that engraving on the wall," Terry said when she stepped inside.

"It wasn't there when we came in here before," Lorcas said. "It's new."

"What does it say?"

"Something about the value of change, I don't remember the exact quote. That engraving is new, too." Lorcas pointed to the geometric bas relief behind the dais.

"Huh." Terry stepped closer and examined it. "Sacred geometry."

"What?"

"It's an architectural plan or style that depends on specific geometric shapes with precise measurements. It's been around since the Middle Ages. Do you know the dimensions of the chapel and the Keep?"

"No, but I could find out."

"Well, I'll bet these two rectangles here represent them. The overlay of triangles and circles show how they're arranged in the scheme. See, there are some other features marked here, although I don't know what they are."

"Cemetery maybe, and the well, and part of the arc of the wall, now that you point it out," Lorcas said, running his fingers over the stone. "Wonder what the part below it is."

"A plan," Terry said. "It's showing you how the rest of the castle is, or will be, laid out. You said there was a basement you were going to take me into some time. If you can do some measurements, I'm sure you'll find that it fits into these shapes. You just have to figure out how to turn the plan, and then, if there are any other levels, how to place those layers within the plan. Then you basically have a map."

Lorcas stared at the wall for a long moment. That would be useful. He had thought Rook was building haphazardly, but obviously he was not. According to the plan, the lower levels were much more contained and squared-off along the sides than he had imagined when he'd been down there, but distances and curves were harder to calculate in the dark. Rook's plan, if that was indeed what it was, seemed to include a number of levels which tended to get larger as they went down, with interesting side features Lorcas couldn't figure out.

"Didn't you know what plan the castle was being built on?" Terry questioned him. "You said you have a controlling interest in this venture. I figured you'd know all about the design and layout."

Of course, Lorcas realized, she still thought the castle was being built by human hands. She wouldn't have any way of knowing that the castle built itself, or that at least the design was dictated by Rook, with no plans, plats, or blueprints having been provided to his human assistants. She probably still thought they were planning on using the castle as a tourist facility in the future.

"No, I'm not involved in the actual architecture," he answered carefully. "There are some unique aspects of the design and planning that are too complicated to go into at this point. Let's just say that the underground parts of this complex are designed to be disorienting, and you probably shouldn't go in there by yourself."

Terry contemplated the plan again. "Yes, it's complicated. And see here, this level is meant to be important." She tapped on a spot in one of the lower levels. "Seventeen levels down, if I'm not mistaken. The outline of this chamber is emphasized."

Lorcas ran a finger over the outline. Yes, it was deeper than the other scratches. It was, he realized, likely to be Rook's chamber. Something he didn't want her to dwell on for too long.

"Power center," he said, hoping that would be enough, and then changed the subject. "What do you need to do now?"

"Just got to get these upper windows sketched in," she said, "then I'll be done."

"Did you sketch the map?" Lorcas asked. If so, she'd done it quickly, and he hadn't seen her do it.

"No, I don't care about the map. Do you have a ladder? I need to get up to the windows."

"Not one that will reach," Lorcas said, "but there's a balcony. We can do the dimensions for the windows we can get to from there and get the other ones some other time, when we can borrow a ladder from Tomash. I can do it for you if I know what measurements you need."

He led her into the door in the north wall and turned left up the ascending staircase. Terry glanced at the descending stair to the right, but did not ask about it. They wandered around the bare upper balconies while Terry measured the few windows she could reach.

"Well, I'm done here," Terry finally announced. "They're all the same size along here, but the end windows look like they could be different. I'll have to get them another time." She pulled out her cell phone and checked the time. "Hmm. Looks like I've got a little extra time. Maybe we should go back down to your place for a bit. If you're up to it, of course. You're still looking a little pale."

She smiled and raised her eyebrows. Lorcas took only a second to pick up on her inference. He grabbed her hand and led her out of the Keep. "Oh, I'm feeling just fine. Let's go!"

After Terry left with her sketches, dimensions, and Lorcas' plan for the window, Lorcas went over to the office to find Tondra and Alan. Tomash was there too. He told them what Terry had discovered about the geometric shapes on the wall.

"That would have been useful in times past," Tomash said. "Too bad we don't have some sort of idea of how he's planning on expanding outside the Cliffview area. Maybe it's not as haphazard as we thought."

"I wonder what the angles are between Cliffview, Seaside Heights, and Lafayette?" Tondra mused. "They might fit into a geometric plan. Rook had to have picked this spot, or his handlers had to have, for some reason. I doubt they carried a rock all the way here from Europe only to plunk it down randomly. Maybe the geometry of the place gives him power."

"Maybe it's time to put the other two stones in the floor," Alan suggested. "Who knows what they might reveal?"

"Good idea," Tondra agreed. "Today would be a good time. Zumar and Raine are here somewhere. They might be able to help if any more text appears."

The four of them walked back up to the castle. Lorcas had not seen Zumar or Raine during his tour with Terry, but they were in the Keep when the group arrived. Tomash and Alan fetched the other two stones from the dais. Lorcas chose Alan's stone first. It was yellow, as glassy as the others, but opaque and shaped like a pentagon. He set it into the matching depression just inside the Keep's eastern door and looked at the walls.

It was the southern wall that started to change this time. Spidery cracks snaked across it, generally following geometric lines like the engraving behind the dais, but on a much larger scale. Tiny squares and rectangles began to appear at the points of a giant triangle. Other features filled in slowly until the entire wall was covered with what appeared to be a huge topographic map, two stories high and nearly the length of the Keep.

180

Alan pointed out the features. "There's Lafayette, there's Seaside Heights, there's Cliffview, complete with buildings, topography, roads, and the whole thing. You were right, Tondra: there's a geometric relationship between the three towns. And I suspect these lines here are the routes Rook's co-opted. There's a faint overlay of shapes, if you look closely. Everything is arrayed along the edges of circles, triangles, and rectangles with arcs inside them."

"Interesting information," Tondra said. "I'm not sure what use it is to us at this point."

Lorcas' attention was drawn back to the yellow stone. It was pulsing slightly, a glow rising and receding rhythmically. He walked back to it and laid a hand upon it, wondering if it was warm. The glow sank into the interior of the stone. He looked back up at the others.

"Hey!" Alan exclaimed. "There's something else happening on the map!"

A bright glow began to develop in the area of Seaside Heights. Another tiny, pinpoint glow showed in the Cliffview area in a square that appeared to represent the Keep itself, and a third tiny light appeared along the coast. The third light was moving slowly.

"I wonder what those mean," Tondra mused. "The third one is moving."

"Maybe there's a clue in the other walls," Alan said. He walked over to the geometric drawing behind the dais.

"I thought I just saw the glow at Cliffview move a little," Tondra said. "Alan, walk around the Keep."

Alan circumnavigated the interior of the Keep while the others kept their eyes on the tiny light. Sure enough, the light described a perfect rectangle corresponding to Alan's movements.

"It's tracking you," Tondra said. "I wonder why."

Alan reached in his pocket and pulled out one gold coin. "I wonder if it's this. This is the first one we removed from Perry's basement. I've just kept it with me as I try to do some research on its origins."

"That would make sense," Lorcas said. "Look, the really big glow would be at Perry's, where the rest of the coins are. Give me yours for a minute."

Alan passed it over and Lorcas walked around the Keep like Alan had. The pinpoint light followed his movements as it had followed Alan's.

"So it's tracking the coins," Tondra said. "The one in Alan's pocket, the ones at Perry's place, and…" She paused and pointed to the third light, the one just off the coast. "But which one is that?"

There was silence. No one could answer her. "I don't know who else has a coin," Alan finally said.

"Well, we need to find out," Tondra said. "When we do, we'll be able to track whoever it is if we want to."

"And anybody else who has a coin, I guess," Alan said as Lorcas returned his to him. "This could be very useful. Er, I think I'll put mine in my desk!" He grinned.

Zumar had walked up very close to the wall and was staring up at the point of light.

"Do you know who it is, Zumar?" Tondra asked.

He shook his head. "No. It's not in any building. It's outside somewhere. Almost as though it's in the ocean."

He backed away, but Lorcas caught him exchanging a quick glance with Raine. He wasn't sure what it was about, but he found it suspicious.

"I guess we should place the final stone," Tondra said. Alan picked it up and unwrapped it, and Lorcas placed it in the depression along the south wall, below the map. It was green and shield shaped. A picture resembling a coat of arms appeared on the eastern wall next to the door in full color, featuring what looked like the star map window in the chapel, against which was set a sword, a rod, a ring, and a key. When the green stone glowed like the yellow one had

Lorcas touched it again. The objects moved slowly into different places. Finally, a castle shaped outline rose out of the floor until it encompassed the shield. Then it faded slowly, leaving the original coat of arms in its first arrangement.

"Not sure what that means," Tondra said. "Kind of anticlimactic after the map."

Zumar studied it and reached up to tap one of the figures. "This one is your sword, Lorcas. Obviously these other two are the key and the ring. This rod isn't the staff, though; it's the caduceus, the cane that's inside the staff when you unscrew it. Rook's showing you that these four things are important for this next phase, but I don't know what it means beyond that."

"I'm sure it means something," Lorcas said. "We'll figure it out eventually. I'll take a look in that book that came in the first crate when I have a minute."

The group started down the hill towards the neighborhood. Zumar hung back a bit with Lorcas, who was bringing up the rear.

"You haven't heard from Rook lately, have you?" he asked nervously.

"No," Lorcas said. "He hasn't gone away as completely as he did before, though. Every once in a while he kind of tickles my mind, like he's reminding me."

"I saw you and your girlfriend in the chapel and the Keep," Zumar went on. "We were in the cemetery. I'm surprised you brought her back up in the tower after what she did to you the other day."

"It was an accident," Lorcas responded. "Or not an accident, but innocent. I can't blame her."

"I can," Zumar said. "You don't just grab someone and start doing this CPR stuff when they're not dead, do you? Raine knows all about it. She was trained in it."

"No, but she thought I wasn't breathing."

"But you were," Zumar argued. "You were fine. She didn't check very well, did she?"

Lorcas stopped abruptly. "What are you getting at?" he snapped, turning on Zumar. He was getting tired of this prodding.

Zumar spread his hands. "Just that the whole thing is a little weird. Do you think it's a good idea to walk her around everywhere, show her all the secrets of the castle? She knows how to get to the balconies now, and she saw the door to the underground. Are you going to take her blob hunting next?"

"She'd probably enjoy it," Lorcas said. "Maybe I will. You jealous? She taking too much of my time? You seem awfully interested in sneaking around in my house when you don't belong there anymore."

Zumar snorted. "I don't need your time, Lorecaster, but don't forget that you might still need me. You have a job to do, remember? Find a sacrifice. Or maybe you have found one?"

"What are you insinuating? That I'm planning on sacrificing Terry?" Lorcas asked incredulously. "You're crazy!"

"Just a thought," Zumar said smugly.

Raine scrambled back up the hill to where they had paused. "Hey you guys, you're not having some kind of argument, are you?"

"Certainly not," Zumar said with a grin. "Lorcas was just saying how he needs to be careful with what he shows his new girlfriend."

"Oh, sure," Raine said. "She's not Fell Ken, and she's just learning this stuff. I remember back when I was a little kid and Tondra started seeing Alan. He had to be introduced real slow."

"Huh." Lorcas crossed his arms.

"They have to get used to things," Raine continued. "Seeing us, me and Andelko, that was way advanced, way too early. It was probably a big shock."

"I'm not sure what she actually thinks about you two," Lorcas said. "She doesn't understand about the castle. She still thinks we're building it like a normal construction project."

"That's good," Raine said, nodding. "There are certain other things you probably shouldn't show her right off the bat."

"Like what?" Lorcas asked. He was interested in what Raine had to say. It might be exactly what Zumar would have told him, but Raine said it better, as far as he was concerned. He could tolerate instruction from her.

"Oh…" Raine frowned and looked around. "Like the little lake, for example. You probably shouldn't let her look in that too long."

"Why not?" Lorcas gazed down the hill at the pond. It was always dark, as though it couldn't reflect the sky. He had never seen much purpose in it, unless it was the promise of a feature to come in the future.

"Well, the lake's a scrying-pool," Raine said matter-of-factly. "If you know what you're doing, you should be able to see future possibilities in it. Not certainties, just options."

"I didn't realize that," Lorcas said.

"Oh, I thought it was obvious the first time I saw it," Raine said, "but that is one of my specialties, so it might be more obvious to me."

"Have you looked in it, then?"

"Once or twice," Raine grinned. "Not for very long. I haven't been back for too long and it saps my energy, so I haven't had a chance to really get in there."

"Can you show me?" Lorcas asked.

"Maybe," Raine said thoughtfully. "I might be able to guide you."

"Go ahead," Zumar said. "I need to get together with Alan. I'll meet you there in a few minutes."

Lorcas followed Raine the rest of the way down the hill, wondering idly what Zumar and Alan had to discuss. He'd never known the two of them to be social, but he figured it was none of his business.

For the first time, Lorcas stood directly on the shore of the little lake, staring down at its dark surface. He'd only seen it from the stairs or up at the chapel or Keep before, but even from there he'd remarked on the oddly distorted reflection. Now, up close, the reflection seemed even odder, more akin to a watercolor painting than an actual image of the buildings themselves.

Raine knelt and stirred the water with a fingertip. She didn't seem to have any issue touching this water; shadow-water, Lorcas thought, as much a part of her world as his. The image rippled and then steadied as the surface returned to a glassy state. Raine remained on one knee, staring fixedly into the pond. Lorcas bent with hands on knees, looking from Raine to the reflection.

"What do you see?" Raine whispered. She pointed to the reflection, and Lorcas squinted at it.

"The castle," he replied.

"Anything different about it?"

Lorcas paused. "It looks like it's up really high, on a taller hill, somehow." He squinted. "We're looking up at it from way below, maybe from back by the edge of the trees. I can't quite see... there's something on top, something moving. Like a flag or..." He paused. For a moment he thought he saw something else, but it was only a flash of an idea, and it was too brief to voice. The castle, when he looked again, had returned to a semblance of its current self.

Raine was grinning up at him. "I saw it, just for a moment!" she said. "If you want to see more..."

"No!" Lorcas straightened. "I don't think I do. I don't want to tire you out. Besides, I think I'd rather just let the future become whatever it's going to become by itself, and be surprised."

"I can understand that," Raine said. "It's more fun."

"And less alarming," Lorcas said. He could see Zumar approaching from the direction of the office.

"You two want to come in for a drink?" he asked. "You can use my computer if you want to."

"I think we'll head back to Seaside Heights," Raine said, "but thanks. Oh, and if you change your mind, don't stare into the lake too long without me. These things can suck you right in. Literally."

"I'll remember that," Lorcas said. He stepped away from the lake. He had no intention of looking in it again. He understood why he shouldn't let Terry look in it, as well.

Chapter Thirteen

When Jack pulled in to the marina Terry was already there, leaning on the side of the *Natural Seize*. Her truck was parked at a haphazard angle alongside. Jack pulled up near the rear of the boat and looked around cautiously. He figured the marina was a lot safer than his office, but he wanted to be sure. He had come up underneath the rocks in the seawall during his journey down Rook's tunnels, so he knew the marina was accessible by Zumar and probably by whoever his ghostly friend was.

He rolled down the window and motioned her over. "Follow me. We're going to a restaurant in Lafayette that's owned by one of our people. I don't want to meet in Seaside Heights at all anymore."

"You could have told me over the phone," Terry replied. "I just drove here from Lafayette."

"I'm sorry," Jack said, "but I just made the decision on the way over. Let's go."

He swung the truck around in the yard and waited until he saw Terry in line behind him. He was being extra cautious not giving her the name of the restaurant, but he didn't want her programming it into her GPS unit or writing it on a piece of paper, on the off chance that Lorcas or another of the Fell Ken might get in her truck and somehow notice it. It was likely they knew which places were the Knights' strongholds, and it would raise suspicions.

When they arrived, Jack pulled around to the back of the restaurant where their trucks couldn't be seen by causal passers-by. He noted that Terry didn't park next to him, but a distance away at the very back of the gravel lot, under a tree. That was an extra precaution he appreciated. At least she wasn't stupid.

Jack waited for her to join him just inside the back door and then led the way to his usual table in the back. It was private, and at that time of day the place was almost deserted anyway.

Terry brought a gym bag in with her which she plopped down on one of the chairs. She took another chair, and Jack scooted in to the bench, facing the door. After they were seated, Terry reached into a pocket of her sweatshirt and then across towards Jack with a closed hand. "Want to see?"

Jack looked at the hand. She hadn't told him why she wanted to meet, but he assumed she'd gotten some information she needed to share. "Sure."

Terry turned her hand over and opened the fingers. A small, dark metal, cross-shaped key lay on her palm.

"Is that…" Jack almost reached for it, but drew his hand back. He didn't want to know what would happen if he, a Knight, touched it.

"Yep. Get this: a couple days ago I went to Cliffview on the pretext of getting measurements for the stained glass window I'm making. Couldn't find Lorcas at his house, so I figured it gave me an excuse to snoop around a little by myself. I went on up to the chapel and up into the tower and found Lorcas in some sort of trance, sitting in his chair. He didn't even know I was there."

"Probably flying his shadow," Jack mused.

"Anyway, it came to me that I had a perfect excuse to get the key. I knew where it was because I saw the scar the other night when, er, he was shirtless. It's pretty obviously key-shaped. And I remembered something from one of those books you gave me: there's an illustration of a person hitting himself on the chest and spitting out a key."

Jack raised his eyebrows. He'd seen the picture himself. It was well-known that Lorecasters generally carried the key 'against the breastbone', as the old manuscripts put it, but he and others had assumed that meant attached to a chain like a necklace, rather than actually within the chest. He shuddered a bit imagining how it could have gotten there in the first place.

Terry continued. "So I hauled him onto the ground and started doing CPR, starting with a big thump to the chest. Checked his mouth and sure enough, the key had popped out. He came back to himself pretty quickly, but he didn't really know what had happened."

"Pretty risky. He could figure it out if he notices the key is missing."

"True, but he didn't seem to notice, at least not right then. He was pretty out of it, confused and sick. I'm not sure if that was from the trance or the CPR. But I figured if it seemed like he did notice it missing, I could tell him it was in his mouth and I didn't want him to choke on it, so I removed it, and I could give it back. But there's more."

Jack waited while Terry unzipped the gym bag on the chair beside her. "He had that staff, the tall one, there with him in the tower, but he forgot and left it there when I helped him back to his house. Then he asked me to go get it. I did, but before I brought it to him I figured out how to unscrew it and took this." She slapped a long, thin wooden rod down on the table. "That's item number two!"

Jack stared at the rod with its intricate, low-profile scrollwork design. He suspected that those designs served as keys to part of the mechanism when the rod, the caduceus, was inserted. A glimmer of hope began to grow in him. Everything he tried always seemed to be a longshot, and so far nothing had worked the way he'd hoped or planned. But now he was beginning to think it might be possible to do this.

"Keep them for now," Jack said. "You might end up being the one who actually uses them. Make sure they're accessible all the time, because as soon as you have all the objects and the opportunity, you need to take it."

"Wow, that's a bit of a change," Terry said with a grin. "Before it's been "we just need information" and "you won't be involved at the end" and "we don't even know for sure what the correct objects are or how to use them." Now suddenly it's "get the objects and use them as soon as you can.""

Jack nodded. "Yes. I know it's a change, but you've exceeded my expectations. I'm beginning to rely on you more. You've become very important to me and to the Knights as a whole." He hoped that some flattery and some honesty as far as her role would encourage her to continue the mission. "I've been studying the books myself, and I'm pretty sure you can concentrate on the first four objects I showed you: the key, the caduceus, the ring, and the sword. Don't risk trying to get anything else, like the silver goblet. And I have a good idea how to use them. I'll show you what I've discovered. We'll practice, so you can do it under pressure without thinking too much about it."

"And if worse comes to worse, I just do it, without it being confirmed," Terry replied. "But why the hurry all of a sudden? You were pretty chill about it before."

"I've gotten word from our people in Europe that some kind of a call has gone out. The Fell Ken from all over the world are packing up and leaving. I imagine they're coming here, and that means something's happening soon."

"Well, I still have to get the other two things," Terry said, "but I know where the sword is. It's in his library, just leaning against the wall. It shouldn't be too difficult to get when I need it. It's the ring that Tomash has that worries me."

"Keep working on things, and we'll figure something out," Jack said. "You're doing much better than I ever would have expected."

Terry sat back in her chair, suddenly serious. "What do you think will happen to Lorcas when, and if, we manage to operate this failsafe?"

"I'm not sure," Jack admitted. "I think Rook will retreat to his cornerstone and the castle will probably fall apart or sink into the ground. Zumar and any other shadow, if they're caught out, might not be able to return to the cornerstone in time, I suppose. They could die, but they're already dead, so I don't know that it matters. Lorcas is a living human being, so unless he gets hit on the head by a falling rock or trapped in the castle, I should think he'll be fine, along with the rest of the Fell Ken. Just disabled."

"You should think," Terry echoed cynically.

"You can back out," Jack reminded her casually.

"And you would send who, then? Kyle? He'd be as much of a bumbling idiot as Korrin was, although maybe not as ridiculous. He'd be sincere, and sincerely dead."

Jack shrugged. In truth, he didn't know how they'd accomplish this plan without Terry. But he didn't want to make it seem as vital as he knew it to be. She already had him over a barrel with what she knew, and he didn't care for it. She could easily blackmail the group or betray them to their deaths.

"Well, I'm in this too deep now," Terry said, echoing his thoughts. "I know too much. I suspect I'd be in as much danger from your people if I back out as I am from Lorcas' folk at this point. Besides, this is the most interesting thing that's ever happened in my life. I work where I grew up, for God's sake. I'm a paralegal and a bike repair technician. Having this whole thing thrown into my lap is beyond my wildest dreams. I'm still in, because I can't imagine going back. Not to mention that Lorcas is by far the coolest boyfriend I've ever had."

"Great," Jack said. "How the hell is that creep "cool"?"

"Are you kidding? He lives in a castle. He can disassociate his shadow and fly it from his body with his consciousness inside it. He hangs out with dead people. In his spare time, he's an artist who reads ancient Slavic languages. And he's a genuinely nice guy, if a little mousy. And when I hang around him I get to stare lustfully at his buddy Tomash as a side benefit."

"You have to be able to betray him in the end," Jack warned.

"Yeah, I know," Terry sighed. "You notice I brought you this stuff which I got by betraying him."

"I notice, and I notice you waited a couple days before telling me," Jack said.

"You don't trust me?"

"I'm trusting you by allowing you to hang onto them. You change your mind, you have the option of returning them. But I think you know what the right thing to do is, ultimately. You save the Earth and all the people and creatures upon it from being annihilated by an alien force."

"That's a heavy load to lay on me, Jack."

"Yes. But it is on you at this point. The rest of us are just your support staff."

Terry fell silent. She gazed at the wall somewhere behind Jack's shoulder for a long moment.

Jack fidgeted. He didn't want her thinking too deeply about the future. "Speaking of support staff, have you seen any more of Zumar?" he asked, hoping to distract her.

Terry's attention snapped back to him. "Oh, yeah. He was in the house when I brought Lorcas down from the tower. In the library, which is where the sword is. He's frankly a little creepy, but interesting. Sometimes those eyes seem like they're looking right inside me." She shuddered a bit. "I guess it's because he's actually dead. But I'd like to find out what it was like to live when he did, just out of curiosity. You know, the little stuff that isn't covered in history books. It's too bad the rest of the world can't know about him. He'd be a great resource."

"And did you see Lorcas' shadow when it came back into the tower?" Jack asked, trying to sound casual. He knew that the state of development of the Lorecaster's shadow could tell him something about Rook's progress, and that the one he'd seen circling above the *Natural Seize* that day had been unusually large.

"Only for a second," Terry said, narrowing her eyes as she recalled. "It disappeared almost immediately. It was weird. I thought you said it was a raven, but it didn't really look like one. It looked too large, and had an odd shape to it for a bird. But I guess 'raven' is just an approximation, anyway. It's not really a raven."

She collected her stuff and got up. "Well, I guess I'll go work on that stained glass, then. And maybe sew up a superhero cape."

"I'm sure we can come up with a superhero nickname for you, something like Stone-slayer or Castle-wrecker," Jack joked. "Keep in touch. But carefully."

He stood up and watched her go. At the door, she turned and stared at him through the daylight dusk of the restaurant with an inscrutable expression. Jack casually picked up his menu and re-seated himself as though he was going to order.

But as soon as she was outside, he threw his napkin aside and strode to the door. He watched surreptitiously as she climbed in her truck and made her way out of the gravel lot. Then he jumped in his truck and followed, at a reasonable distance but close enough so he wouldn't lose her.

It wasn't that he didn't trust her. Much of what she did seemed like what he would expect a dedicated ally to do. But her behavior puzzled him. Some of what she said, or the way she said it, seemed to indicate that she was, in fact, having second thoughts, or at least was conflicted. He wasn't sure what he expected to find out from following her; anything she did could be explained away with a bit of thought. But he felt the need to see what she was doing anyway.

She headed northwest on the highway and then exited towards Seaside Heights. She had said she was going to work on the stained glass. He didn't know where her studio was, but he had assumed it was in Lafayette. Of course, she could have changed her mind, but he found it just a bit odd.

He followed her until he was sure he knew where she was going. He hung back as she turned off the main street of Seaside Heights along a road south of his office that he knew wound up a small hill. He took a second route, and parked where he could see what he believed to be her destination.

Although Seaside Heights was a small town, it featured one interesting historical building: a stone church some 120 years old, with newer stained glass windows added during rehabilitation. It had been established, Jack knew, during the height of timber harvesting in the area, when it was thought Seaside Heights would remain a major center. The town had been supplanted by Lafayette, further south and inland, the center of the farming and ranching community, serviced by a larger riverway, on flatter terrain, and with easier access. Seaside Heights was now only a tourist stop for those seeking coastal access. The church was still used, and sported a historic designation plaque on the front near the door.

He could see just the back quarter-panel of her truck after she parked. In a minute, she came around the front and entered through the large wooden door. Jack sat leaning on his steering wheel, considering. She could have been taking a look at the stained glass windows. Or she could have come seeking some sort of guidance, having encountered phenomena that would shake anyone's belief system. The Knights were, after all, the religious arm of those involved with Rook, those who had believed Rook to be the embodiment of an evil demon, although Jack and his cohorts now believed somewhat differently. Many of them had sought such guidance in the past, and, they believed, received it.

Either way, it was really none of his business. She would either get the inspiration she had come from in the windows, or she would make peace with her God. He was confident that she would come down on his side.

He started the engine and made a U-turn. He would leave her alone and take a quick trip past Perry's shop before heading to the office. He made his way through town and pulled up a little way beyond the shop on the far side of the main street. It was a spot his spies used regularly. He kept his window up and idled the engine, ready to pull back onto the road if necessary. He had to twist in his seat to see, a bit of an uncomfortable position.

He noticed a large rock just to the front and side of the house, and as his eyes adjusted to the gloom of the overhanging trees around the place, he saw that the old statue that had at one time been fastened to one of Rook's stones that had been brought back to Seaside Heights and installed. Someone was trying to create a garden or landscaping, apparently.

Suddenly a figure appeared from around the side of the house, near the statue. Jack sat up straighter. He knew that figure immediately: it was Zumar, the Messenger. Jack considered Zumar his arch-rival now; it was as though he embodied the arrogance and confidence of the Fell Ken and Rook in particular. He felt the burn of rage rising inside him at just the sight of the shadow.

Zumar actually wasn't much of a shadow, now, and Jack took note of the fact that he had walked around the house rather than simply stepping through its boards. He stared at Zumar much as he had when they had met outside his office. Zumar stretched and stared pointedly back at Jack. It was obvious he knew Jack was there; whether by recognition of the truck or just by feel Jack wasn't sure. As Jack watched, Zumar turned and ran his hands suggestively up the semi-nude statue, pressing himself to it in a blatant show.

Jack turned away in disgust, yanked the steering wheel, and pulled out into traffic. Would Zumar tell the rest of the entourage he had been there? Were they aware that Perry's shop was being watched now, or would this be news to them and make them more careful?

He wasn't too concerned; they would continue to watch whether it was in the form of undercover spies or more open harassers. Nevertheless, the encounter ate at him as he pulled up outside his office. And it had been stupid to follow Terry that obviously, he thought. She could have noticed his black truck behind her in the small town and realized that he didn't trust her as much as he had pretended. That could affect her willingness to interact openly with him. He had to let her do what she was going to do and trust the decisions she would make.

As he walked into the office, he turned the gold coin in his pocket restlessly. It had become almost a talisman, a reminder of how he'd narrowly escaped Rook's clutches and come out triumphant. He needed to look at those code cards. That evening, he promised himself. He'd stay late at the office and see what he could make of things. That would make up, in his mind, for the stupidity of following Terry and revealing himself to Zumar.

Thus occupied, he almost ran into Jason Japert. He pulled up abruptly and hoped the irritation he felt at seeing Japert at his office again didn't show on his face.

"Mister Japert," he said calmly. "What can I do for you?"

"Just a couple questions, won't take a minute of your time," Japert said with his usual friendly grin. "We don't even need to go in your office; I'll be out of here in a minute."

"Well then, shoot," Jack said. He kept his hands stuffed deep in his pockets to cover the restless fidgeting.

Japert leaned against the wall of the building. "So I happened to notice that you know the young lady who's the girlfriend of Lorcas Felken, the main stockholder of Cliffview Estates," he said.

Crap, Jack thought to himself. How in the heck did this busybody know that?

"Oh, you mean Terry? I wasn't aware of her relationship," he said casually.

"Mm-hmm, pretty new, I think. How are you acquainted with Ms. Bell?"

"She's a paralegal and her firm did some work for me," Jack said truthfully, getting more comfortable. "She dated my nephew Kyle for a short time."

"Right, Kyle Bright, Korrin Bright's brother," Japert mused. "But they're not dating anymore."

"No, but I run into her once in a while, and I always thought she was a promising young lady, so I've kept in touch. I figured I could give her a good reference if she needed it."

"I see," Japert mused. "Do you think Mr. Felken knows about this convoluted relationship?"

"Oh, I bet he does," Jack said. "Like you've pointed out, it's a small town, small area. A lot of people know each other, and these things tend to happen."

"Right," Japert said. "Just wanted to get my ducks in a row, since I'm going back up to Cliffview to poke around a little bit more here pretty soon."

Jack shrugged. "Well, whatever you can do to find out what happened to Bob and how it's connected to anything that might be going on up there, I'm all for it. You just let me know if I can be of any more help."

Jack stepped around Japert and continued quickly on towards the door of the office without looking back. Japert was going to have to yell at him if he had any more questions. But he reached the office door and slipped inside with a sigh of relief. He could only hope that Terry would tell Japert the same general story if he questioned her and that Japert wouldn't mention the connection to Lorcas.

He took a look out the big ground-floor window that faced the parking lot, just to check and make sure Japert was going. He could see the investigator standing by his car in the lot apparently drawing something on a large pad of paper, almost like an art pad. From the motions of his hands, he seemed to be drawing lines out from a central spot. Jack realized he was likely drawing a map of relationships between all the people involved in his investigation, developing a kind of web to help him visualize the connections. Jack felt a new prickle of nerves.

He was too distracted to work. He pulled out the old Knight/Fell Ken book and hopefully removed the code cards from their envelope. On the inside front cover of the book was a set of characters in a block approximately the same size as the code cards. The characters were unfamiliar, of no language anyone had discovered on Earth, and it was tradition amongst the Koen that they represented the language of Rook and had been developed specifically to record information secret and important to the Fell Ken. It had never been deciphered.

Jack laid one of the code cards over the block of text. Characters showed up in the holes in the card, perfectly aligned. Even better, he noted, there were several alignment holes in the card, shaped like the letter L and located at each corner. As he moved the card, he found a spot over the text where all of the alignment holes were filled by underlying marks in the text.

Jack grabbed a pen and paper and carefully copied each of the text characters that showed up in the holes of the code card. He noted where there were blanks, as well. Those usually indicated a break in the word. There were three code cards in all, each one slightly different, and he copied their characters into three separate blocks on his paper. He left spaces underneath each copied line.

Next, he removed the final piece of vellum from the envelope carefully. It was fragile and old. There was a single block of text written in old Slavic characters upon the page. Jack slid the first code card over the text and copied the characters once again, this time lining them up in the spaces underneath the lines copied from the book's front cover. He did this for all three cards, once again, then sat back and surveyed his work.

There was quite a bit of text, probably 1500 'words', or separate sets of text, altogether. Once translated, that would give a sufficient vocabulary for a simply written manuscript. The book didn't appear to be that simple, although it was written in large letters and heavy on the illustration. Jack leafed through it carefully, and noticed something: there were other blocks of text of the same size as the block inside the front cover throughout the book, about one per chapter. He sighed. Each chapter would require the use of the code cards prior to translation. It would take some work.

The next step was to get the Slavic text to someone who could read it and figure out how each Slavic word corresponded to the alien word above it. This was the specialty of his nephew Kyle, and had also been Korrin's forte. Kyle would be able, he hoped, to read the old Slavic text, translate it to a newer Slavic language and thence to English, and create a dictionary that would allow the book to be read. Perhaps he could even create a computer program to help with the task.

Once the book, and particularly the chapter concerning the failsafe, was translated, he could confirm what they'd only been able to guess at before. He could figure out exactly how to use the four items, what the consequences would be, and any other vital information necessary to cause Rook to return to his cornerstone. Like putting the genie back in the bottle, he thought. Then they could mount a full-scale assault, with the certain knowledge of where the stone was located, who the people involved were, and where the parts of the castle that survived could be found. That was in the future, but he allowed himself a moment of satisfaction. The fact was, they were closer to destroying Rook than the Knights of Earth Natural had been in generations, hundreds of years. He really bore little ill will to most of the entourage, but he knew what the Lorecaster was destined to become better than perhaps anyone else. And of course, there was Zumar, dangerously corporeal and disgusting in his living death. Jack couldn't wait to be rid of him.

Chapter Fourteen

The day after Terry's short visit, Lorcas decided to distract himself by hiking up into the state forest along the cliffs overlooking the ocean. She probably wouldn't be able to visit that day, and he was feeling restless. He needed to do some hiking anyway; he knew Terry liked it, and he wanted to be in shape to at least be able to keep up with her, if not out-hike her.

The wind came up from the ocean, rising against the cliffs, bringing the smells of kelp and fish and salt water with it. It would be nice to fly off those cliffs, he thought, but he was outside Rook's influence and besides, there were people around, non-Fell Ken. He found himself hoping that Rook would eventually take the rocks there, too, but not, he considered, cause any real changes to the environment. Of course, he himself might have some say in that matter. He wondered if he could dictate which environments to save and which could be used or abandoned. He didn't care about power over people so much, but the idea of having the power to save the places he cared about was intoxicating.

He returned by turning inland and following the UTV trail back through the woods above the barred window. From there he cut back to the west rather than following the base of the hill, and strolled through the woods where he and Tomash had practiced archery. He walked through the cemetery and was brushing a bit of dirt off Bishop the Cat's marker when the sounds of unfamiliar voices drifted to him from the direction of the Keep.

He knew no one was working in the Keep. Lately nobody had been doing anything as far as building, since Rook seemed to want to concentrate on creating tunnels, and he didn't need any help for that. Besides, the cadence and tone of the voices didn't sound like someone working.

He walked quietly up to the northern door of the Keep and carefully opened it a crack, just enough so he could see into the interior. Sure enough, there were three people there: kids, probably new Fell Ken from the neighborhood. One of them, a boy of about eleven, had stationed himself in Tomash's chair on the dais. A girl of about eight examined the stone in the floor in front of the throne, and a small boy of three or four stood near her. Siblings, he guessed, or they wouldn't be hanging around each other.

They could do little harm in the Keep, but Lorcas knew that kids weren't allowed up at the castle, and he was concerned about their safety. After all, the castle had dumped him down stairs, into dungeons, and opened the floor up to swallow his mother with no warning, and he had a personal relationship with Rook. Lorcas opened the door and stepped in.

The boy scrambled immediately off the chair and dais and scurried over to his brother and sister, where all three stood staring at Lorcas, the older boy with a look of defiance, the girl with a look of horror, and the little boy with nothing but curiosity.

"Hey, guys," Lorcas said as he approached them. "What are we doing?"

"It's the Lorecaster," the girl hissed. She dropped her eyes to the floor, only raising them to cast desperate glances at her brother.

"I know, stupid," the boy said boldly. He had a stick in his hand, which Lorcas guessed he'd been using as a sword. Despite his self-assurance, the boy's eyes were wide.

Lorcas was more amused than irritated. He decided to break the ice a little bit before kicking them out of the Keep; there wasn't any reason for kids to be afraid of him.

"So you know who I am," he said. "Lorcas Felken, the Lorecaster. Now, who are you?"

"I'm Dirk, and this is my sister Karabela and my brother Saber," the older boy said. His tone of voice suggested he was hanging on to the edge of self-control.

"That's... nice," Lorcas said, processing the fact that all three of them appeared to be named after edged weapons.

"We are in so much trouble," the girl whispered, glancing at her brother once again.

"I won't tell if you won't," Lorcas replied. He bent over with his hands on his knees to get closer to eye level with them. He wasn't around kids very much, and they made him realize how tall he was, or how tall he must seem to them.

"He sat on your chair," Karabela told him, addressing him directly for the first time, barely flicking her eyes up from the floor.

"It's not his chair," Dirk snapped. "It's the King's chair. That's Tomash, the guy that came to our school and showed us the bows."

"But the Lorecaster found the chair, didn't you?" Karabela pressed. "We learned all about how you got all the pieces to build this whole place." She gestured around, growing bolder.

"I did find it," Lorcas said. "It belonged to the Fell Ken in the past. So did all the rest of the stones in this building."

"And you found them all because you're magic," Karabela agreed.

"Well, kind of," Lorcas said with a laugh. He hadn't heard anyone use that term before, but he guessed it did apply. He didn't feel magic, though. "Now, what's your last name? Who are your folks? Have I met them?"

"Katzbalger," Dirk said. "We just moved here a few weeks ago. Everybody's moving here now because this is where It's At. That's what my dad told me."

Lorcas wondered if "It" referred to Rook or just circumstances in general. "Did your dad tell you not to come up to the castle alone, too?"

Dirk flushed. "Yes."

"It's not safe up here. Strange things happen here without any warning. I know it looks like fun, but this isn't a place to play, okay? It's a weird place."

"I know all about it," Dirk assured him. "I'm not afraid."

"Neither am I," Lorcas said with a chuckle, "but it doesn't care if I'm afraid or not. It still dumps me down stairs and traps me down in dark basements whenever it feels like it. It's not pleasant."

"We promise we won't come up here anymore," Karabela said hurriedly. "It was Dirk's idea."

"Alright, then," Lorcas said. "Better sneak back out and get down the hill."

The three of them scrambled for the door, but Dirk paused there and turned back to Lorcas. "When is Rook going to build the moat?"

Lorcas was a bit taken aback by Dirk's direct reference to Rook, but of course he probably had been educated about the castle all his life. "I don't think there's going to be a moat," he answered. "There's a pond, though."

"I've been studying my books, and there's supposed to be a moat," Dirk said confidently. "I know he's going to make one soon. I can feel it."

Lorcas raised his eyebrows. "Is that right?"

"Yes." Dirk frowned and lowered the stick. "I could always feel Rook, even when I was living in Las Vegas. It wasn't my imagination."

"No, probably not," Lorcas said diplomatically. That was a long way away to feel Rook, though, he thought.

"It's all of our job now to protect Rook, and I'll do it if I need to," Dirk continued seriously. "I'll protect you and Tomash and Tondra. I swear fealty."

"Well, thanks," Lorcas said, suppressing a grin. "If I need a personal bodyguard, I'll remember that!"

Dirk nodded briefly and disappeared out the door, following his sister and brother down the hill.

Lorcas returned to the northern door and pulled it shut. As he turned back, he glanced at the map on the southern wall, with its glowing coin pile and the two smaller, independent tracks. He squinted. There were actually three extra points now. There was the unknown one in Seaside Heights, and there appeared to be two very close together at Cliffview. He knew Alan carried one of them. Perhaps he'd given Tondra another, or taken another himself for some other reason.

The two at Cliffview appeared to be moving in his direction. He waited for a minute, and Alan came through the southern door into the Keep.

Alan smiled as he greeted Lorcas. "Hey. I saw the Katzbalger kids coming down the hill. I was going to chew them out, but it sounds like you already sent them packing."

"No harm done," Lorcas said. "What's the deal with Dirk?"

Alan glanced at him with a brief expression of approval. "You figured that out, huh? He's really strongly connected to Rook, but we don't know what that means for the future. For right now, we're making sure he has plenty of contact with Tomash and plenty of training, but of course we don't want him to be vulnerable, so we're leaving some stuff out."

"Sounds like he already knows a bunch," Lorcas noted. He gestured at the map. "You've got two coins now?"

Alan nodded. "I picked one up the other day thinking it could be useful, now that we know what they do."

He paused for a moment, then pointed at the single light on the map. "We know who has the other one, now."

"We do?" Lorcas asked, with a brief feeling of irritation that there seemed, once again, to be things he was being left out of.

"Yeah, sorry, we just figured it out."

"So? Who is it?" Lorcas asked. After all, he had been out hiking all day, and he couldn't fault Alan for not telling him if he hadn't been around.

"The other coin is with Jack Bright," Alan replied.

"With Jack? How the heck did he get one?"

"We don't know. Maybe the Koen have always had one, and we just didn't know until we got the map. But we're sure the extra one is him. Useful, huh?"

Lorcas nodded. "But how did you figure it out?"

"Zumar did. You know he and Raine have been tracking Jack's every move, at least when he's within range of some part of Rook. So they were able to figure out that Jack was always in a particular location when the coin showed on the map as being in that location."

"That must have taken some careful documentation," Lorcas said with some admiration.

"Not really. I gave Zumar a smart phone."

Lorcas turned to Alan abruptly. "What?"

"Yeah, he can carry the phone and use the screen now. Helps out a lot. So we'd set up a time for him to be watching Jack, and me to be in the area of the castle. You know cell phones don't work inside the Keep or the chapel, so I still had to run back and forth in and out of the Keep to look at the map."

Lorcas turned back to the wall. "So Jack is at his office now," he said, studying the area of Seaside Heights.

"That's right." Alan paused again, and Lorcas could hear the two coins clinking in his pocket as he handled them. "So when is Terry coming back for a visit?" he asked, changing the subject abruptly.

Lorcas shrugged. "We had a little visit yesterday. She said she's almost done with the stained glass window for my office, so I guess she'll bring it up here next time she's off work."

"Ah, well, good, glad she hasn't sworn off us permanently. By the way, Tondra wants to schedule another meeting pretty soon. We have a few things to discuss."

"Let me know. It's not like I'm doing anything."

"You feeling okay?" Alan asked suspiciously.

"Just still a little sore. It doesn't mean you can't keep me in the loop about things."

"Sorry, we'll try to do better. Sometimes we assume you know stuff that you don't, or can't. Or we figure you just don't want to be bothered. Traditionally your role has been kind of removed from day-to-day operations. The Lorecasters were supposed to be off to themselves, studying and improving their skills and knowledge. But, of course, this isn't the past."

Lorcas took a last look at the map, and he and Alan left through the southern door, shutting it firmly behind them.

Almost as soon as he left the Keep, Lorcas got a message on his phone. It must have come through while he was inside, he realized. He pulled his phone out of his pocket and checked it. It was Terry, telling him she was done with the window, and she'd be at work the rest of the day, but she'd like to come up the next day before work and see if they could install it.

"Speak of the devil," Lorcas commented to Alan. "It's Terry. She'll be here tomorrow."

"Good deal," Alan said. "I'll see you later." He headed towards the office, leaving Lorcas standing on the side of the hill texting back to Terry. Lorcas felt a lift in his mood almost immediately: things were getting back to normal, and he'd have some more time with Terry. He'd have to dig up wood and tools to make a frame to fit the casement and window, but it would be easier to access things in his garage now that the statue was gone. Tomash had hauled it away to Perry's shop at Zumar's request. Better there than at Cliffview, Lorcas thought. He'd never liked the thing, although no one else had been willing to just haul it to the dump for him. They all seemed to think it was connected to the Fell Ken somehow, though nobody could say exactly what they thought that connection was.

After a shower Lorcas felt pleasantly tired but focused, and he thought he could spend some time in his dad's library working on the books. It was really his library now, he considered as he opened the door. He was beginning to make it his own, to rearrange and add and subtract according to his liking. He still thought of it as his father's space, though.

The book taken from the crate in Perry's basement sat on the desk. Lorcas opened the heavy curtains over the back window, allowing some natural light into the room, and seated himself at the desk. As usual, he pulled out the pipe and the package of herbs, now new stuff collected from Rook's garden rather than the stuff his dad had left behind, and had a quick smoke before starting. It no longer caused him to want to go antique hunting. Now he recognized it as a way to access Rook's consciousness, and it helped him translate the old script he'd been studying and match his father's notes to the text.

The new book, or rather, the old book they'd recently acquired, was quite different from the other books in the library. The inner bindings of the covers were decorated with scales, bringing to mind the layout of the library itself. Following that, the chapter titles were embellished with copies of certain sections of those scales; he could tell they were each unique due to minor differences, obviously placed there to differentiate the sections.

Fine, Lorcas thought, the book was connected to the layout of the library. But what did that mean? He stood up and took the book, laid open on one hand, to the shelves, and compared the pages to the physical layout. There was a numerical code at the beginning of each chapter, and he soon realized that, if he was looking at a section as specified by the pattern of scales in the chapter's title, he could pick out a specific book from that section based on a number he could use to specify a shelf and a book's position. He wasn't sure he was interpreting things correctly, but he went with it, trusting himself and the contents of the pipe. He realized, with some satisfaction, that in the past he might not have been able to do that. He had learned.

Eventually he had picked out a book to correspond to each chapter in the new book, which he now thought of as the Library key. He laid them out in order on the desk, after clearing it of objects he might knock off. The sequence in the book's chapters also specified what Lorcas guessed was a page number. He opened each book to the noted page.

Now what, he thought. He studied the Library key again. Each of the first pages in each chapter was laid out oddly, he noted. There was a pattern there, but it didn't make much sense. Finally he began turning the book from side to side, and quickly realized that the pattern, when turned sideways, looked like a block of text with certain sections left blank. He isolated the page and awkwardly held the book up to the light of the window, keeping the bulk of the book away from the single page. When he looked at it that way, without the bulk of the book behind it, he could see that the areas where the blanks were located were translucent. He could also see a faint line of perforations along the inside of the page.

Lorcas tried to position the page over one of the books on the desk, but he couldn't get it to lay flat enough. The bindings interfered with each other. Grimacing, because it galled him to damage a centuries-old book, he gingerly pulled the page free along the perforations. Then he laid it over the text on the correct page in the book corresponding to that chapter. Words in the text fit precisely into the blank spots. The words almost glowed through the page, as though illuminated.

Lorcas took a deep breath and carefully tore out the title page from each chapter. He laid each page over its corresponding page in the associated book. He could feel his heart pounding with excitement as each set of words slipped into place. This was obviously important. The message would be vital.

When he had all the pages laid out, he set the Library key aside and grabbed his laptop. He had created a character set representing the old Slavic text many of the books were written in to help him as he translated. Now he used that set to type in the words showing in the translucent spots, in order according to the chapters.

When he was done he used the vocabulary he had added to his computer to help him translate. It wasn't exact; he wasn't sure of the nuances of some of the words, although Zumar had helped him as best he could, and his father's notes had given him some clues. As was often the case, the paragraphs were awkward and left much to be interpreted. There were a few blanks as well, words he had never encountered before.

He read the whole thing over several times carefully. It was confusing. What he read had to do with the window in the chapel, the one with the map of Rook's homeland star system and the moving gears. It also had to do with what Rook had described as a 'sacrifice'. As best he could tell, there was a hidden mechanism near, or under, the window. It had been designed with Rook's help, but it was purely a human device. The mechanism was intended to give the human entourage some control over Rook's development and disclosure. It could be used in an emergency to cause Rook to retreat to his cornerstone, abandoning whatever building he had created.

This was something he apparently needed help to do, and the mechanism was designed to provide him with that aid. It sounded to Lorcas like it would cause any above-ground structure to sink quickly into the earth, then contract into a mass of stone, through which Rook could travel to a safe spot, where he could dwell until such time as he could be revived.

But there was more. The mechanism could be triggered by a Fell Ken using four objects in Lorcas' possession: the key, the ring, the sword, and the caduceus from inside the staff. The procedure was shown by the shield in the Keep. It implied that the Lorecaster would be the one to make the decision to use the mechanism. If it was triggered in an emergency, Rook would return to the cornerstone as noted; but under certain circumstances, the mechanism could instead trigger a huge surge in Rook's power, the next step in his development. Exactly what would happen was unclear; the book once again pointed to the shield in the Keep as depicting the results.

But, the text warned, if the mechanism was triggered by someone not Fell Ken, it could be disastrous. Lorcas frowned. More disturbingly, the Koen were aware of the existence of the mechanism, or had been aware in the past. The sequence was written in a book they possessed. It had been given to them prior to, or near the time of, the fracturing of the families. But here the text became more cryptic.

"They are those who broke the compact in the past, and thus they will be those who bring forth the power in the end, by their own hand," Lorcas muttered, translating aloud.

He sighed and sat back in his chair. As usual, there was a chunk of information provided to him which he didn't truly understand. Rook was little better in person, and Zumar had never experienced this stage of development, so he was of limited help. No one else in the entourage could help, either. A few things were clear, though: the four listed items were vital to the next step, and the

Koen could not be allowed to obtain those items, or the results could be disastrous.

He realized it was late. It was dark outside the window now. He needed to get some sleep so he could enjoy his time with Terry. Maybe he would be able to interpret the text better after he had slept on it. After all, he'd accomplished quite a bit that day. It was nothing to be ashamed of or frustrated by.

Terry showed up early the next day. Lorcas had done nothing else with the book other than take a second look over everything in the morning light. He was still working on a cup of coffee when he heard the truck pull up outside the wall.

Terry had packed the window in the bed, wrapped in horse blankets from her parents' farm and encased in cardboard. The two of them moved it carefully to the bed of the UTV. Then Lorcas loaded tools and lumber from the garage while Terry had some coffee.

"You look better than you did when I was here a couple days ago," Terry commented as she watched him load. "More color."

"I feel fine," Lorcas said, truthfully. He felt much improved, energized. Rook was even cooperating by allowing a little bit of sun to shine through the fog.

"Good. I still feel really bad about what happened up there. I feel responsible."

"It wasn't your fault at all," Lorcas assured her. "Besides, you made up for it. Let's get this stuff up there and see what we can do about installing it. I'm excited to see what it looks like."

"Hope you like it," Terry said. She slid into the passenger side of the UTV and Lorcas started off carefully, trying not to bang the window around in the back.

He drove up towards the state forest on the two-track and then up the hill at its lowest slope, where there was a construction road reinforced with gravel. This brought them up near the graveyard and the Keep. As they trundled by, Alan stepped out of the Keep's main door.

Lorcas pulled up near him. "Good timing. I could use some help getting this thing up into the tower."

"Sure," Alan said with a grin. "Hi, Terry! Zumar's here too."

"I don't think he'll be much help," Lorcas said, but Terry interrupted him.

"That's fine! He doesn't freak me out. I'd like to get to know him anyway, maybe see if he'll tell me about what it was like living in his time period."

"I wanted him to take a look at some translations in the library," Lorcas said. "He could do that while we're installing the window, and we can talk to him later."

"Sounds like a plan," Alan said. "I'll meet you in the chapel."

Getting the window up the narrow staircase all the way to the third level was difficult. Lorcas and Alan had to keep switching the positions in which they held the window in order to get it around corners. Fortunately, Terry had added a sturdy wooden border around it already so it wouldn't flex and crack, and it was well-packed in cardboard.

Finally they set it down near the open casement. Terry started unpacking it while Lorcas and Alan caught their breaths.

"I made it in two sections so it can be opened easily," she said. "It's on a special hinge that allows it to slide back after it's been opened, so it will sit fairly flush with the side of the casement and won't be in the way in the room."

She pulled the final wrapping off, revealing an arched double panel in rich colors, with dark, reclaimed barn wood forming the frame.

"Nice!" Alan said. "That must have taken a lot of work!"

Terry nodded. "I've been working on it in most of my spare time. It's modeled after some of the windows in the old church in Seaside Heights. Do you like it, Lorcas?"

Lorcas knelt on one knee in front of it, staring. His drawing had been brought to vibrant life. There were the rock cliff, the dark trees, the hint of ocean below, the mottled sky with clouds scudding across the blue. A large raven swooped through the left panel. The edge of the castle seemed to continue from the casement into the glass. The small figure stood in silhouette on the cliff edge. At the bottom of the right panel there was a small plaque reading, "In Memoriam: Condra Felken."

He felt a welling of emotion and reached out wordlessly to touch the panel. Terry crouched down next to him and he drew her in close. "I love it," he managed to mutter.

Alan remained tactfully quiet until Lorcas regained his composure. "Let's fetch up the tools and get to work installing this thing," he said when Lorcas regained his feet. "Did you bring a rock drill?"

"Yes," Lorcas said. The three of them trooped back down the stairs and hauled up the lumber and tools, and together they managed to build a sturdy frame in the casement. Then they separated the two panels and Terry showed them how to install the hinges. When the window was mounted it fit snugly, and the light through it gave it even more dimension.

Lorcas jumped as he caught movement out of the corner of his eye and discovered Zumar at his elbow.

"Nice job," Zumar said. He examined the window more closely. "Perfect. A work of art."

"Thanks, Zumar," Terry said, coloring a bit. "Lorcas, do you know what time it is? I have to work at noon, so I won't be able to stay long."

"It was past ten when I left Lorcas' house," Zumar said.

"I'll have to go soon, then," she said, "but I wanted to see this installed as soon as possible. It's very satisfying."

"Didn't you want to ask Zumar a few questions?" Alan reminded her. "If you've got a few minutes, Lorcas and I can put the tools away and put the blankets back in your truck while you two talk."

"That would be great," Terry replied, then put her hands on her hips. "I had planned to take a look at one or two of the end casements in the Keep and get some measurements today, too. I don't trust that the higher ones are exactly the same size as the ones along the balconies. I guess I won't be able to do that."

"If Lorcas can unload the tools by himself, I can take you to the Keep and get you a ladder," Alan said. "There's one in a storage room in there. You can measure and talk to Zumar. That will kill two birds with one stone. Sorry I don't know how to drive the UTV, Lorcas, or I'd do it."

"That's fine," Lorcas said. Actually, he didn't mind unloading by himself, if it meant Alan would remain with Terry and she wouldn't be alone with Zumar. He didn't trust what the shadow might say or suggest, but he knew Alan would be careful and respectful and he could shut Zumar down, too.

"I'll be down to say goodbye in a few minutes," Terry assured him.

Fifteen minutes later, Terry stopped by the house. "I have a couple days off coming up. Can I come visit for a bit longer?" she asked with a smile.

"That would be great," Lorcas said. "Thank you for my window. It really means a lot to me."

"You're welcome. I'm glad you like it. See you soon," Terry replied.

Lorcas watched as she turned the truck around and rumbled out of the neighborhood. He turned around to find Zumar right behind him once again. "You're really starting to bug me with that," he snapped.

"I can't help it if you can't hear me coming," Zumar said. He looked unusually serious as he gazed after Terry's truck.

"What did she want to know?" Lorcas asked.

"Oh, just normal stuff. Mostly she just measured. We tried to make her feel welcome."

"Good," Lorcas said. "Now can you show me what you learned from that stuff in the library?"

"Real mess you made, tearing up a perfectly good book," Zumar said. "Come on, I'll tell you what I think of the translation, but I'm not sure it clarifies anything much."

"Great," Lorcas sighed as he followed Zumar inside. "Business as usual: foggy, with no chance of clarity."

Chapter Fifteen

Two nights later, Lorcas woke suddenly in the middle of the night. Terry, in bed beside him, sat up as well. Lorcas reached for the light.

"What the heck is that?" Terry asked.

"Not sure," Lorcas said. "I'll go see."

He pulled on a pair of jeans and T-shirt hastily and headed for the stairs. Terry was right behind him, also in T-shirt and jeans.

Lorcas opened the front door cautiously. The rumbling sound that had awakened them grew louder. Outside it was dark and foggy. He took a tentative step out, but he couldn't see anything. The stones of the walkway felt damp beneath his bare feet, and he could feel the tingle of vibration through them.

Tomash appeared from around the corner of the house, looming out of the dark. "What's going on?"

"I don't know. I can't see," Lorcas said.

Terry lurked in the doorway, arms crossed over her chest.

"Should we go and try to figure it out?" Tomash asked doubtfully.

"I suppose. I want shoes and a flashlight first, though. And the sword," Lorcas added.

"Meet you back here in a minute," Tomash agreed.

Lorcas stepped back in the house and grabbed a pair of socks and shoes. He sat on the couch to put them on. Terry sat on the chair and put on her own shoes.

"If you think I'm staying in this house alone with that noise going on outside, you're crazy," she said. "I'm coming with you."

"Okay," Lorcas agreed. He didn't see much point in arguing, and he wasn't into some sort of false chivalry. Besides, the house was well within Rook's influence, and it likely wasn't any safer there than outside. The two of them donned windbreakers at the door and Tomash joined them in a minute.

The rumbling seemed to be coming from a distance away. Their flashlights proved useless; the light simply bounced back in their faces off the fog. It wasn't pitch black out, though, once their eyes got used to it. It was light enough to see general features close in front of them.

They went cautiously through the gate in the wall near Lorcas' house and out of the neighborhood. From there it was difficult to tell where the sound was coming from, but they elected to turn towards Rook on the east side. Moving slowly, they approached the hill upon which the castle sat.

Tomash, who was slightly in front, stopped abruptly. He took a few more tentative steps forward. Lorcas, just behind him, raised the sword in anticipation.

"Huh," Tomash said. "It's a ditch."

Lorcas and Terry joined him. Directly in front of him was a brand-new, rock-lined trench of indeterminate depth. The rumbling seemed to be caused by the trench itself opening slowly within the ground. It was not wide, perhaps ten feet. Steam and the odor of soil and roots rose from it.

"Not just a ditch, a moat," Lorcas answered, thinking of Dirk's question.

"I wonder what all it runs around?" Tomash asked. "I can't see how far it goes."

"No way to tell tonight. We can explore in the morning when we can see and won't fall in it."

"Yes." Tomash turned to him. "This is definitely a sign that things are progressing. He hasn't done anything this big, at least not on the surface, for a long time." He stopped and glanced at Terry.

"We'll talk in the morning," Lorcas said. "We'll get Tondra and Alan out here too, and see what Zumar can tell us. Alan can call him on his new phone."

"Maybe," Tomash said with a grin. "I hear Raine's on it all the time browsing the Internet."

They made their way back to Lorcas' house, where Tomash said goodnight. Inside, Lorcas tossed their clothes in the dryer so they'd be ready the next morning. The heavy mist had made everything damp and clammy. He was happy to climb back into a nice, warm bed with a nice, warm person beside him.

In bed, in the dark, they listened to more rumbling at inconsistent intervals from outside. "Is the castle doing that by itself?" Terry asked with a note of puzzlement.

"Yes, it is," Lorcas admitted. "We built the chapel and Keep by hand, but things like the basement and this trench happen kind of automatically. We don't really control that part of it."

"Freaky," Terry said, but she didn't ask for further explanation.

In daylight the next morning, they joined Tomash, Tondra, and Alan at the trench. It was not a continuous ditch, and resembled a moat only superficially. It was drastically steep-sided, with the side nearest the castle paved with smooth stone and the outer side left rough and rocky. It had not widened during the night, but a slender walkway now arched over it from the neighborhood to a point part way up the hill, above and to the side of the pond, giving quick access. It could also be skirted to the east where a second trench, not attached to the first and shorter, had appeared. One could also walk along the top of the wall where it had been built along the edge of the cliff and bypass the ditch that way. A permanent miasma leached out of it, adding to the lowering fog that swirled around the castle. Somehow the mood was ominous. Lorcas felt as though something was about to happen, but he didn't know what or when. It put him on edge.

He paced the rim of the trench, brooding. Rook tickled in the back of his mind, but there was no specific call. Tomash, Tondra, and Alan seemed to be looking to him for answers. They stood quietly watching him.

"You should try and find out what Rook needs," Tondra suggested.

"I suspect I know what he wants," Lorcas answered darkly. "The next step is up to me. I just have to be able to accomplish it."

"This thing has a different feel to it," Tondra said. "We should discuss it, and I think it's time to open the rest of the crates in Perry's basement and make sure we know what's in them. Things are moving along quickly."

"Rook is preparing," Tomash said. He met Lorcas' eyes pointedly. "He needs one more thing to take the next step. We'll have to provide him with what he needs, and we'll have to do it soon. I think he's getting impatient."

Lorcas didn't answer, and Tondra frowned. "Yes, but I don't know what he needs at the moment. Do you, Lorcas?"

Lorcas shrugged. "I'll see if I can figure it out." He shot Tomash a dirty look behind her back.

Terry seemed chilled and uncomfortable. "I should get back to Lafayette," she told Lorcas. "I think I may have caught cold, and I don't want to infect everyone."

"Sorry, I hope it wasn't the dampness here," Lorcas said. "I'll call you this evening and see how you're doing."

He was disappointed that he wouldn't have another day with Terry, but they hadn't made any kind of plans, and he thought his mood, affected as it was by the new development, might be unpleasant. He didn't want to inflict that on her. And he needed to consider the trench and its implications and discuss things with the rest of the Fell Ken. They would be freer to do that without her there. Much as he would have preferred to spend the time with Terry, he recognized that the entourage needed him now, and that was his first responsibility.

Terry headed back to her truck. The rest of them explored the new bridge, pausing on top to check out the view.

"We have a whole new group of Fell Ken arriving this afternoon," Alan said. "Supposedly they're bringing something important. Maybe it's connected. We should be here for that. Let's make any meeting this evening at the earliest."

Lorcas heard a big truck arriving just after lunch and joined the rest of the entourage, minus Zumar and Raine, at the gate to welcome the new arrivals. Alan directed the truck to back up to an area near the base of the new bridge. Once the back was open, a number of people climbed inside and began maneuvering a large wooden box onto the hydraulic tailgate lift. They had to turn it sideways to fit it on.

Alan suggested that Lorcas bring his forklift to remove it from the tailgate. Lorcas fetched the forklift from his garage and slid the forks under the box, which had a gap underneath the middle portion, being supported on the ends by wooden rails. Instead of depositing it on the ground, he left it on the forks for the time being.

"Do you know what's in that thing?" he asked Alan as he joined him again.

Alan nodded. "Yes. It's Zumar's coffin."

"What?" Lorcas frowned. "Zumar was thrown into a pit and covered with the stone that became the cornerstone of Paracel's castle. He doesn't have a coffin."

"Apparently he does," Alan replied. "We didn't know about it until recently, either." He gestured at the men who had moved the box from the truck. The men were talking among themselves, not in English.

"When the betrayal of the Koen occurred, only a few Fell Ken escaped. They later returned and secretly rescued the cornerstone, after the castle was destroyed. That much we knew. It was hidden and passed from one place to another, and finally brought to this country, where it was thought it would be safer.

"But according to these guys, when their ancestors removed the cornerstone, they found bones beneath it. They recognized those as the earthly remains of the Messenger and decided to inter them out of respect and also with the idea that they might be useful or necessary at some point. They were collected and a stone ossuary was created for them. That was passed down through the Fell Ken families over the generations. Now that things are ramping up, it was felt that the bones should be brought here to be interred in Rook's graveyard."

"What does it mean for Zumar?" Lorcas asked.

Alan shrugged. "It might give him more connection with the material world, but I'm not sure. His shadow's been disassociated from his body for so long it might not matter."

"What shall we do with it?" Lorcas wondered. He realized the ossuary must be quite large, given the size and weight of the crate.

"I suppose we bury it in the graveyard. Rook will probably prepare a grave where he wants it to go."

"In the past, sometimes people were buried beneath the floor of castle buildings, if they were important," Lorcas pointed out.

"We'll see what Zumar wants," Alan said. "For right now let's just get it up to the castle."

The men from the truck jumped down at Alan's request and pried off the wooden crate, leaving the ossuary sitting on a single slab of plywood. The box was nearly the size of a coffin, big enough, Lorcas thought, for the bones of a short man like Zumar to be laid out in approximately anatomical position. It was not decorated, but made of rough-hewn rock with a slightly rounded lid.

With the coffin revealed, Lorcas jumped back in the forklift and made his way to the base of the new arched bridge. It was wide enough to drive across, but just barely, and the grade was steep. He was a little nervous, but the span held, and he drove right up to the rear double door of the Keep and deposited the box inside, against the northern wall, beneath the quote. That seemed appropriate, with its final sentence of "Here lies death and life."

As he left the Keep, he paused. It suddenly occurred to him how bizarre the scene laid out in front of him was. The neighborhood, bustling with people, in the shadow of the castle; the creeping fingers of stone wrapping around the houses; the strange spikes like the tops of steeple roofs starting out of the earth at random intervals; the oddly opaque little lake in the persistent mist; and the smoking rents in the earth. The whole scene looked dark and otherworldly, as, indeed, it was, he realized. He wondered if eventually the whole Earth would look like that, and the thought made him shudder. There needed to be sun and living plants, not just stone and mist.

Then his eye lit on something else and he cursed under his breath. A sedan he recognized was pulling up outside his house: Jason Japert.

He took a deep breath and drove the forklift down the hill, retracing his route. He pulled up next to Japert, who was standing by his car with an incredulous look on his face.

"What the hell?" Japert asked as soon as Lorcas shut down the forklift, without any pleasantries.

"Er, construction is coming along," Lorcas said lamely.

"Talk about creepy," Japert said, "this is about the creepiest thing I've ever actually seen in person."

"It's supposed to be creepy. You know, mystery weekends and fantasy role-players and such."

Japert glanced at him briefly. "Bullshit. There's something else going on here. There's something else going on in this whole place, this whole..." he made a sweeping gesture, "area. I don't know what it is, but this place is practically unnatural. It freaks me out, and I don't get freaked out easily."

"Sorry," Lorcas said. There wasn't much else he could say.

"And the two of you, you and Jack Bright," Japert continued. He turned to face Lorcas, and the friendly veil he usually maintained dropped, leaving his eyes icy. "I don't know what's up with you. You obviously don't like each other, but you've got connections upon connections upon connections. I've actually started drawing out a chart, and it's like a spider web. People Jack knows come up here and they disappear, but he's not pointing fingers at you. People you know die left and right, and there are suggestions he's involved, but you're not pointing fingers at him. You're killing each other like the Hatfields and McCoys, but you've apparently got each other over a barrel. And neither one of you thinks this place is creepy or unusual at all."

Japert turned back to the castle. The ground rumbled slightly, and Lorcas felt it under his feet. Japert looked down briefly, and Lorcas wondered what he thought about that.

"It's like Cliffview Estates has its own personality, like it's a thing, not a corporation," Japert muttered. He shook his head, then he took a deliberate step and swung around, with his back to the castle.

"Let me tell you something," he said. "Everyone knows it's immoral to protect someone who's done wrong to other people. And it's immoral to protect yourself when you've done wrong to someone else; you have to own up to it. But there's something else: it's immoral to protect someone who has wronged you, personally. That's right: you have a right, even an obligation, to accuse and expose someone who has hurt you, and to let society judge that person as they will. You can't just shut your mouth and concentrate on revenge. That's vigilantism. "

Lorcas avoided Japert's eyes. He was getting very uncomfortable.

"If Jack Bright is that person to you, then you have an obligation to reveal what he's done, and how. You can't let him go around committing crimes that affect not only you, but the people you're connected to and love and the people you count as friends," Japert continued pointedly. "And whatever is going on here… no matter how involved you are, you have a moral obligation to not allow it to adversely affect the environment, or the resources, or the area and the people who depend on this place for their livelihoods or who just like it the way it is."

He paused and took a breath. Lorcas stood still, feeling a bit like he was getting a scolding from one of his parents.

"You seem like a pretty nice guy to me, Mr. Felken," Japert went on in a softer voice. "Think about it. Think about what I've said. Think about where you're going and what you're doing. And if you decide that you need to talk about Jack Bright and what's going on around here, you can call me any time, day or night. I'll support you. But if you don't… I'll find out anyway. I'm almost there. Just a few more pieces to fit together. Starting with an interview with Miss Terry Bell. So it's soon, or never."

Lorcas, looking over Japert's shoulder to avoid looking at him directly, noticed a figure in the center of the new arched bridge, paused and peering over the side into the trench. For a moment he thought it was Tomash, but then he realized that the size was wrong. It was Dirk, the kid from the neighborhood.

"I have to go," he said abruptly, meeting Japert's eyes for the first time. He gestured to Dirk. "I have to get that kid off the bridge. He's not allowed up there."

Japert looked at Dirk for a moment and nodded. "You do that. That's a good thing to do, Mr. Felken. Save the kid. But don't lose yourself. Remember my offer. It still stands, and it will stand, until one day it'll be too late and it won't be available anymore."

Lorcas didn't bother to answer. He didn't want to allow Japert's implications to penetrate his mind. He turned his back and strode to the neighborhood wall, jumped over it, and trotted to the bridge. Dirk still stood at the top of the arch, looking now at the castle itself rather than the trench.

"Dirk!" Lorcas called out to him as he made his way up the bridge. "You know you're not allowed up here."

"I told you about the moat," Dirk said softly. "You didn't believe me."

"You were right," Lorcas said. "But you can't be here on the bridge. It's not safe."

"I have to go," Dirk pleaded. "I can feel him calling to me. I want to meet him."

Lorcas felt a cold shiver run up his spine. He knew that feeling well. Why was Rook calling to a young boy? Why was Dirk so connected to him? Alan had admitted they weren't sure about Dirk's role. A suspicion struck Lorcas. Could it be that Dirk was intended to be the sacrifice Rook had demanded? Surely Rook wouldn't require Lorcas to give him a kid, someone who hadn't even reached his teen years yet. He'd rather throw Japert in there, somehow. He wondered if "someone who means something to you" could be interpreted as "someone who irritates you and makes you feel guilty".

One way or the other, he couldn't allow Dirk to go to the castle. "I understand what you mean. I feel him too. I'm used to it, and you'll get used to it too. I tell you what: next time I talk to Rook, I'll ask him if you can meet him somewhere safe. Then you can go to the castle with me and maybe Tomash and some other people."

Dirk looked up at him hopefully. "Like Zumar?"

"Sure," Lorcas said. "If you promise not to go up here alone again, I'll arrange for you to meet Zumar, and maybe even Raine."

"That would be cool," Dirk said.

He turned and Lorcas followed him off the bridge, that crisis averted for the moment. He glanced over at the forklift, but Japert's car was gone. Somehow, some way, something was going to have to be done about Japert. He couldn't succumb to Japert's moralizing now: it would be futile. He could accuse Jack Bright and the Koen all he wanted, could explain Rook and the Fell Ken 'til he was blue in the face, but none of it would be credible. He was trapped, and the only way he saw forward was with the Fell Ken.

Alan and the new arrivals had apparently gone to the office for check-in, so Lorcas headed that way. The office was packed, but Tondra caught his eye and motioned him over.

"What do you need, Lorcas?"

"Just wondering when you wanted to hold that meeting you were talking about."

Tondra shook her head. "Much as I would like to, I don't see it happening any time soon. I'm too busy." She paused. "We need to unpack those crates, though. There could be other things in them we'll need. Of course, it's not necessary for all of us to be there to do that. If you've got some time, you could buzz down there and unpack them and bring the contents back yourself, unless there's something too big to handle alone."

"I could do that," Lorcas said. It was something to do, and Tondra rarely suggested he go to town, or anywhere, alone. But he wasn't going to mention it now. Besides, with all the Fell Ken in the general area, including Seaside Heights, perhaps she wasn't as nervous as she had been about it.

After some consideration he decided to take his car. The flatbed would hold the crates better, but he couldn't get the crates up the ladder himself, so he'd be unpacking them, and the contents would likely be small. He pulled out of Cliffview within minutes, before Tondra could change her mind.

He'd been expecting to meet Zumar and Raine at the shop, but neither of them was there when he arrived. He did notice someone sitting in a vehicle across the street, which made him nervous. The shop was still under surveillance. To be on the safe side, he pulled the car up with the back end right against the back stairs, and went in and out on the alley side where he was not visible from the street.

He'd forgotten about the small crates of coins. They were heavy, and the best method for getting one up the ladder seemed to be balancing it on each rung and moving it up one step at a time. Once he had the box at the top, he shoved it out into the room.

There were, however, a bunch of crates of coins. He realized pretty quickly that he wasn't going to be able to move all of them up the ladder that way without taking a bunch of time and wearing himself out. They would just have to come back for the coins in a group and form a chain, or figure out some other way to get them out, perhaps repackaging them.

He cracked the lids on the other crates. The contents of those crates were packed in smaller, lighter boxes and bundles. He didn't open most of those, but he did peek in one small box, which appeared to be full of seeds, and a flat container that had what appeared to be candles in it.

The car was riding low on its shocks by the time he had it loaded. It had taken a couple of hours, and when he peeked around the corner he saw the person in the car was still there, but now standing outside, looking bored.

Lorcas jumped in the car and took off for Cliffview, leaving the spy behind. He felt a buzz of adrenalin; he'd avoided a confrontation with any of the Koen, and now he was heading out with thousands of dollars of gold in his car. Plus he was out of the fog for the time being: it was nice and sunny in Seaside Heights. He cranked up the radio for the cruise.

It occurred to him that anyone looking at the map in the Keep right now would see a large glowing area moving along the highway, or at least he assumed so. He would check when he got back and see if it had relocated itself on the map and how accurate it was. He knew that at least Alan's coin was pretty accurate.

When he pulled up to his house, he left everything in the car and headed for the Keep out of curiosity. It was different getting there over the bridge; he was used to just walking up the hill when things were dry, or up the steps otherwise. The south door was open and he walked in to find Alan and Zumar there. Both were staring fixedly at the map.

"Did you see the pile of coins moving up the highway?" Lorcas asked with a grin.

Alan nodded. Zumar said nothing. They both continued to stare at the map. A bit irritated, Lorcas checked it himself. Sure enough, a glowing spot sat in front of his own house now. Very near it was a single spot he figured was Alan, and the other two spots were further away, in Lafayette, huddled together.

He frowned. Obviously Alan no longer had the second coin. He must have given it to someone, and from the looks of it, it was someone connected to the Koen.

"How did you manage to do that?" he asked, gesturing to the double spot on the map. "You get close enough to drop one in some Koen's pocket?"

Once again, neither Alan nor Zumar answered. Lorcas glanced at them, puzzled. Alan stared fixedly at the point as though ignoring him, but he swallowed once; Lorcas could see his Adam's apple bob. Zumar moved away and stood on the far side of Alan, looking more at the floor than at the map.

"There's something we need to tell you," Alan finally said. He turned reluctantly to Lorcas. "You see that second coin, the one that's now next to Jack Bright's coin?"

"That's what I was pointing out, yes," Lorcas snapped, getting impatient.

"Well, that one is one of the two I was carrying. You can see it's a slightly different color. I'm guessing that when a Fell Ken or Koen has one, it's bright yellow, and when someone else has one, it's more of that orange color."

"Uh-huh," Lorcas said. He glanced at the map again. Sure enough, one of the two spots in Lafayette was yellow, and one was more orange. The two were still together, in some building he couldn't identify off the beaten track. But that wasn't enough to make Alan and Zumar as tense as they seemed.

"So? Who is it? Who's got the other coin?" Lorcas demanded.

Alan glanced at Zumar, who avoided his eyes. "Well, Lorcas, that one there…" he tapped the map with one finger, "that one's Terry."

It took a moment for that to sink in, and when it did, Lorcas felt a rising anger. "What do you mean, that's Terry?"

Alan took a deep breath. "Zumar and I gave her a coin the other day, the morning we installed the window, when we were with her in the Keep and you had gone to put the tools away. That's why we wanted to get her alone. We knew you'd be pissed off that we didn't trust her."

Lorcas stared from one to the other. "Pissed off? That's putting it mildly!"

"I know, Lorcas, and I'm sorry," Alan said. "I really am. But Zumar and Raine had seen her truck in some places that made them suspicious, like the marina near Jack's boat. We had to know. This was an easy way. We told her it was a sign of acceptance and to keep it on her so the Fell Ken could identify her in case of emergency. We figured she'd show it to you at some point, but I guess she didn't."

Lorcas shook his head. "So she's in the same place as Jack Bright right now. Doesn't mean anything. It could be a restaurant."

"It is a restaurant, one that's owned by the Koen and used as a Koen meeting place," Alan confirmed. "After she left here on that day when we put in the window, she went straight to Jack, not to work. And today after she looked at the trench, she did the same thing. Went straight to Seaside Heights, stopped just outside town, then pulled back onto the highway when Jack's coin was nearby. Then the two of them went to Lafayette, and they've been at the restaurant ever since. She must have called him."

"I don't believe it," Lorcas said firmly. "Why would she have put all the labor into making that window? She's sleeping with me, for God's sake."

Alan looked back to the map. "I don't know. But there's a way to confirm it, I think. We know that the Koen want some of the items the Fell Ken see as treasures, property of the Lorecaster. They're those Rook usually bestows himself, and we know they're important. Zumar confirmed that the other day when he looked at your translation of the book from the basement, and we've seen it here in the Keep." He gestured to the coat of arms on the eastern wall. "One of them is the sword; the Koen had that, but they lost it when Korrin attacked you. Another is the ring. We know you still have the sword and Tomash has the ring. The other two are the key and the caduceus, the one inside the staff."

Lorcas brought his hand to his chest and rubbed the scar there, remembering the day in the tower.

"Lorcas, do you still have the key?" Alan asked bluntly.

"I'm not sure," Lorcas admitted. "I've felt weird ever since that day in the tower. I thought maybe things had been damaged in there due to Terry doing CPR on me." He was pretty sure the key wasn't there. He tried thumping himself gently on the chest with no result. It had originally been difficult to get the key out, but recently it had become easier. Now, however, there was no result.

"What about the staff?" Alan asked.

"I still have it," Lorcas confirmed. "I had it that day in the tower..." he paused, remembering. He'd left it there, and asked Terry to get it for him.

He turned and strode hurriedly from the Keep. Alan and Zumar followed him. Lorcas jerked the door of his house open and grabbed the staff from its place in the entryway. He unscrewed it and pulled the two halves apart. It was empty. The caduceus was gone.

Chapter Sixteen

Jack had just arrived at the office when he received a call from Terry. She sounded flustered, in a way Jack had never heard from her before. She told him she was in her truck heading away from Cliffview towards Seaside Heights and asked if they could meet. Jack turned and walked straight back out of the office. He told her he'd head for Lafayette and she could meet him at the restaurant. If she waited at the intersection of the road to Cliffview and the highway, she could follow him down.

He called Don as soon as he hung up with her and asked him to meet them at the restaurant as well. It seemed like things were coming to a head, and he suspected they were going to have to make some decisions. Terry's voice told him that much.

He saw her pull in behind him as he passed the turnoff to Cliffview. He went straight to the restaurant, pulled around back, and walked inside without waiting for her. Don's Hummer was already there, and Jack joined him at their usual spot in the back, with a nod to the waitress.

Terry came in a minute later. She sat down in her usual chair. Jack thought she looked a little disheveled. He had seen her each of the last two days, once when she'd met with him after installing the stained glass window, and once the next day, briefly, when she'd told him she would be spending a couple days with Lorcas and asked if there was anything specific he wanted. Things had seemed to be going fine then. He was curious what had happened to change that.

"What's going on?" he asked without preamble.

Terry blew out her breath and ran a hand through her hair. She explained quickly about how they'd been awakened in the night, about her trip into the thick fog with Lorcas and Tomash, and about viewing the trench early that morning. She described it as best she could, then paused and shook her head.

"For the first time, I'm feeling freaked out about the castle and this entity you all call Rook, and Lorcas himself," she said. "The way that trench appeared was just violent. The earth ripped itself apart like an earthquake. I would've thought it was an earthquake if I didn't know better at this point. And none of the people at Cliffview seemed to have any control over what was going on. They all just stood there and said it was a big thing and looked to Lorcas to explain it. And he couldn't. I've never seen him dark and brooding like that, scowling and pacing along the rim of this trench while smoke from the bowels of the Earth leached out around him."

Jack couldn't help but smile briefly at her florid description, but he sobered quickly. Don remained serious, his hands working a cloth napkin as though he was about to tear it in half.

"I have to say, I'm surprised you haven't felt this before," Jack said. "I figured it's because you aren't Fell Ken or Knight. But I would have thought anyone would have an instinctive dread of whatever lurks within."

"Well, I do now. Frankly, this is so bizarre: I've been consorting with the undead, walking within a building raised by supernatural power, sleeping with a man who speaks to an entity whose motivations are at best suspect. What am I doing?"

"You're doing the most important work you could possibly do," Don stated. "You're saving the Earth from invasion. Don't freak out now. We need you, and if this development means what I think it means, we'll need you soon."

Jack raised a hand to silence Don and smiled encouragingly at Terry. "Let's not get too heavy. Did anyone say anything that seemed meaningful while you were there? Any comments about what they thought about this trench?"

"Yeah," Terry said thoughtfully. "They seemed to think this is a definite sign that Rook is ready for the next step, whatever that is. Something passed between Lorcas and Tomash; I saw it. But I don't know what. It was almost as if they have some secret and they were keeping it from me, but also maybe from the rest of the people there. Lorcas seemed sure about what he needed to do to take this next step, but he didn't seem happy about it. And nobody else seemed sure at all, except Tomash."

Jack sat back in the booth. "Well, there are a series of phases in the development of the castle which serve to increase Rook's power. The first one occurs when he identifies a new Lorecaster and directs the Messenger to make contact and start pulling the Lorecaster in to his world. In some cases it's probably easy; with someone like Lorcas it was difficult, because he hadn't been raised knowing about this stuff, and he had to be introduced to it slowly, fooled into taking care of the tasks he needed to do.

"The second step is when the castle starts being built. The Lorecaster gathers stones and other objects as instructed by Rook and builds one or more enclosed stone buildings. This allows Rook to expand and begin to grow. The Messenger becomes more corporeal in order to provide guidance until the connection between Rook and the Lorecaster can be solidified. They also assemble the entourage at this point. The third step starts when the coronation takes place and the entourage dedicate themselves to working for Rook. Following that, there's a period of apparent hibernation or gathering of strength. We don't know exactly what happens during this time, but the end of this period, this third step, is signaled by the creation of a moat or trench, according to our sources. The fourth step is said to be a huge accumulation of power and revealing of Rook's true nature. If he's not stopped and he manages to complete this fourth step, it will be much, much harder to contain him. It may very well be impossible."

"And what completes this fourth step? Other than the trench, what needs to happen?"

Don and Jack exchanged glances. "We're not positive," Jack said slowly.

"But you have some idea." Terry leaned over the table. "You'd better tell me, or I'm getting up and leaving right now."

Jack sighed and studied the table for a moment. "You understand that all our information is old, hundreds of years old, and subject to interpretation. Plus, it's not complete. All of this happened out of our view, and those who were recording it in the past could only state what they saw and suspected. This stage never happened in the most recent incarnation, in Zumar's time. Our information about this part is nothing but legend."

"You're stalling," Terry said.

"You know by now that Rook uses the shadows, the shades, you might say the souls, of dead people to accomplish some of his purpose. He needs a Messenger, that is, Zumar, who can pass back and forth between worlds. And Rook's connection to the Lorecaster is managed in that way, too: he takes the Lorecaster's shadow and connects it to himself, but in this case without killing the body of the Lorecaster. That's how Lorcas can do what he can, and how he communicates with Rook, and why the others depend on him to translate what it is Rook wants."

"And?"

"In order to complete the next step, Rook will need another shadow. This shadow will be used to pull him into the physical world, out of the stones. It may be a process that consumes both the body and the shadow in the end, unless the person is very strong. That's why the Fell Ken are so concerned. They know they're going to have to find another shadow soon."

"But 'find another shadow' is a euphemism. You mean a sacrifice," Terry said, sitting back. "You're saying Rook needs to take another life so he can use that person's shadow, his soul, for new purposes."

"That's what we think," Jack admitted.

"And who do you think this person is going to be?"

"It has to be someone strongly connected to Lorcas, someone he cares about and has invested himself in, or the shadow won't be strong enough. Maybe somebody from the entourage, maybe Tomash or Tondra, since they are co-rulers and really only one is needed."

"Or maybe me. We have a relationship, you know. I'd say he's 'invested himself' in me. Did you think about that?" Terry demanded.

"It crossed my mind," Jack said simply.

Terry flung an arm over the back of the chair, crossed one leg over the other, and contemplated Jack with what appeared to be an expression of mixed disgust, amazement, and amusement.

"Do you think Lorcas has been using me while I've been thinking I was using him?"

Jack shook his head. "I doubt it. He's not duplicitous enough."

"But there's a possibility," Don put in. "He did take to you pretty quickly."

"Or maybe he took to me because he actually likes me," Terry said. "I hope so. I hate to be deceived. But besides, despite being a little freaked out by him, I like him. And I'd hate to see him injured for the sake of this stupid castle."

"It's hardly just a stupid castle," Jack corrected. "It's the embodiment of evil."

"Baloney," Terry retorted. "You know what I think about evil, Jack. I told you when we were out on the boat that first time, when we hiked up to take a look at the castle and the boat came loose. Evil isn't a thing. Evil is what people do to other people. Murdering people's family members would qualify."

Jack gestured impatiently. "Whatever you want to call it, this is an exterior force seeking to destroy the Earth as we know it. You can see me as an evil person if you want; I don't care. But what I've done, and what I'm willing to do, are very, very minor in the face of what Rook will do if he gains the power he's seeking." He paused to collect himself before his temper got out of control.

"So the question is," Jack began again after a moment, "can you keep going with this or are you done?"

Terry slowly readjusted herself and leaned forward across the table once again. She fixed Jack with a penetrating gaze. "I'm not done with "this". The question really is, are you done with me?"

Jack stared back for a moment, digesting that. "Do you mean you'll stay loyal to Lorcas if and when the shit hits the fan?" he asked bluntly.

"I'm not sure I'll know that until the moment comes," Terry admitted. "If he tries to throw me in some deep, dark pit or slit my neck over a stone altar, consider my relationship with him over. Providing I escape," she added. "Until then, I will do what I can to collect information for you, and if the opportunity comes to get either of the other items we need, I will."

"What if the opportunity comes to actually use them?" Jack asked. "That's the real thing. I don't think we've got a lot of time to mull it over. I think things will be happening in the next few days, and we'll sink or swim. If you refuse, we're basically doomed. Being a Knight in an Earth ruled by Rook and the Fell Ken won't be pleasant."

Terry drummed her fingers on the table. "If I can get the other items and you can show me how to use them, I'll see if I can arrange an appropriate time to do it. But it'll be at my discretion: I'm not blowing up, or imploding, or whatever, this place if I think a lot of innocent people are going to be killed along with it. I'm now not counting Lorcas or any of the entourage as innocent, by the way, since it seems they're aware of this practice of sacrificing humans to Rook at regular intervals. I assume I'll have time to escape myself?"

"I assume so," Jack said. He relaxed a bit. Terry was still on board. Deep in her heart, she knew the right thing to do. Perhaps her visit to the church had helped solidify that resolve.

Terry ran her fingers through her hair, rearranging it and tucking it away from her face. "There's one other thing," she said. "I keep getting these messages on my phone from some guy named Jason Japert, some investigator. He wants to talk to me for some reason. It sounds like it has to do with Cliffview Estates. What do I tell him?"

Jack grimaced. "Ignore him. Don't call him back."

"I'm not going to be able to avoid him forever," Terry said. "I think that's kind of suspicious."

"Well, put him off for a while. If you do have to talk to him, tell him as little as possible, but tell him as much of the truth as you can in your answers, obviously leaving out the stuff about Rook. That's so we don't trip each other up or get caught in lies."

"Okay. So, what's next?" Terry asked in a businesslike tone.

Jack signaled the waitress, relieved that she seemed to be returning to the cocky, confident person he was used to. "Coffee?"

"Sure," Terry agreed. "You're paying."

"Of course. And after we relax a bit, you and I will go to my office, carefully, and take a look at the book I've been translating. It has a bunch of illustrations that show how to operate the mechanism, and I can read most of it now. That is, it's been translated by Kyle. We'll work on you memorizing the steps and you can practice them until you feel like you could do the whole thing under stress. Then we'll take a break and meet back this evening to talk over some possible methods of getting the ring from Tomash. The sword is less of an issue, I think."

"Okay," Terry agreed. "Maybe I could drug him or something and take the ring while he's out."

"We do have some expertise with drugs," Jack said. "In fact, Lorcas' mother tried to use one on him at one point. And that's an idea to keep in mind for emergencies. But I think that would be a last resort with Tomash. He would obviously realize what happened as soon as he woke up. There must be a better way."

"Well, we'll think it over and talk about it tonight, then," Terry said. "Let's get to that book."

The three of them reconvened at the restaurant later that afternoon for an early dinner. Terry, after spending a couple of hours with Jack, had gone home to shower and change, and she looked calmer and more put together than she had that morning.

"There are a few other things that indicate some changes are coming," Jack said as they received their meals. "As you know we've had spies watching Perry's shop and tracking the Fell Ken as they move about. This afternoon one of them saw Lorcas arrive by himself at the shop."

"It would have been a good time to take him out," Don mentioned.

"Our spy is not an assassin, and wouldn't have made that decision himself, anyway," Jack reminded him. "Lorcas was there for a couple of hours, loading stuff into his car. I'm guessing it was the stuff from the basement that I saw when I came through there, because I can't see any of the junk in the shop being worth anything to them."

"You were in the basement of Perry's shop?" Terry asked.

Jack nodded. "It was an attempt by Rook to swallow me up, I think, but I escaped and popped up in the basement. There were a number of crates in there. I took the time to open one and found a number of items, most of which I left to avoid attracting attention. That's where I got the code cards and this." He removed the gold coin from his pocket and set it on the table.

Terry laughed. "I have one of those!" She pulled hers out of her pocket and set it down next to Jack's.

Jack raised his eyebrows. "Where did you get that?"

"Alan and Zumar gave it to me." Terry shrugged. "They said it was a symbol of acceptance into the Fell Ken."

Jack considered for a moment. "Lorcas didn't give it to you?"

"No. Alan made some joke about keeping it to myself, that Lorcas might get offended that he'd given me one, so I haven't told Lorcas yet. It was just the other day."

"Well, there's a whole load of these down in the basement, crates full," Jack said. "I figured they're laundering them to back Cliffview Estates. But it's kind of weird that Alan and Zumar would give you one and specifically tell you to keep it quiet from Lorcas. I wonder what that means?"

"Maybe nothing," Terry said, but Don shoved his plate aside and pulled the coins closer.

"It means that Alan and Zumar wanted you to have something that Lorcas would disapprove of you having. He'd be offended that they gave you one? That's a lame excuse. There's something special about these coins. Lorcas would realize what it was and be pissed off."

"Why?" Jack wondered. He thought for a minute. "Because whatever it is, it would call his judgment into question, specifically about Terry, that's the only thing I can guess. Alan and Zumar are standing back, looking at this relationship and seeing something Lorcas isn't. So they give you this thing to prove a point, and tell you to keep it from Lorcas. They're buying time. They want to be able to tell him what they've done themselves, and show him what this proves."

"But what does it prove? I'm not spending it. I'm just carrying it around."

"Right, like I am. I've grown kind of attached to mine," Jack admitted.

"Carrying it around," Don growled. "You both are. You both like them. You want to have them with you. Jack, you said you're attached to yours. Terry, you're wearing different clothes than you were wearing earlier. So you specifically took it out of your old pocket and put it in your new one."

Both Terry and Jack stared at the coins. Don slapped a hand over them and scooped them up. He jostled them in his hand, then rolled them back onto the table. "Which is which?"

Quickly, Jack reached out and took one of them. Terry took the other.

"You sure?" Don asked.

"Absolutely," Terry replied, and Jack nodded. "I can tell which one is mine. I can just… feel it."

"These coins want you to carry them. They form an attachment to whoever has them," Don continued. "Now why would Alan and Zumar give you something that they're pretty sure you'll carry all the time?"

Jack paled. "It's a tracking device."

Don nodded. Terry looked from one to the other. "I've only had it for a couple of days," she stammered.

"And in that time you've met with me three times," Jack pointed out. "If they know I'm carrying one, and they can track it and tell which one it is, and they know you're carrying one, they would be able to tell that we're spending time together. A lot of time."

"And three times is enough," Don said. "I'll wager they've either told Lorcas, or they're going to tell him soon."

Jack shoved his plate aside. "And of course there would be a way for him to check, if he didn't want to believe them. He would only have to look for the key and the caduceus. Once he finds them missing, he'll know."

"Damn," Don said.

"Call him," Jack said immediately. "Call him right now. If he doesn't know yet, you have to distract him while we put things together. You have to keep him away from Alan and Zumar. And for God's sake get rid of that coin. Leave it at home or something."

Terry pulled out her phone. "What should I say?"

"Just tell him you want to get together. Go out for dinner. Go to his house. Something so he won't find out yet. Keep him busy."

Terry pulled up Lorcas' number and put the phone to her ear. Jack could hear it buzzing. But there was no answer. It went to Lorcas' voice mail.

"Lorcas, give me a call. I'd like to get together," Terry said. "I guess I don't have a cold like I thought. I feel better now. Talk to you soon." She ended the call and looked at Jack. "I'll text him, too. But he usually answers when I call."

She put together a quick text and sent it. "Maybe he's in the shower or out in the castle. There's no reception there, you know. Let's give it a little time."

They sat without conversing in the restaurant, each of them picking at their food from time to time. Don ordered a beer and Terry another soda, but Jack stuck with water. His stomach was beginning to turn with the realization that this could be it. Lives hung in the balance, including his own.

When forty-five minutes had passed Terry tried again, another call and another text. But still there was no answer. As a last resort, Terry tried Alan's phone: he'd given her the after-hours contact number for Cliffview Estates, which was his own cell phone, in case she needed something and couldn't get hold of Lorcas. But Alan didn't answer either.

"I think we have to consider that the game is up," Don said. "They know about Terry, they know about the key and the caduceus, and they'll guess at our plans. Certainly they know about the failsafe as well, and how it works. Now we're going to have to act, and act fast. They'll try to finish this next step in a hurry, before we can stop them."

"Do they need the key and the caduceus to do it? They'll have to get them back from us," Terry pointed out.

But Jack shook his head. "I don't know. But we need them, and we need the ring and the sword. We have to put together a plan. And you have to be a big part of it. You're the only one who knows your way around Lorcas' house. You're the only one who knows your way around the castle. And you're the only one Rook is apt to let in there, if the Fell Ken haven't managed to warn him somehow."

"But if they know about me, there's no way anybody who sees me will let me in there," Terry protested.

"We'll create a diversion, don't worry," Jack said. "But you might be able to use your relationship to your advantage. Obviously Alan and Zumar think Lorcas is in too deep with you, that's why they didn't include him in their plan. You might be able to get him to listen to you."

"And betray him in the end," Terry said bitterly.

"Save his life, and the lives of all his kinfolk at Cliffview," Jack pointed out, "or at least, save his soul. Consider that, and which is more important."

After Terry left and Don had gone to prepare himself for what was to come, Jack sat in the dark corner of the restaurant thinking. He had not wanted it to go this way, but there were other people, both Fell Ken and, possibly, Knights, who would have to give up their lives. Last time, for every Fell Ken person that died in the Keep, a Knight had died in the slump when the cliff collapsed. Bob and Korrin had both sacrificed themselves in that effort, as well as Lorcas' mother.

He hoped the toll would not be as great this time, but the stakes were higher. He accessed his cell phone, and, hesitating only a minute, set in motion the chain of communication that would rouse the Knights and bring them together to organize before the assault. But he put in a special message to Kyle.

Don, Knight that he was, would need a page, or rather, a squire. A squire was the next step up on the way to becoming a full-fledged knight in medieval history, and Kyle had earned that distinction. Jack regretted that the young man might not live to become an actual Knight in the Knights of Earth Natural. But he would be willing, Jack knew. Despite Terry's dismissal of Korrin and Kyle as inept, Jack knew that Kyle was dedicated and true of heart, and thus, he believed, capable of doing what was needed. He would be prepared to back up Don as a personal servant and to take the banner, so to speak, if Don fell. If both fell, they would be remembered as martyrs in the fight against the creeping menace.

Jack considered his own role. As leader of the Knights, he knew his place was there on the scene, facing the castle and the Fell Ken, leading the charge. He would not go blindly; he would make his plans, and if possible, live to see another day, to continue the struggle should Rook survive and to celebrate, but not for too long, should Rook subside. His personal day of reckoning was near.

Cornerstone: The Delving

Chapter Seventeen

Lorcas sat slumped in the center of his couch. The radio was on, loud in the silence. The channel featured a segment of folk songs and the haunting strains of an old lament wafted out through the room. The radio had belonged to his mother, and he hadn't turned it on in years before today. Or rather, the night before; he'd been sitting there all night, and daylight had come once again.

There had been no recriminations, no "I-told-you-so" from Tondra. Instead, she'd optimistically noted that Terry had not got the ring, and that she probably didn't even know where it was. The Koen might have won a battle, or part of a battle, but they hadn't won the war.

Zumar had made himself scarce, probably guessing that Lorcas would direct some of his anger towards him for the audacity of finding a traitor in their midst. But Lorcas didn't feel the resentment Zumar had predicted. He had been through the betrayal, the anger, the disbelief, the fear about what she might know. But his mind skipped around over the members of the entourage and the Fell Ken, and felt nothing. The only thing he felt was a jolt in the pit of his stomach whenever he came back around to Terry.

249

He could trust no one who wasn't Fell Ken. He never had been able to, and he should have realized that. He was bound up in Rook and Rook's future, and he knew it. There had been times when he had struggled to extricate himself, but there would be no more of that. He belonged to Rook now.

He had to wonder why he had not seen it, had not felt something wrong. Was there nothing real between them? What about their trip up the coast? What about the window? Was there no truth to any of it? Or were his senses so clouded by Rook that he couldn't tell? The pain he felt now seemed to indicate otherwise.

Whatever he had once dreamed for himself, it was no longer available. He had drifted for ten years with Carol, kidding himself that he was heading someplace, when in reality he had been meant for a different fate. Perhaps he was trying to recapture that with Terry, to deny what he was, to deny what his future was, to deny how others saw him. There was no use pretending anymore.

He would go to Rook, would open himself up to whatever Rook wanted or needed from him from now on. But he needed a sacrifice, and now he felt little remorse about choosing one. He would like it to be Terry.

He was aware that planning had continued on without him after he'd retired to his house, so he wasn't particularly surprised when he heard a knock on the door, despite the early hour.

He didn't feel like getting up. He didn't feel like talking to anyone, either, but he heard someone test the door. He had left it unlocked; he rarely locked it at Cliffview. He didn't even bother to look over his shoulder at the entryway.

Alan shut the door behind him and walked into the living room, where he stopped opposite the couch, fully within Lorcas' view. "Hey, come on, Lorcas, we're all going down to Seaside Heights to get the rest of the coins," he said with an encouraging smile. "Tondra thinks we should move everything important up here for now, including Zumar and Raine. The Koen might have gained some power with the key and the caduceus." He shrugged apologetically.

"What do you need me for?" Lorcas groused, not moving.

"We need your muscles, bud," Alan said. "You're a vital link in the chain."

Lorcas sighed. Alan walked into the kitchen uninvited, and Lorcas could hear him tinkering with the coffee machine. A couple minutes later Alan handed him a steaming mug.

"Get any sleep last night?" Alan talked over his shoulder as he returned to the kitchen and made himself a cup.

"No," Lorcas replied. He was too tired to lie about it.

"I'm sure we can come up with something to help, if you need it," Alan said. He seated himself in the armchair and sipped his coffee. "Marek and Wyne will have something useful."

Lorcas shook his head and sampled his own coffee. It hit his stomach hard; he hadn't eaten last night, either. Nevertheless, he drank it down. Then he pushed himself up off the couch.

"I'm going to take a shower and change. I can meet you guys down there."

"No," Alan said. "I'll drive. You shouldn't be driving when you haven't slept."

"I hate to keep everyone waiting," Lorcas said, hoping Alan would leave and he could then just not go. He didn't feel particularly social.

"It's just me and Tondra. Tomash went down to do some work on the skirting around the side and front of the house, so he's already gone. Zumar and Raine are there, of course. So it's not a problem. I'll wait."

Alan settled himself deeper into the chair. Lorcas shrugged and headed upstairs. "Help yourself to more coffee if you want it."

Alan raised the mug in acknowledgment.

When Lorcas came back downstairs Tondra was there as well. She and Alan had brought in the single crate of coins and the other packages from Lorcas' car, which he'd left there the day before. They were engaged in unwrapping them.

"Interesting, but I'm not sure how important," Tondra said. "Unless you can tell me different."

Lorcas knelt down on one knee and sorted through the items spread out on his living-room floor. There were more books, but a quick skim through them didn't point to anything particularly important. Some of them appeared to be old hymnals or poetry books of some type: probably valuable monetarily, but with no significance that Lorcas could see. Most interesting was a set of large candles made of a substance he couldn't identify. They were white and waxy, but much harder than wax. They were accompanied by several candelabras of different sizes, all made of iron and wood.

Lorcas studied them, but eventually he shrugged. At the moment they were just stuff, and he couldn't seem to find the energy to guess at their use. If Tondra and Alan had hoped to engage him in something that would pique his interest, they had failed.

"This stuff either isn't all that important, or it's not important now. We can stow it in the spare room, since Zumar's not staying there. Or is he?"

"No," Tondra said. "He and Raine can have their own place, one of the new trailers."

They cleared the floor, moving the items into the spare room off the living room. There were still many other items in there that Lorcas' dad had collected or that he himself had picked up, but that he hadn't found a use for yet. It seemed like there was too much stuff for the size of the chapel and Keep, unless Rook wanted him to start decorating the lower levels.

Alan brushed his hands off. "Well, let's go, then."

Lorcas climbed into the front of Alan's car and pushed the seat back to make room for his legs. Tondra took the back seat. Lorcas noticed that a bow and quiver were already in the car.

"Expecting trouble?" he asked.

"You never know," Tondra said. "I take these whenever I leave Cliffview. Although Tomash is really better with a bow; a sword is more my style. But it doesn't have the reach."

When they arrived in Seaside Heights, they turned off as usual before reaching Perry's shop in order to access the alleyway that ran along the back side. Perry's shop was in the middle of the block, with a good amount of room on either side allowing for parking. As they turned off, Lorcas glanced down the road that ran past the front of the shop, and barely registered that there was an SUV parked in a slightly unusual location in front of the neighbor's house. He also saw Tomash, who looked up from his work around the front and waved. In the shade of the large firs that overshadowed the building Zumar and Raine relaxed, ready to slip away should a vehicle pass by in front.

Alan continued on to the alley and turned right, slowing to negotiate the potholes in the gravel. They crunched along until they reached Perry's. Tomash had parked with the rear of his truck backed up to the back steps, ready to load the crates of coins, so Alan pulled up on the grass to the side. The three of them got out and headed to the front to meet Tomash and check out the repair work.

Just as they came around the corner, Lorcas registered that two other people were approaching. In fact, they were approaching fast, at a run, with one in the lead. They were coming from the direction of the oddly parked SUV. He heard Tondra yell. Tomash stood up as though puzzled, a hammer dangling from one hand. From the corner of his eye, Lorcas saw Zumar and Raine start to move as well.

The two men came up close along the front of the house near the new garden, avoiding the firs. Lorcas realized that the one in the lead was Don Bright. In a flash, Zumar jumped out in front of them. He could do little to stop the onslaught of a charging human body but, just as Don arrived, Zumar crouched, making himself into an obstacle in Don's path.

Don tripped and went down, but shoulder-rolled to his feet. He paused briefly as Zumar made a futile grab at him. Don's arm slashed out and Lorcas saw the bright flash of a knife blade. To his horror, a clean slice appeared in the side of Zumar's neck. The Messenger staggered backwards. Raine grabbed him by the arm and disappeared into the side of the house, but Zumar, too solid to pass through, slammed back first into the boards and collapsed on the ground.

The second man, blocked by the conflict, stopped for a moment. As he turned to avoid Don, he came face-to-face with the old garden statue. It almost seemed that the statue reached out and grabbed him. In a moment it fell heavily forward, bearing the man to the ground. One arm flopped out from beneath.

Don barely paused. Instead, he launched himself forward and hit Tomash at a dead run. Lorcas had the impression of one arm moving in and out and a flash of metal. Tomash doubled over and fell heavily to the ground.

Don loomed over Tomash and looked up and around quickly. Then he grabbed the chain around Tomash's neck and, with a quick slash of the wickedly curved knife he held, severed the chain and yanked the ring away. At the same moment, Lorcas heard Tondra yell again. There was a buzzing noise near his ear, and an arrow appeared low down in Don's abdomen. Don turned and began to stagger towards the SUV.

As what was happening began to sink in, Lorcas started to run towards Don, with no idea what he would do. He heard Tondra yell again and ducked. Another arrow buzzed over his head, but it missed Don, who took a dive and completed another shoulder roll, despite his injury. It slowed him down long enough for Lorcas to catch up with him. He grabbed hold of Don's shirt, but Don swung around violently, his elbow slamming Lorcas in the ribcage.

Lorcas went to the ground with the force of the blow. The wind was knocked out of him, the ribs damaged by CPR flashed pain. He saw Alan make a grab for Don, but a quick slash from the knife left blood spurting from Alan's wrist. Don doubled back before Lorcas could gain his feet and powered towards the SUV.

Lorcas forced himself up and staggered in Don's direction, clutching his ribs. It was then that he noticed Raine, who had reappeared from the house. Raine bent for a second over Zumar, then stood and turned to Don. With no more than a second's hesitation, she ran towards the SUV. Lorcas dimly heard Tondra screaming, "No! Raine, stop!" and realized that she was on the very border of Rook's influence.

It seemed at that moment as though she dived forward, and as she did, a column, almost a splash, of rock, shot out of the ground, propelling Raine onward. The rock barreled into Don, throwing him heavily to the ground. But once again he crawled to his feet, gained the safety of a fir tree, and then he was at his vehicle. Lorcas stopped short as the SUV roared out onto the road, narrowly missing him. Don and the ring were gone.

It had taken only seconds. Lorcas turned to the scene behind him. He hardly knew where to go. Tondra was kneeling next to Tomash, screaming at him in a voice he'd never heard before. Even from there he could see the bright red blood staining Tomash's shirt. He lay very still.

Alan sat nearby on the grass, holding one wrist with the other hand. Blood leaked from between his fingers.

"Call 911!" Alan yelled at Lorcas. "I can't do it! Then get Zumar inside! The emergency crews can't see them!"

Lorcas pulled his cell phone from his pocket as he went to Zumar's side. He almost told the operator that three people had been stabbed, but corrected himself. No emergency crew could do anything for Zumar.

The operator wanted him to stay on the line, but Lorcas slipped the phone back into his pocket. He knelt beside Zumar and took his first good look at the damage. Zumar was breathing heavily. His gray eyes locked on Lorcas'.

"I didn't think he could do that," Zumar gasped. "A Koen knife, that must be it."

Lorcas looked back at the stone wave in the front yard. He knew that it was an extension of Rook and, as he watched, Raine slowly materialized at the bottom end of it, as though pulling herself up and out of the rock.

Lorcas slid his arms under Zumar's legs and back and lifted him easily. Zumar weighed no more than thirty pounds or so, though Lorcas was surprised he weighed even that. He heard, and felt, his ribs cracking as he stood and lifted the weight in front of him.

He could hear ambulance sirens as he hurried around back. The door was standing open, and he maneuvered Zumar in and laid him on the couch in Perry's front room. Raine followed and knelt down next to him.

"I'll be back," Lorcas assured them.

He ran back outside and knelt down next to Tondra at Tomash's side. He had no idea what he could do. Tondra clutched her brother's hand, but Tomash was pale and unresponsive. Don's curved knife, Lorcas knew, must have slipped in under his ribcage, maybe finding a lung, his diaphragm, other internal organs, even his heart. An assassin's knife, it could even have been prepared with poison to finish the deed.

Lorcas glanced briefly at the hand protruding from under the statue. It was unmoving. The body appeared to be locked in a fatal embrace.

A fire truck arrived first, followed quickly by an ambulance, and then a second. Two police cars arrived next. Tomash was bundled off quickly and Tondra went with him. Alan was taken in a second ambulance. The fire crew checked on, and then began to extricate, the man under the statue, but their pace was unhurried. Lorcas was sure the man was dead.

Lorcas was left alone with the police. Just as one of them started to interview him, he saw a familiar car pull up. Jason Japert got out and headed in his direction with a purposeful stride.

The officer deferred to Japert. Japert took Lorcas by the arm and steered him off towards the side of the house, near Tondra's car and away from the extrication work. In the shade of the firs there, he paused.

"Now's the time, Mr. Felken," he said quietly. "You remember what I told you at Cliffview the other day? This is what I was talking about."

Lorcas nodded. "I remember. I need to get to the hospital. One of my friends might be dead and another one's been seriously injured. I got knocked around myself. But I'll tell you something before I leave: I'm not sure who that guy is under the statue, but I'm pretty sure you'll find that he's connected to Jack Bright. And the guy who stabbed Tomash and Alan was Don Bright. He should be injured, so he might show up at a hospital somewhere. And just one more thing: you might want to talk to Terry Bell next time you see her."

Japert studied Lorcas for a moment. "Thanks. You're doing the right thing identifying this criminal. I know you want to get to the hospital right now, but I'll need to get a more complete statement at some point. Some point soon."

"I'll call you."

"Okay. If you forget, I'll find you somewhere, at the hospital or at Cliffview. Do you need a ride?"

"No, I'll drive my friend's car," Lorcas said. He knew where the extra key to Tondra and Alan's car was, and he doubted they'd mind if he drove it. He hurried around back and shut up the shop to keep prying eyes and the curious away. He felt bad about leaving Zumar and Raine, but he needed to go to Tomash.

257

Lorcas found Tondra in the Emergency Department waiting room, alone. Her clothes were stained with blood. He sat down next to her. "What's going on?"

"They took both Alan and Tomash to surgery right away. Alan will be okay; he'll have some emergency work done and then he'll go to a hand surgeon for further repair. Tomash -- I'm not sure."

"Did they tell you anything?"

"He has a punctured lung and some other internal damage, I'm not sure what. They won't know everything until they get in there. But they did say they were amazed he was still alive and that his vitals were remarkably stable considering. That's encouraging."

"He'll be okay. He's strong and Rook probably protected him to some degree," Lorcas said, disbelieving his own words. He had seen the amount of blood on Tomash's shirt, the grim haste of the emergency crew. "Damn Don! What should we do?"

Tondra looked at him sharply. "Where's your sword?"

"At my house, in the library. Why?"

"It just occurred to me that none of us, none of the entourage, are at Cliffview now. This would be a perfect time to make some sort of strike. They have the key, the caduceus, and the ring. All they need is the sword."

Tondra jumped up and pulled her cell phone out. "I have to stay here! I have to be here for Tomash and for Alan. I'm going to call Cliffview and put everyone on alert. There's nobody there to guide them, but they may be able to do something. You need to get back there as soon as you can."

She paused and stared at Lorcas. "What about Zumar?"

"He was alive, so to speak, when I left, but it looked bad. I'm not sure what's going to happen. I need to go back and check on him. I can't just abandon him there."

"No, but you need to get to the castle, too." She rubbed her eyes with one hand. "I can't think. Just do what you need to do. Do what you can for Zumar but get back to the castle as soon as you can. I'll keep you informed about what's going on here."

"Are you sure you'll be alright here by yourself?" Lorcas asked.

Tondra nodded, and Lorcas gave her a quick, firm hug. Then he hurried out of the hospital. He'd forgotten to tell her he was driving her car. He took it again anyway and sped back to Perry's shop. He could feel a knot in his stomach as he unlocked the door and went in. What would he find there?

Zumar and Raine were where he had left them. Raine sat on the floor, holding Zumar's hand. Zumar looked to be asleep; the gash in his neck showed in ghastly relief, but as Lorcas approached he opened his eyes.

Lorcas bent down on one knee and put a hand on Zumar's shoulder. Any animosity he'd felt in the past towards the Messenger was gone. He felt only the connection, the way their lives had become intertwined.

"What can I do for you?" he asked.

Zumar met his eyes. "Get me back to the castle. Put me in the casket in the Keep with my bones. Make me whole again, even if it's only in the end."

Lorcas sat back. "Zumar, how am I going to get you there?" he asked gently. "You can't ride in a car. You'd be outside Rook's influence."

"You can fly him!" Raine said urgently.

Lorcas turned to her. "What do you mean?"

"Take him with your shadow! You can do it! Your shadow is strong now, no longer just a bird. I see it every time you stand in the sun. You can carry him. Take him, please!" Raine laid a hand on his arm. "Don't worry about me. I'll come along as fast as I can. Please, do it quick! He won't last much longer! That Koen knife was like poison!"

Lorcas stood up. He had never traveled as his shadow starting from any point outside the chapel tower. There was an armchair in the living room, and he sat in it and tried to make himself as comfortable as he could. He closed his eyes and concentrated until he felt the familiar pull and tug on his psyche.

His point of view changed, and he could see Zumar clearly. Zumar always looked more corporeal when Lorcas was in shadow form. He was surprised that his point of view seemed to be taller than he remembered, from nearly the height of a man rather than from the height of a bird. Raine, he could see, was staring at him wide-eyed.

Lorcas went over to Zumar, stepped easily up to the arm of the couch, reached out a talon, and grabbed him. He gave a few powerful flaps and dragged Zumar off the couch. He pulled towards the back door, barely passing through it sideways. On the back step he flapped his wings more strongly and grabbed Zumar with his second talon as he became airborne. He could feel the power of his wings now, and he pumped them strongly, gaining altitude until he could bank and soar over the tops of the firs. He headed north along the coast, following the strip of Rook's influence. The route was familiar after his previous flight. Zumar dangled beneath him, unmoving.

He could see Cliffview from a distance. Steam and smoke seemed to roil from it. Clouds gathered and split apart in bizarre formations. He could hear the rumbling of the ground even from his height. Rook was angry, and it showed. He felt a swell of righteousness over Rook's anger, the inevitability of what would happen next.

As he entered the neighborhood, Lorcas saw with a jolt that there was a red truck parked near his house, as well as a sedan. He swooped down low to confirm it: Terry's truck and Japert's car, though neither vehicle was occupied. The neighborhood was bustling like an anthill; Fell Ken ran around, forming groups that seemed to be heading towards the castle. Outside his own house Lorcas saw a familiar figure: Dirk, his arms crossed defiantly, stood in front of the door. He stared up open-mouthed as Lorcas swooped overhead.

Lorcas lifted himself higher and headed for the Keep. The double back door stood wide open and he glided in, feeling the tips of his wings, to his surprise, brush on either door jamb. The stone ossuary was closed and Lorcas wasn't sure he could open it in his state, but, just as he slowed, two familiar figures darted in: Wyne and Marek. Marek threw the lid up on the ossuary and Lorcas stalled and dropped Zumar in gently. He saw the Messenger's body relax through and into his own bones, alive, dead, or something else, he did not know. Marek slammed the lid, and Lorcas lit on the top.

"What's going on?" he demanded, not knowing if Marek could understand him in shadow form.

Marek gaped at him and swallowed before answering. "The Koen are assaulting the castle. They came in from the north, through the forest. They're trying to kill as many Fell Ken as possible in hand-to-hand combat. I think they believe that if they kill us with Koen knives and weapons we won't be able to come back as shadows. They may be right. Jack Bright came up the coast via boat. We saw him climb to the top of the cliff. We wanted to engage him, but Tondra called and told us not to try, but to be available to help you. I think she wants to get him herself."

"Have you seen Terry or Jason Japert?"

"Yes. Japert was with her for a while near your house. We knocked him out with a poison dart and stowed him in Tomash's garage."

"You didn't kill him, did you? He's not Koen. He doesn't have a stake in this."

"I doubt it," Marek shrugged. "The woman split while we were dealing with Japert."

Lorcas fell silent for a minute. Terry was in the castle, of that he was sure. Had Dirk prevented her from getting his sword? If so, he would need to have it with him, himself. It was his only real protection, especially against Koen knives. He didn't dare try and take on the Koen with his physical body disassociated from his shadow; he wasn't sure what would happen if his shadow was wounded or his body was disturbed, but his last experience told him it would be unpleasant at the very least. He couldn't handle the sword as his shadow-self. And Terry must have a plan, one that included the sword. Was she looking for him? What would she do if she found him?

"I have to get my physical body," Lorcas told Marek, the decision made. "Seaside Heights isn't that far. Tell everyone to hold the Koen off as best they can, but don't worry about the exterior too much. If worse comes to worse, fall back behind the trench and hold them off there. I think they're trying to distract us as much as anything else. I'll be back as soon as I can."

Lorcas turned and rose into the air with a few flaps. He gained height as he passed through the door and headed back towards Seaside Heights as fast as he could. He felt his speed increase as he continued to push himself.

Finally he ducked back in the door of Perry's shop, almost crashing into various pieces of furniture, and quickly re-assimilated. Then he jumped up, ignoring the dizziness and nausea and the pain in his ribs. He ran out to where he'd parked Tondra's car and in seconds he was headed back to Cliffview. He pushed the speed limit the whole way, going as fast as the car and the road would let him.

He didn't bother to enter Cliffview itself, but parked outside the wall near Terry's truck, burning with anger. Tomash was wounded, maybe dying; Zumar the same; Alan was seriously wounded; and it was Terry's fault! She was in the castle looking for him -- perfect. He would find her, or let her find him. And then Rook could have his way.

He vaulted over the wall and ran to the door of his house. Dirk stood aside as he came.

"Dirk!" Lorcas stopped and put his hands on the boy's shoulders. "Did anyone get in here?"

"No, sir," Dirk replied. "There was a lady who wanted to, but I wouldn't let her!" He raised a hand, displaying a short, sword-like blade. "She didn't want to mess with me!"

"Good job," Lorcas said, for the moment unconcerned that the boy held a blade. "Did she ask about me?"

Dirk nodded. "She saw your car and asked where you were. I didn't tell her you were gone. I told her you were in the castle. I figured Rook would take care of things if she went in there."

Lorcas smiled grimly. "Did anything else happen?"

"Marek came and took care of the guy she was with, and she ran towards the castle. And, sir," Dirk paused and fished in his pocket. He brought out a gold coin and offered it to Lorcas. "She gave me this and told me to give it to you if I saw you."

Lorcas took the coin and turned it over. Then he handed it back to Dirk. "Keep it," he said. "It belongs to the Fell Ken. You might find a use for it someday."

Dirk flushed as he took the coin. "Thank you."

"Don't go away," Lorcas said, considering what would be safest for Dirk. "Your place right now is to keep guarding my house. If worse comes to worse and you're in danger, run inside and lock the door. Then go in the library. You understand?"

Dirk nodded. Lorcas ran inside and into the library, grabbed his sword, and ran out again. Leaving Dirk behind, he charged up the hill towards the new bridge and over the bridge to the Keep.

Chapter Eighteen

Lorcas skirted the dark pond. He gained the foot of the bridge and ran up over the arch. From there he could hear shouting coming from the north beyond the castle and various clangs and bangs, the source of which he could not guess. The ground trembled beneath his feet and steam billowed from the crevice, which appeared to be glowing red in its depths.

Just as Lorcas approached the Keep, he felt a vibration in his pocket. He paused and pulled out his phone. This would be the last time he had any reception until he emerged from the castle, if indeed he did emerge.

There was a text from Tondra. *Tomash out of surgery. Stable but guarded. Alan OK too. Dead man under statue was Kyle Bright. Police guarding rooms. Don not found yet. BE CAREFUL! I am heading to castle but need car.*

Lorcas glanced around to make sure he was in a safe location for the moment, then returned the text.

Sorry took car. Tomash truck at Perry's. Can you get there? I'm at castle.

265

Will take cab to Perry's. Will take control of forces at castle unless you want to?

You do it. I'm going in. Terry is inside already.

Be careful, Tondra texted again. *Use your head. Trust Rook. I care about you.*

Lorcas paused for a moment. He considered Rook's entourage his best friends, but he had sometimes clashed with Tondra. Her words meant a lot to him. He felt a surge of confidence. He stuck the phone back in his pocket. Then he hefted the sword again, and entered the chapel.

He could see at once that no one was in the chapel. It was only a single room and there was no place for someone to hide. He moved cautiously to the door to the tower, sword held out in front. If someone was up there and came down at him it would be a bad place to be trapped. There wasn't enough room to swing the sword, but perhaps he could stab with it. He moved quietly, keeping to the outside of the curving staircase to see as far ahead as possible.

He paused in the first room, trying to still his breathing and listen. He heard nothing but the sea below, crashing on the cliff, and the yells from outside. He went slowly up the next flight, and the next, then climbed the ladder to peer into the top floor of the tower. No one was there.

Lorcas paused for a moment in his study, allowing his heart rate to return to somewhere closer to normal. He studied the stained glass window, trying not allow his pain to distort his appreciation of it as a memorial. He felt a momentary urge to smash it, but he held himself back. It would remain as a reminder of misplaced trust.

Instead he unlatched it and leaned out the casement. It occurred to him that he could fly his shadow and get an overview of the scene outside for Tondra, but he quickly realized that he would have to leave the sword behind. While there was no one in the tower at the moment that was no guarantee that someone would not make their way into it in the future, and the sword would be the ultimate prize. He gripped the hilt, indecisive. While he obviously couldn't leave it unattended, perhaps he should use it against the Koen outside. He grimaced as he imagined swinging it, chopping into some body. He had no desire to do such a thing, but it was his responsibility to do what he could to protect Rook and the rest of the Fell Ken.

He turned and hurried down the steps, pausing at the bottom to check that someone hadn't come into the chapel while he was upstairs. No one else was in there, but the window was in motion, the gears rotating around themselves like a radio-controlled clock resetting itself at Daylight's Savings Time.

Curious, Lorcas walked closer to the window. Below it was a large sill and block of stone. It had always been there, but now it looked different. He could clearly see a slot in the top. He recalled the objects moving around on the shield graphic in the Keep. Cautiously, he raised the sword, tip down, and slid it into the slot. It fit perfectly, but nothing happened.

He withdrew the sword and looked more carefully. There were other openings on the block: a keyhole that he felt sure was meant to fit his key, another slot of about the same size and shape as the caduceus, but he did not see a place for the ring.

There was a wooden bench directly beneath the window. Lorcas stepped up on it and looked more carefully at the window itself. It was beautiful and fascinating in its movements, a piece of art as well as a functional control center. The glass swirled like liquid, the stars twinkled and danced alluringly. Multi-colored lights shot out into the room, like a kaleidoscope with its own source of illumination.

In the middle of it Lorcas saw a depression. It was the correct size and shape for the ring. He stepped down off the bench and turned his back to it. Once all four of the elements were in place, Rook would be helpless to resist, stuffed back into the cornerstone with all progress lost. As for the Fell Ken, without the support from Rook they would all be vulnerable and in danger. He tightened his grip on the sword. Whatever happened, he couldn't let Terry get the last element.

Lorcas left via the back door and headed resolutely for the south door of the Keep, which stood ajar. He peered into the Keep quietly. It would be a logical place for Terry to be, looking for him, having not found him in the chapel or the tower.

Instead, he saw that the lid of the ossuary had been thrown back again. Curious, he stepped further into the Keep. It was oddly suffused with light, given the gloom of outside.

Marek and Wyne were still there. They stood in a far corner near the dais, with Raine and a young man Lorcas immediately recognized, although he looked quite different. Other than the times when he'd been in his flying form, Lorcas had never seen Zumar as a completely solid, corporeal being.

"Zumar!" Lorcas lowered his sword and entered the Keep.

"Hey, Lorecaster!" Zumar greeted him. "You like my new form?"

"You look completely solid," Lorcas replied. He reached out tentatively and put a hand on Zumar's shoulder. He could see no mark on Zumar's neck, and the shoulder felt like that of any other human being.

"Good as new, and even better. I haven't felt like this in, well, several hundred years," Zumar said. He slapped himself on the chest. His body threw a dim shadow on the floor.

Lorcas stared at first the shadow and then at Zumar. "Does this mean you're mortal? I mean, can you actually die?"

Zumar shrugged. "I don't know. But I never wanted to live forever, anyway. If that's the price I pay for being whole, complete again, that's okay. I'll live out this life and be done with it."

Raine, Lorcas thought. Zumar had taken her shadow, or convinced Rook to do so, for his own reasons. What would become of her if Zumar was no longer able to interact with her, if she was the only shadow left in the castle? Would her sacrifice have been in vain? She had risked her existence for Zumar, thrown it away with no guarantee of protection there at Perry's shop.

She noticed Lorcas looking at her and smiled bravely. "I did what I did of my own accord, Lorcas," she said. "I love Andelko, and that won't stop even if I can't touch him. My hope now is for Rook's next phase to become reality."

Lorcas took two steps towards her and put his free arm around her. He knew that he alone, now, could touch her, and her body felt nearly solid to him. "Whatever happens, you'll always have your place here with us," he assured her. In fact, he considered, it was more likely that she would survive should their efforts fail than anyone else; she could hide in the cornerstone with Rook. Zumar, now corporeal, would never have that option again. His life was in as much danger as that of anyone else.

"Thank you, Lorcas," she said, smiling up at him. "There's not much I can do to help you now, in this form. But I can stay here and raise the alarm if anyone comes in. I can use Zumar's cell phone and call Tondra, or run outside and get help."

"Be careful," Lorcas said. "If anyone does come in here who's not Fell Ken, it's likely that person will have some Koen weapon or my sword, and those can touch the shadow-world."

Raine looked around and then grinned. "I'll hide!" She pointed to the ossuary, then glided over and settled herself within it. "How do I look?" she asked, crossing her arms over her chest and closing her eyes.

"Dead," Zumar said. "Don't do that. It's a good place to hide, though." He removed his cell phone from his pocket and placed it on edge of the ossuary where Raine could access it. He and Raine held each other's eyes for a long moment, but finally Zumar broke away.

"Did you see Terry come through here?" Lorcas asked.

"No," Marek said. "She must have gone below before we got up here after dealing with Japert."

"I was in the ossuary until Wyne and Marek let me out," Zumar said. "I heard someone run through, but I couldn't see."

"Well, I need to find her," Lorcas said. "She has a few things that belong to us. But she'll be looking for me, as well."

"We'll go with you," Marek said. "It's a hunting party!"

"Yes," Lorcas said, "but perhaps we should help outside instead. I do have the sword. That should put fear into a few of the Koen."

Wyne shook his head. "Your responsibility is to protect Rook. He's not in danger from the puny Koen outside. Only we, the humans, are. The threat to Rook is from inside."

Zumar nodded and fixed Lorcas with a purposeful stare. "I agree. Once it's clear Terry has failed, the rest of the Koen will flee. Their purpose is only to distract us. And you know you have to deal with Terry. You know what Rook needs."

"We can deal with the Koen," Wyne continued. "We can stand behind the trench, and there's no way any of them will be able to cross it or the bridge. They haven't dared crossed the wall into the neighborhood, either. They're making short forays towards sections of the castle, the graveyard, and the woods, trying to draw us out. But there's no reason for us to respond the way they want us to. We'll defend the driveway and make sure Tondra can get here, then we'll make a decision as far as what we're going to do."

"'We' will?" Marek asked. "I thought you were coming into the castle."

Wyne shook his head. "You go. The three of you should be able to take on Terry. I'll be of more use outside. I'd like to get close to Jack Bright. He's down at the southern edge of the neighborhood in the trees, directing his groups by cell phone. I'd love to get a dart in him and give him a taste of his own medicine."

Marek looked dismayed, but he didn't argue. "Be careful out there."

"Be careful in there," Wyne replied with a smile. "Now you had better go."

"Are you armed?" Lorcas asked Marek and Zumar as Wyne slipped out the door.

"I have my little darts," Marek answered with a grin.

Zumar shrugged. "I have nothing. But I know the castle and I can feel Rook. That hasn't changed. And the Bob-blobs can't hurt me now."

"Let's go, then," Lorcas said grimly. "But please don't just kill Terry right off the bat if you see her. I may need her alive." At least temporarily, he thought.

He led the way through the door in the wall of the Keep, noting that it stood ajar. Below, the caverns and tunnels were dim and the grumblings and vibrations more intense. It seemed that the walls or ceilings could collapse from the shaking at any moment and, indeed, small chunks of stone rattled down on them as they went. But Lorcas didn't care if the ceiling did collapse. He was filled with a burning rage at the Koen and at Terry in particular, and Tondra's texted words were in the forefront of his mind: Trust Rook.

They moved quietly but quickly. Ahead of them they could often hear scuttling sounds as some creature scampered out of their way. There was the tinkling of dripping water, and the passageways became damper. Odd sounds like rolling boulders, dragging weights, and the scraping of heavy bodies on stone floors met their ears from time to time. The whole underground of Rook seemed alive and active, suffused with sound and motion.

Suddenly, from behind them and to the side, down a tunnel, a bright beam like that of a flashlight crossed the opening, then disappeared. Footsteps echoed as a figure fled. With a yell, Zumar and Marek plunged down the tunnel, leaving Lorcas to bring up the rear as he turned to follow them.

A tickling in his mind made him stop. Rook was there. *Trust Rook*, Lorcas thought. He honed in on that feeling, that call, like a beacon, and began following it through the tunnels alone. At each intersection he turned surely down one or the other passageway, picking up his speed as he went. He encountered broad stairs in the dark with the feeling of cavernous space above: perhaps the stairs he'd fallen down into Rook's chamber. He ran down them, turned, followed a balcony around open space, darted up over an arched walkway, and passed odd window-like insets and fountains in the middle of nowhere. Slick, glazed tiles reflected the glow of ambient light in some rooms. Eventually he passed out of the more refined areas of the catacombs and into caverns, with walls of rough rock and the odor of damp earth. Here he could feel the strange ebb and flow of the wind that signaled that Rook was near.

He could tell that he was very near the chamber in which Rook lurked. In the low light his hearing and other senses seemed more acute. He slowed and moved more cautiously. He doubted his footsteps would be heard, given the movement of air and the other strange noises, but he quieted his steps anyway and held his sword at the ready in both hands.

As he stepped into the chamber itself, he saw Terry standing near one wall. In the dark recesses of the other side Rook lurked. Terry seemed to be peering at that corner, but Lorcas doubted she could actually see Rook. Rook would seem to be a strange, thick mist, perhaps one that moved in unusual ways. But the underground was full of strange shapes now, and there was nothing to identify this one as anything special to anyone but him.

His movement caught her eye. She turned to him. "Lorcas! I've been looking for you."

"I bet," Lorcas said, moving a bit closer. He did not lower his sword.

Terry took a few steps towards him, then stopped. "Lorcas. What are you planning to do with that sword?"

Lorcas laughed shortly. "I'm hoping I won't have to use it. But right now I'm not sure."

"Have you been planning this all along?" Terry asked. "Were you always going to sacrifice me to satisfy some crazy notion?"

Lorcas shook his head. "Oh, no. I never had any such plans for you. You had plans for me, though."

"It's not what you think," Terry answered.

"I think you betrayed me," Lorcas replied. "Is that not it?"

Terry hesitated. "That's not exactly it. Or it doesn't have to be. Please, put that sword down and let's talk."

Lorcas lowered the sword a bit and transferred the weight of it to one hand. "I imagine you want this sword," he observed. "You have the key, the caduceus, and I suppose you have the ring, too. Only one more thing to get."

"Only one more thing for the Koen to get, you mean," Terry said. "I'm not Koen, as you must have guessed, or I wouldn't have gotten this far. I do have those other three things. I didn't give them to Jack or to any other Koen. I kept them out of their hands."

"Then why did you take them in the first place? And why are you here?" Lorcas asked bitterly.

"Because I was worried about you, even though I thought you might have been using me all along," Terry said, ignoring the first question. "Really. I'm not such a cold fish that I don't care about you. I heard what happened at Perry's shop, and I was afraid for you. I thought you might have been injured or be terribly upset. So I came to find you. I checked at your house, but there was a kid there who wouldn't let me inside. He said you were in the castle, so I came here. I've been wandering around in this dungeon trying to find you."

Lorcas lowered the sword so that the tip scratched against the stone floor. In the background, Rook roiled and hissed.

"I don't believe you," Lorcas said hollowly. "I wish I could."

"I believe you. What can I say to make you believe me?" Terry asked, taking another couple of steps closer.

273

Lorcas stood his ground. "I don't think there's anything."

"Oh, Lorcas." Terry put a hand over her eyes for a moment. "Listen, why don't we go somewhere and talk? We could leave this place. We could go to your house. We could go to my house, for that matter. Leave this place behind forever. We could sit down, have a beer, and I'll tell you everything. Anything you want to know about the Koen. I want to earn your trust again. I want us to trust each other again."

"Are you kidding?" Lorcas growled. "Do you know what's going on outside? It's a full-scale assault out there. Tomash is in the hospital, he may be dying. I saw him stabbed right in front of me! Don Bright nearly cut Zumar's head off! Alan was seriously hurt. Don was hurt, too, you know. And Kyle Bright -- he was killed right there. All of this to get you these four objects so you can murder the rest of us."

An expression of pain crossed Terry's face. "I knew Kyle Bright too, you know," she said quietly. "He's the reason I even met any of them. I used to date him, until I threw him over for you. Now he's squashed flat under a marble statue."

Lorcas felt a quick flash of guilt. He hadn't known about Kyle and Terry's relationship, of course. He wondered briefly what he would feel like if that had been Carol. He knew that even though their relationship was over, he wouldn't feel good about it. But she had admitted that she had "those other three things". That meant she had the ring, and she could only have gotten it from Jack or Don himself. She knew what had happened, she hadn't renounced the Koen right then, and Kyle's death couldn't be news to her.

"I'm sorry about Kyle," Lorcas said, "but it doesn't change anything. The people you're hanging out with want to rid the world of me and my friends in any way they can, and they're willing to resort to murder to do it. If it's guilt by association, I'm sorry, but you're as guilty as they are."

"Think about the window," Terry urged, taking another step towards him. "The effort, the time, I put into that, as a memorial for your mother. Do you think any of the Koen had me do that? I did it myself, for you."

Lorcas took a deep breath. Could she have created something like that without putting some emotion, some consideration, into her work? As far as he could tell, the window had no special Koen significance. It was only a thing done by her, for him. He wavered.

He focused on Terry. She wore a knapsack in which he assumed the three objects had been stowed. One hand was curled unnaturally, and he could tell she held something in it, too large to be either the ring or the key. His mind flashed back to a day in the Keep, alone with his mother, and the attempt she'd made to stop him from following this path. That poison had come from the Koen, and he suspected that was what Terry held.

Much as he wanted to, he could not trust her. He felt a pain deep in his chest, the pain of loss and rejection, of betrayal. He could not allow the scene with his mother to replay itself. But in the end, would he be the same as Jack and the Koen, who thought nothing of sending their own people to their deaths? Would he be the same as Terry, who betrayed him? Could he betray her to her death to preserve his way of life?

He knew what he had to do, whatever the consequences. He turned from Terry and moved towards Rook, dragging the sword. He felt Terry's eyes following him, but he knew she would not understand what transpired.

The mist swirled around Lorcas, blurring Terry's outline and the rest of the cavern. He felt Rook as strongly as if he had stepped inside his mind.

"I see you have finally brought my sacrifice," Rook hissed.

Lorcas glanced at Terry in defeat. "Yes. But now I can't let you take her."

"I do not refer to the woman," Rook answered evenly. "I refer to you. You are, and always have been, the sacrifice, the only one who will be able to successfully bring this next stage to fruition."

Lorcas raised his head. The words echoed in his mind. He knew the truth of them intuitively. It was obvious now. All of Rook's plans had been leading him to this conclusion.

"Throw down the sword, Lorecaster. You will have no further use for it."

Lorcas looked at the sword in his hand. "Rook, she has the ring, the caduceus, and the key. If she gets the sword she'll have all four. She's trying to destroy you!"

"Throw down the sword."

"She's a Knight, whether by blood or by association. I may not want you to take her, but I can't let her destroy you and all of what we've made together, either."

"It is of no consequence, Lorcas Felken, Corax Lorecaster. She will not destroy me. I am not so stupid as that. Do you think me so?"

Lorcas shook his head. Of course, Rook was far from stupid.

"Lorecaster, think back on how you have come to this point. Think of the Messenger. Even he deceived you, to lead you along this path for your own good. And he has no such wiles as I have. I have been able to deceive for many hundreds of years and plan far in advance, and even to use the Fell Ken themselves in that deception. Long ago I set up a deception with the Lorecaster you call Paracel. You denigrate him, I have heard your kind say that he was not strong in mind or ability. Yet it was through him I set up this deception, anticipating this future. Even the sword you hold in your hand has played its part."

Lorcas glanced down at the sword. He knew that the sword had been forged and the ring, key, and staff had been created during Paracel's tenure as the Lorecaster. The books had told him about the mechanism that Paracel had set up. He had assumed that those things had been made following plans laid out by Rook. Was it possible Paracel had played a larger part?

"We knew we were unlikely to be able to continue our growth at that place and at that point in time," Rook continued. "The development of your kind was not advanced enough, and we anticipated a backlash against us, which we knew we would not be able to resist. It was not Paracel who was lacking, but the rest of the Entourage. They had not the knowledge to be able to see past their own small planet into the vastness of space and time, and the Messenger was young and inexperienced. And so it was Paracel who suggested a way we might deceive your kind in the future, in anticipation of future attempts. Alas, I was unable to save him in the end."

Rook sighed, the only expression of emotion Lorcas could remember hearing from him. Understanding was beginning to dawn in his mind. "The books, the ones I have and the ones the Koen have. They're intended to deceive. And they were set up to be complicated and difficult to decode so we would believe we had found the truth once we did decode them. You had to deceive the Fell Ken as well as the Koen to make sure the Koen could not find out the truth through obtaining the Fell Ken's books or through torture or betrayal of the Fell Ken themselves."

"You are perhaps smarter even than Paracel," Rook said, with the tone Lorcas had learned to associate with humor. "Paracel devised the books, assuring me that your kind holds such written records in high regard. He also created four items for me and I placed part of my own being within each of them. Smaller amounts I placed into other items, such as the goblets and each of the stones of the chapel, and the window. So it is that when all of these objects are gathered together in the chapel, when the time is right, when the strength has been developed by the Lorecaster and the Entourage and the sacrifice is made, there will be a great increase of my power.

The woman will not be able to use the items to her own advantage. Indeed, the advantage will be ours. But it is necessary for her to place them, for I have need of you here. And besides, it gave me pleasure to plan this thing so that the traitors, the Knights, would have a hand in their own deception. Throw down the sword."

Lorcas hesitated a moment, but then he tossed the sword to the side. It clanged on the stone floor and skittered towards Terry in the dark. He saw her take a few steps towards him, puzzlement on her face. Then she reached down, took the sword, and backed carefully out of the room. In a moment she was gone, heading, he was sure, for the chapel and the block of stone under the window.

He felt the dark mist of Rook's power envelope him. It seemed to him he was breathing it, feeling it deep in his lungs and stomach. His heart hammered.

"Are you afraid, Lorecaster?" Rook hissed.

"Yes," Lorcas whispered.

"You are afraid of death," Rook answered, "but it will not be that which you fear. I do not ask the sacrifice of your body, but of your shadow. For this I returned it to you after I took it the first time. I imbued it with a great part of my own essence, and it has grown stronger, as you have seen, through your own growth and development. No longer is it a mere raven, but a thing of power. It has become a reflection of me. It is now ready to be used, in conjunction with Paracel's objects, to complete me. You have carried the Messenger, and you have now the strength to bring me forth from my womb of stone into the light."

Rook drew closer, tighter, darker. "Our time is limited, for should the woman place the items before the sacrifice has been made, before I integrate your strength with mine, their power will dissipate and I will be unable to claim those parts of my essence. Release your shadow. There will be no pain. You will never have your shadow again; it will become a part of me and I will move into it. In return, the lifespan of your body will be greatly increased, and when it does come to die, that which you identify as self will return to me. I will grant you great powers. You will have access to my memories, my knowledge. And I will remove myself from the depths and strike fear into the hearts of our enemies."

The mist wrapped around Lorcas more tightly, squeezing him, thickening in his throat. Despite Rook's assurances, he felt death like a raw presence. What did Rook know, or care, about the death of a human? Did Rook even understand what death was? What, in fact, did his shadow represent? Was it that thing others identified as soul? He did not know. What Rook said sounded like mere platitudes, answers that were not answers, assurances that reassured him not at all. He had no idea what might be coming.

"Are you ready?" Rook hissed in his ear. "Are you ready to become the sacrifice?"

"Yes," Lorcas whispered. "I'm ready."

The squeezing intensified, and Lorcas felt himself losing consciousness. He wondered briefly if he would ever wake up again, and if so, in what form.

Cornerstone: The Delving

Chapter Nineteen

At first, Terry wasn't sure if Lorcas had thrown the sword at her intending to hurt her or if he'd just tossed it aside. She sidestepped out of the way as it skittered across the floor. Given how easy it was to avoid, she decided it hadn't been meant to do damage. She eased over to it and bent to retrieve it, heart hammering, keeping one eye on Lorcas. She still wasn't sure if he had originally intended to sacrifice her or not, or if he might change his mind. She kept the little injector vial of poison clasped in the other hand, just in case.

She stood for a moment watching Lorcas. She wasn't sure what was going on, but he seemed wrapped in the roiling fog in the corner, and he was ignoring her. The fog, which she assumed was the entity Jack referred to as Rook, ignored her as well. It had done nothing other than exude a vaguely sinister hiss since she'd arrived in the chamber. She didn't like it; from time to time, though she tried to suppress it, that creepy feeling she'd gotten standing at the brink of the trench washed over her. On the other hand, she wasn't terrified of it. It didn't seem very potent, and she couldn't see how it could wreak the havoc Jack accused it of in its current form. Besides, she'd stuff it back in its place soon enough.

She had all four objects. The realization dawned on her and she looked down at the sword in her hand. She tested the weight of it. It was heavy; no wonder Lorcas had held it in two hands. She was glad she'd procrastinated injecting Lorcas with the poison while he stood there communing with the thing in the corner and that he'd thrown it aside of his own volition. For one thing, he was now not unconscious, as he would have been had she used the vial, and that gave her hope that he might still escape on his own when she placed the objects. She was disappointed that she hadn't been able to talk him into coming with her to the upper part of the castle, though. She had hoped to talk him into returning to the Keep or chapel, where he would undoubtedly be much safer even if she had to use the poison to obtain the sword.

She backed slowly out of the room, wondering if the thing in the corner or Lorcas would react. But neither seemed to care; they were involved in each other, at least for the moment.

As she reached the entrance to the chamber, it occurred to her that perhaps Lorcas was distracting Rook on purpose. Perhaps he was giving her a chance to escape, to use the objects. Perhaps he didn't really want Rook to succeed. One way or another, her path was clear: since she had not succeeded in turning Lorcas away from Rook, she needed to do what she could to stop the thing in the corner from whatever it intended to do, and perhaps she could get Lorcas out of the mess he'd gotten himself into at the same time. She dared to consider what things could be like afterwards: the castle nothing but a heap of stones, Lorcas released from the power of the thing in the corner and a normal, if interesting, person, grateful to her for saving him from his grim future indentured to an evil interloper from another place and time.

She turned and hurried up the ramp that led out of the chamber, making her way in the semi-dark until she felt that she was in a safer location. Then she paused and threw the pack off her shoulder. She fetched her flashlight out of the front compartment and pulled a folded paper from her back jeans pocket. She unfolded the paper in front of the light, just to check herself before starting off.

It hadn't been that hard to figure out the plan of the castle. It had been easy to surreptitiously take a photo of the sketch on the wall of the Keep with her cell phone, which she held under the sketchpad she had been using. She'd been surprised later to find that it hadn't come out, but it didn't matter. She had a good head for things like that, good spatial orientation that helped her with her stained glass art, and it hadn't been hard to draw the main parts of the plan from memory.

She had seen the pattern even while standing in the Keep. The top three levels were oriented with the front of the pattern to the west; after that, the pattern shifted with the front to the south for three levels, then to the east, then to the north, then back to the west, and finally to the south again, for a total of eighteen levels. But the eighteenth level was incomplete; instead, the seventeenth level appeared to have special significance. This didn't surprise her; she'd noticed an odd incidence of the number seventeen in the castle. There were seventeen large stars in the window with the gears in the chapel; seventeen small windows in the Keep, with six on each long side and five on the front; and seventeen steps between each level in the tower.

Now she stared at her sketch of the plan in her flashlight beam. She had only to retrace her steps, avoiding the other two men who she knew were in the castle as well. They were likely the same men who had taken Jason Japert down by Lorcas' house with some sort of dart, and there could be others inside now, too. But they didn't seem to know the castle plan. This didn't surprise her too much. Lorcas obviously hadn't understood how it was designed, and she doubted any of the others did, either. The plan had been known only to Rook, and he'd disclosed it in the sketch to people unfamiliar with the particular geometry he was using. But she, a stained glass artist who had studied the history of art, had recognized it immediately.

She had realized another thing from her look at the sketch that day in the Keep: around the outer rim of many of the levels were a number of odd casement-type insets at regular intervals, as well as openings in various locations that led to an outer passageway. Each of those outer passageways traveled along the long side of the level, then ended at a second door. They were like long, underground balconies. Knowing this enabled her to bypass other people in the hallways and chambers, and she could hide in the dark casements if she was caught in an area with no balcony access. She had used that knowledge to trick the men who she had lured with her flashlight beam into following her the wrong way, while she had doubled back along a balcony.

She folded the paper again and stuffed it into her pocket, turned off the flashlight, stowed it and the cylinder of poison in the pack, and slung the pack on to her back again. She stood up and hefted the sword. She needed to travel using ambient light to avoid attracting attention. But she had the map of the place in her mind and as long as she kept track of what level she was on and noted the front of each level as she went by to confirm her location, she would be alright.

She tuned in to her hearing as she hurried up a flight of stairs. She really wanted to get out of the place, now. For one thing, it was possible that Lorcas understood the plan as well as she did. He had seemed puzzled by it in the Keep that day, but he might have figured it out. She had assumed, when the boy told her Lorcas was in the castle, that he had headed straight to the important chamber on the seventeenth level, obviously not a 'power room' as he'd told her but Rook's room. She had stuffed down her fear of being buried in a collapse, braving the pebbles that rained down from the ceiling and the nerve-wracking quaking. But when she'd arrived, Lorcas had not been there. He'd come in after her. That might mean he'd bypassed the main route, or possibly he knew some secondary route she hadn't figured out. So she had not encountered him on her way down, and he could cut her off and confront her again if he left the chamber after his discussion with Rook.

The weight of the sword began to tire her arm, and she switched it to the other hand. Ahead, she heard whispered voices and footsteps on the stone. She ducked through a dark door, ran down a passage as quietly as she could, and paused at the door at the other end, listening intently. The voices were now down the hallway from her. One of them had the cadence and tone she associated with Zumar. She slipped out and continued up, sometimes along a ramp and sometimes up a flight of stairs.

She thanked God her legs were strong from hiking and biking. It was like scaling a mountain. None of the levels were the height of a normal building, and many were very tall, adding to the length of the climb. Her breath came hard and she began to feel the burn in her leg muscles.

Finally she saw true daylight from the door leading into the Keep's northern wall. She tried to still her breathing as she peered cautiously into the Keep itself. It was empty. She stepped in with relief. She began to cross towards the southern door, but her eye was caught by an object. Someone's cell phone was balanced on the edge of a large, open stone casket. She paused and thought for a moment. What if it was some sort of monitor or had been left there for some purpose? She strode over to the casket and reached for the phone.

Just as she laid a hand on the phone, her eye was drawn by motion within the casket. The woman named Raine lay within like a corpse. Terry's hand closed around the phone, but she felt the shock of adrenalin as Raine's eyes popped open and tracked hers.

Terry turned and fled towards the door. She glanced over her shoulder to see Raine rising like a ghost from the casket. Raine moved towards her with surprising speed. Terry halted and swung around. She raised the sword and waved it threateningly at the shadow, doubtful that it could have any impact on someone as insubstantial as Raine. But Raine stopped abruptly, then silently darted towards the back door and disappeared through it. Without the phone, Terry realized, Raine would have to alert someone in person. But, given her speed, that wouldn't take long.

Terry stuffed the phone in her back pocket and ran along the stone walkway between the Keep and the chapel and in through the back door. The gears in the front window rotated crazily. She threw her pack off below it and stood for just a moment, catching her breath. Her thoughts turned to the stained glass window in the tower above her. She had made that for Lorcas and his mother, Rook and Jack be damned. It had taken a lot of hard work. She hesitated. She did care for Lorcas. She hoped she would not be an instrument of his destruction, but of his salvation.

She turned back to the window. The block of stone Jack had showed her in pictures was there beneath it. She bent and opened the pack and pulled out the three objects stowed therein. First the caduceus, according to the pictures in the book. She stepped up on a bench positioned below the window and looked. There was a hole the same size as the caduceus, and she inserted it, pressing it down until she felt a click. Next she placed the ring in the slot in the window. This was not easy, as the spot where it fit kept moving, but she finally got it set. She paused and waited for a moment to see if anything happened, but nothing appeared to change. She placed the key in the keyhole on the front of the stone and, finally, slid the sword into the obvious slot on the top. Then she stepped back, not sure if she should flee or wait.

Nothing changed. She gave the sword a tug towards her; some pictures seemed to show the sword tipping forward with a pull. It did not budge, and in fact seemed stuck in the rock. She frowned. Was there something else that needed to be done? The caduceus was now stuck irretrievably in the stone, and the ring couldn't be moved from its spot in the window. But the key, when she gripped it, felt loose.

Perhaps the key needed to be turned. She felt a rising panic. She needed to hurry: Raine was raising the alarm. Would the Fell Ken simply kill her on the spot if they caught her? Or would they take her captive? She shook her head and focused on the key. Which way should she turn it, and how many times? She glanced up at the window; the stars seemed to be rotating clockwise, and, of course, as she had previously realized, there were seventeen of them. She took a deep breath to calm herself and turned the key to the right. It clicked. She turned it again, and it clicked a bit further. She counted and turned seventeen times. The last turn produced a much louder click and the block of stone seemed to settle and separate from the wall behind it.

She reached up and grabbed the hilt of the sword. This time the entire block tilted towards her. She jumped off the bench backwards as it came. Finally it ground to a halt at an angle, and just at that moment all of the quaking, the rumbling, the grinding, came to a stop. The gears in the window halted abruptly as well.

Terry stood for a moment in the sudden silence, hearing voices from outside but nothing else. And then she knew she needed to run. She abandoned her pack on the floor, scurried to the back door, and darted along the south side of the chapel. Below her she could see a group of people heading for the bridge across the trench. She had taken that bridge to access the castle before, but she would have to take a different route now.

She scrambled for the edge of the cliff and the wall that ran along it, her mind turning unpleasantly to the fate of Lorcas' mother on that very cliff. Ignoring her fear, she leapt up on top of the wall and used it as a path to take her down and away from the castle, along the side of the neighborhood. The cliff plunged away to her right. A misstep would send her plunging to the rocky seashore below. She slowed enough to risk a glance into the neighborhood, to see who might be trying to cut her off, but to her surprise most of the people seemed to have halted and stood in place, staring up towards the castle.

Ahead of her, standing on the wall, she saw a figure. She knew it was Jack; he had promised her he would be there to take her to the *Natural Seize* below, to rescue her from the maelstrom to come if she could not get to her truck. He had handed the ring over to her along with the grim news about Tomash, Zumar, and Alan, telling her that Don had been passed over to the care of other Knights, a hunted man, and that, if he lived, she would never see him again. He had also told her that for Kyle there could be no hope, suggesting that she hold her grief at bay until a time when she could afford to feel it.

But Jack was not alone. A figure lurked by the side of one of the lower houses, down on one knee, working at something in his hands. It was the Fell Ken man she knew as Wyne, and she'd seen him and his partner, Marek, take Jason Japert out with some sort of blow-dart.

"Jack!" Terry screamed. She pulled to a stop and waved her hands frantically, pointing at the man. But there was nowhere for Jack to go. If he stepped backwards, he'd plunge off the wall and over the cliff. Forward off the wall would bring him closer to Wyne, and either way along the wall made him a perfect target, silhouetted against the sky.

She spun around, weaponless herself, searching amid the chaos for another of the Knights to help, but she saw no one near them. Some of them were fleeing to the east, away from the castle, and others were near her truck, but they had cleared the neighborhood and halted their assault. Her attention was drawn to a lone figure. A man staggered out from the shadows of one of the upper houses. It was Jason Japert. Japert looked around, bewildered, then seemed to see Terry and headed in her direction, his steps unsteady but becoming faster as he moved.

A moment later he veered. As Terry watched helplessly, Japert barreled full-speed into Wyne, knocking him into a roll that left him sprawled on his back, his tools scattered on the ground. Japert barely paused. He continued on along the base of the wall south towards the tree line. Jack leaped off the wall ahead of him. Terry started off again, following the wall down towards its end near the two men.

She halted at the edge of the trees near Jack, not far from where the trail wound down to the sheltered cove below. She stared back at the castle, leaning over, hands on knees, catching her breath. Members of the Fell Ken stood around the neighborhood, staring up at the building upon the hill. Some of them pulled children to them. She could see Tondra among them, the bow that had injured Don gripped in one hand. Next to her stood the boy from Lorcas' house, holding a short sword.

She saw the castle shudder like a dog shaking off water. Even from that distance, she could see bits and pieces of stone and mortar beginning to fall. And then it began to move. The earth around it erupted. It took her a moment to register that it was not sinking into the ground as she had expected. Instead, it began to rise. As she stared, dumbfounded, the steeple of the chapel shot into the sky. The ramp to the dungeon, once underground, shook off its layer of dirt and revealed itself to be a turret-edged roadway looping from the Keep. The bridge became a flying buttress. The Keep itself rose ponderously, becoming nothing more than the topmost few stories of a gigantic structure. The odd spires protruding around the area were in fact the tops of towers. The entire hillside peeled away, cleaving along the edge of the trench, the inner wall of which was now revealed to be the outer wall of the new castle. The expansion stopped just feet short of the closest houses in the neighborhood and the stoic Fell Ken, none of whom moved a step except to balance themselves on the trembling ground.

Terry's eyes traveled up the looming walls. Several figures appeared on various balconies of the new, gigantic building, looking over the sides. They were Fell Ken, she realized, who, instead of perishing within, had ridden the structure from the depths of the Earth to the heights it had now acquired. They stood upon the very balconies she had used as secret passageways when they had been buried underground. She scanned to the topmost spire, that which had been the tower of the little chapel. From where she stood, the curve of the coastal cliff allowed her to just see her window. As she watched, the window burst open, and the figure of a man emerged, standing in the casement without fear hundreds of feet above the sea below, his arms resting on the tops of the window frames.

Behind him, from within what had been the Keep, a much larger figure emerged. Even from that distance she could identify the form, a thing of legend and nightmare. Stone-colored except for its giant yellow eyes, it shook itself and spread immense wings as if stretching. Then it clambered ponderously onto the top of the chapel, breathing steam, claws clutching the spire. Its tail thrashed and threatened to bring down the Keep behind it. She could hear the scrape of its scales on the roofing tiles, like the tip of the sword on the stones of the dungeon floor.

It wrapped its neck around to bring its head next to the window and the man that stood within. A single one of its teeth equaled the man in scale, but he leaned out and laid a hand upon it. The immense head continued on past the chapel and turned towards two men on the balcony. One of them stepped boldly up on the rail, even with an eye.

And then the eye nearest to Terry seemed to focus more narrowly. She knew in an instant that it was focused upon her and Jack. A spike of terror shot through her and she stepped back under the limbs of the trees, though she felt sure nothing could hide her from that gaze.

Terry tore her eyes away as Japert staggered up along the edge of the trees. Japert fell nearly into Jack's arms, clutching at him.

"What on God's green Earth?" Japert gasped, his eyes wild.

"Nothing of God's Earth at all," Jack replied. He grabbed Japert's arm and dragged him to the cliff's edge. Together they scrambled down the steep, rocky path, Jack supporting Japert as needed.

Terry followed them step for step, the eye burning into her back like a laser. As soon as she gained the top of the rock, she yanked the quick-release knot on the boat's bowline and pulled the boat in close. Jack shoved Japert across the gap and jumped aboard. He swung into the cabin and started the engines.

Terry jumped onto the front deck and scrambled back to the cabin. She leaned out, gripping the cabin's support strut as Jack backed the boat out of the cove. She half expected the thing to be there, its wings beating the sea to foam.

"What do you think happened to Lorcas?" she asked grimly.

"Do you care?" Jack asked.

Terry studied him for a minute. "Yes, I care. I had hoped this would turn out differently."

"Don't worry," Jack said bitterly. "Rook wouldn't harm him. Didn't you see that figure in the window?"

Terry squinted at what had been the chapel, the spire now easily visible above the cliff's edge. Perhaps she had been wrong. She had been taught that evil was a thing that men did, but the creature upon the castle put the lie to that belief. Its eye bored into her and it spread its wings and thrashed its tail once again, as if on the verge of launching itself into the air.

Bitterly she had to admit that Lorcas was likely lost to her, if not to the world. While the whole thing had started out as a kind of game, and she had never really believed herself to be in danger until the very end, she now felt the loss of that relationship much more keenly than she had imagined she would. Had she made the right decision there in the bowels of the castle?

It was too late now. The decision was made, and her lot had been thrown in with the Knights, with Jack Bright and his kin. She could only transfer her anger to the thing that had ultimately taken Lorcas from her, too early in her relationship for her to make the kind of commitment she would have had to make to change the results.

"This isn't over!" she shouted at the being upon the chapel spire. "We've got the whole of the U.S. military, jets, bombs. You can't stand against that! You can't win!"

But Jack shook his head. "Nobody will believe us," he shouted over the noise of the engine as he yanked back the throttles and spun the wheel. "To everyone else it just looks like a castle, an eclectic stone construction on a cliff. Nobody else can see what we, what you, now, can see. You have to believe it first."

Terry glanced at Japert, who stared glaze-eyed at the castle and the destruction wrought by its ascent.

"I knew there was something weird going on here," Japert whispered.

Terry put a hand on his shoulder. She wasn't sure what Japert could perceive or what he would remember, given that he had been poisoned by one of the Fell Ken. She caught Jack's eye.

"Guess we have a new ally," Jack said. "He saved my life back there."

Terry pulled her cell phone out of her back pocket and set it on the bench seat so she wouldn't crush it as she sat down next to Japert. It was, she realized, the phone she'd taken from the Keep, not her own phone. Her phone had been left in her pack in the chapel. So now they had one of the Fell Ken's phones, and the Fell Ken had one of theirs. She laughed abruptly.

"How long will it be?" she asked as the boat got up on plane.

Jack glanced at her. "You mean, before Rook can co-opt all the rocks in the Earth?" He shrugged. "Years, decades, longer than that, maybe. Likely you and I will be dead long before it happens."

"Then we've got time," Terry muttered.

Jack didn't answer. The waves grew choppy with a squall moving down off the cliffs, dark and menacing, rolling up behind them as they fled down the coast.

About the author:

K.A. Krisko is the author of epic - medieval and modern - contemporary fantasy fiction novels, literary short stories, and mysteries. She grew up living in national parks, where her father worked as a ranger. Her mother, a William and Mary graduate in English Literature, encouraged her to write, read, and recite poetry competitively. Her father took her on star walks and taught her about lightning. Later she became a ranger herself, and worked in parks from Texas to California. She now lives in northern Colorado with her two Australian Cattle Dogs, Page and Carter. She enjoys walking and hiking with her dogs, skiing and snowshoeing, and reading and writing.

http://www.kakrisko.com

Other works by K.A. Krisko:

Novels:
Cornerstone: Raising Rook (Book One of the Cornerstone Series)
Stolen (Book One of the Stolen Trilogy)
Crypt of Souls (Book Two of the Stolen Trilogy)
Hyphanden's Box (Book Three of the Stolen Trilogy)
The Stolenworld Companion
AFTERThought: A Derange Mystery

Short Stories:
The Snow Deer and Other Stories (short story anthology)
One Wet Dog (stand-alone short story, also in Happy Endings II)
Almost A Dog (Happy Endings I)
The Possessed RV (American Blue: Real Stories by Real Cops)
Mother Bear (Wisdom of Our Mothers)
Finding Mandel (Of Words and Water 2013)
The Name of the Dog (Of Words and Water 2013)
The Natural Seize (Of Words and Water 2014)

www.ingramcontent.com/pod-product-compliance
Lightning Source LLC
Chambersburg PA
CBHW071257170626
46809CB00001B/259